Dead Fit

Dead Fit

Stephen Cook

St. Martin's Press
New York

Library of Congress Cataloging-in-Publication Data

Cook, Stephen.
    Dead fit / Stephen Cook.
        p.   cm.
    ISBN 0-312-08756-X
    I. Title.
PR6053.O5242D4   1993
823'.914—dc20   92-21216
                                                   CIP

First published in Great Britain by Macmillan London Limited.

First U.S. Edition: April 1993
10 9 8 7 6 5 4 3 2 1

DOCKLANDS SQUASH AND WEIGHTS CLUB — ground floor

SQUASH COURTS

1

2

3

4

BAR SEATING AREA

stairs to upper floor →

Spiral stairs up

MEN'S CHANGING

BAR

RECEPTION DESK

SHOWERS

SHOWERS

Security door

WOMEN'S CHANGING

notice board

OFFICE

LOBBY

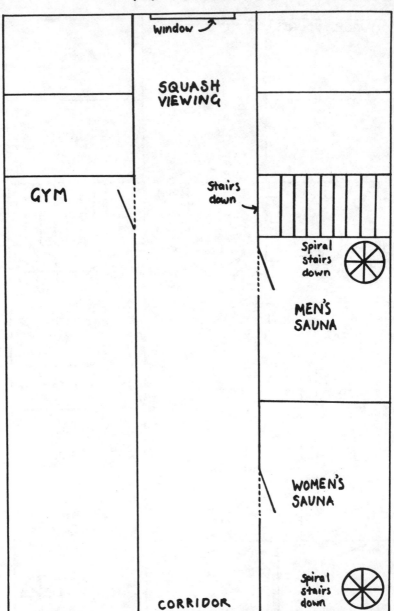

Dead Fit

CHAPTER 1

It was like looking into a tank of tropical fish: the grimacing specimens, in day-glo leotards or exotically cut-away vests, pumped the weights up and down with the slowness of submerged creatures, or floated around with hands on hips, mouths gulping and chests heaving. Some would come up to the glass and stare expressionlessly out, cheeks rising and falling like a parrot-fish or a guppy, before turning and drifting away to some gleaming, padded piece of apparatus. The scene was swamped with harsh neon light, and Judy half-expected to see an aeration tube in the corner, pushing out a column of frothy bubbles. Only the occasional crash of a poorly controlled column of weights was audible above a thudding soundtrack with a girl singer moaning: 'All nigh-igh-ight, I wanna do it all nigh-igh-ight.'

Judy, watching through the glass wall from the dim corridor outside the gym, had never before seen the cult of the body taken to such lengths. She'd always been sporty and gone in for running and swimming and even done a bit of circuit training, but this was something completely different. The last gymnasium she had seen was full of reluctant, shivering schoolgirls with dresses tucked into their knickers climbing stiffly up wallbars or falling off wooden horses with lumpy brown leather tops. Now she watched in fascination as a muscular Asian in a wide leather weight-lifter's belt drew the chrome handle of a machine slowly up to his chin, looking down longingly at his swelling sweat-streaked bicep as if it were the cleavage of a woman brushing past him. A white girl with an Afro hair-do sat on a rubber mat with straight legs wide apart, slowly and impassively lowering her face on to one knee and then the other, as if performing the obeisance rituals of a primitive lost culture. On a bicycling machine with a screen of blinking read-outs between the handlebars a bulky, bulging youth toiled away, face down, sweat dripping to the floor like copious tears. Next to him a blond man in bright red shorts pedalled steadily, his face trance-like. His white T-shirt bore the scrawled instruction 'Scream!', and Judy felt immediately that there was something strange about him.

She looked again and saw that, every few seconds, his eyelids fell halfway over his eyes for a moment, reminding her of the sleepy, sinister blinking of caged reptiles: a water-snake, fallen among the tropical fish, biding its time. As she watched, waiting for the next blink, she suddenly had the feeling that the eyes were not sleepy at all, they were alert, missing nothing, and gazing straight back at her through the screen. She took an involuntary step back, as if moving out of range, and wondered if it was possible for him to see her properly, out here in the shadows.

'Gotcha!' Two sets of bone-hard fingers dug into Judy's diaphragm just below her ribs, and she jumped and wriggled with a frightened squeal.

'Clinton, you bastard!' she gasped, falling back into the embrace of a laughing young man and trying to jab him with her elbow. 'It's creepy enough here without you playing bloody silly tricks.'

'Sorry, darling, just trying to give you a nice surprise,' said Clinton in his lazy south London accent, switching on a charming grin.

'You might have got quite a surprise yourself,' she said, narrowing her eyes and locking her fingers round his neck. 'These hands are lethal weapons.'

'OK, officer, I'll come quietly.'

'That sounds nice, Clinton. Got some new talc, have you? You smell like a tart's bedroom, as my colleagues would say.'

They walked, hands linked, down the stairs to the bar of the Docklands Squash and Weights Club. They were a good-looking pair, at ease with each other and moving comfortably together. But Judy had a self-contained air and a look of wariness which seemed out of place among her open features and slightly snub nose. Clinton was a neatly built man, medium height, with bright eyes, gleaming dark skin and a built-in smile. They reached the bottom of the stairs and before them was the open-plan bar, where some of the dozen or so people turned to watch their approach.

8

'What d'you think, then?' asked Clinton theatrically, behind his hand. 'Full of yuppies, like you were worried about?'

The wariness was all over Judy's face now. 'Dunno about yuppies – more like zombies. People in that gym are in a world of their own, you know. They don't look at each other or speak to each other, even.'

Clinton laughed. 'They probably feel so stupid about what they're doing they don't dare look at each other. I always feel a fool when I go in there. And the music's too loud to hear yourself think.'

'That's right, and when I was watching at first, they were playing Sex Machine, you know, really heavy beat, and they were all bumping and grinding away. Then some joker in charge of the tapes suddenly changed the music to La Bamba, and they all started jerking too fast and dropping their weights. You could see the panic in their eyes.'

Clinton pointed and nodded at a free table near the corner. 'Yeah,' he said. 'I've always thought you could have a nasty accident with them weights. Trap your fingers or your foot in them easy. I never go near 'em – just go in there to ride the bikes a bit.'

Judy gave him a private smile. 'You needn't bother, you know, Clinton. I keep telling you – it's not the size of your muscles that makes you attractive to women.'

While he went to buy drinks, Judy sat down self-consciously. She was wearing jeans and a white sweat shirt, and the half-dozen men in the bar appraised her more or less covertly as she pulled off her black leather jacket. She was used to male attention, more for her lean and well-proportioned body than her grey eyes, pale blond hair and unmade-up face: sometimes she felt like some peculiar headless creature as a room full of men studied her intently from the neck down.

In the two months she'd been going out with Clinton, though, their attention seemed to contain a new and unpleasant intensity. She knew what they were thinking, and that her colleagues at work would say things out loud if they got to hear that she was going out with a black man. Her neck flushed a little as she stared out at the deserted, dimly lit riverside walk outside. It was a dank November evening, with mist crawling up the Thames. A hundred yards away was the great bulk of New Falklands Wharf, a recently completed up-market apartment block garnished with round windows and brightly painted bits of unnecessary ironwork. Few of the windows had lights in them.

As she waited she caught whiffs of conversation from adjoining tables. One man in loafers and jeans with sharp creases down the front was explaining confidentially how his flatmate had walked in just as he and a girl were about to 'close a sale'; another, bearded and wearing a sweater bulging with muscle, was relating in a lounge-lizard drawl how the bank had called in one of his company's loans, causing 'a serious willy-clutching experience'.

But what really caught her attention was the exchange at the next table between a gorilla-like youth in a track suit and a wiry, middle-aged man in flimsy shorts with streaks of hair plastered sparsely over his perspiring skull.

'I nearly 'ad 'im in the fourth, but then I stopped seeing it and 'e kept coming back at me and then I didn't 'ave the legs,' complained the skull, bouncing his racket irritably on the floor between his feet. A large pearl of sweat fell off the sharp tip of his nose.

'Well, on a good day, when he's stretching into the balls a bit, he's definitely got the strokes,' replied the gorilla, in a surprisingly plummy voice. 'Lays them off beautifully in the corners.'

'I'm not stretching anywhere,' said the skull bitterly. 'This new racket's got too much ping in it, I reckon. I get wrist lock.'

When Clinton arrived with pints of orange juice, Judy greeted him with relief and complained that the place was populated entirely by overgrown schoolboys and squash zombies. 'I don't think I could cope with being a member,' she said. 'I think I'd feel terribly inferior, surrounded by all these rich toffs and people with big biceps.'

'You don't want to worry about it, Jude,' said Clinton, setting down his glass with a grin. 'They've all got spotty arses and blow their noses in the shower.'

'But who are they all?'

Rich City types in New Falklands Wharf, genuine cockneys from the old council estates, owner-occupiers like her from the more modest new houses and flats set back from the river in Rotherhithe – all of them, he assured her, human beings underneath. She'd soon fit in; besides, squash was safer than running in a track suit round the dimly lit byways of Bermondsey or

10

ploughing up and down in the chlorinated soup of the local swimming pool.

Sean, the bluntly spoken little Irishman who had just given Clinton a close run on the court, joined them. His face was still scarlet and his bulbous hand contained a pint of lager.

'You see,' said Clinton. 'Another example of the amazing variety we get round here. Sean's part of the furniture, really, here every night.'

Sean was uncomfortable, looking twitchily round the room rather than at them.

'Watch yer bleedin' lip,' he muttered eventually, and wandered off for a conversation in squash-speak with a couple of men who had just come in, dripping and panting, from the courts.

'Charming,' said Judy, raising her eyes to heaven before returning to the easy banter with Clinton which had become the staple of their relationship. They'd met when he'd come to install the phone in her flat, and she had found no reason to resist his beguiling, inoffensive familiarity: he was entertaining, undemanding, and appeared to bear no grudges in life. Just to exist and have the sun rise each day seemed enough to make him happy, and her more sombre world absorbed some of that enjoyment of things. At the same time, her carefulness protected him from the worst consequences of an impulsiveness which bordered on naïvety. So he made her laugh, she stopped him chatting to dodgy characters in pubs, and they were already spending two or three evenings a week together. From time to time she reminded herself that it might not last, that he might revert at any moment to more familiar masculine behaviour, with its possessiveness and aggression.

'Hi, Clinton. Who's your friend?'

It was a light-toned voice, expressionless but insistent. Judy jumped a little in her seat and looked up at the figure standing next to her chair, casting a shadow over her. One of the ceiling lamps was directly behind his head, so she couldn't make out his face very clearly, but there was enough light on his features for her to see his eyelids drop for a moment, half-hooding his eyes. She felt a small tremor in her spine, something between fear and excitement. It was the blond man who'd worn red shorts in the gym and stared back at her from the bicycle. He was now wearing

11

a navy blue Guernsey sweater and jeans. Clinton was suddenly tense and waved his hand in an irritable gesture of introduction.

'Judy, this is Duncan Stock. We have the odd game together in the leagues. You all right then, Dunc?'

Duncan stared at Clinton for a moment, as if he didn't understand the question or was about to reply with some sarcasm. Then the eyes went vague again.

'Sure,' he muttered, subsiding with an ambiguous smile into the tatty blue-upholstered chair between the two of them, and looking at them expectantly.

Clinton started a faltering conversation about recent matches, while Judy studied Duncan surreptitiously. His face, well proportioned but without notable features, was handsome in an unspecific, anonymous way, and his blond hair was neatly trimmed; the things which registered most with her were his pallor and his expression, which hovered between disdain and sleepiness and somehow suggested that it was up to you, rather than him, to make the running. And every so often the eyelids drooped for a second or two, and again she was reminded of the eyes of a snake. He'd just finished telling Clinton how easily he'd won his game tonight, and now the eyes turned on her.

'So you're going to join?'

'Thinking about it. Having a look around. Not sure I can compete with these super-fit squash types.' She took a nervous pull at her drink.

'You look pretty fit to me.' An ambiguous little smile accompanied the drop of the eyelids, and she saw that a couple of his lower teeth were discoloured. 'What do you do for a living, Judy?'

'I'm a policewoman, actually.'

She'd even practised in front of the mirror, but she'd never learned to say it easily or naturally. She'd asked Clinton not to tell people at the club if possible, but she could hardly avoid it when asked a direct question like this.

Duncan suddenly looked alert, coughed, and sat up straight. Judy saw Clinton grinning; the twitchiness which overcame most men when they heard about Judy's job was amusingly familiar to him.

'What about you?' Judy put him out of his misery, knowing he'd find it easier to talk about himself.

12

'Er, financial services. Firm in the City.'

Judy nodded. Although she didn't wish it, Clinton seemed to have been excluded from the conversation and was studying a sick-looking pot plant on a nearby table, his foot in its white training shoe tapping nervously at the floor.

'How's business in the City, then?'

'Fine, fine.' He suddenly seemed more animated. 'In fact, pretty good at the moment. Bit of a shake-out going on, of course, but nothing like a couple of years ago. Just been promoted, actually.'

'That's nice.'

Clinton jumped up, asked them briefly what they wanted, and went over to the bar for more drinks. Duncan declined alcohol, saying he was 'in training', and ordered some obscure designer glucose drink with lots of x's and t's in the name. With Clinton gone, he leaned towards Judy with more details of his recent successes. She looked at his bland, boyish face and guessed that he was probably in his late twenties, like her. He was in charge of a department now, hiring and firing, and he also had a new car – up from a 3-series BMW to the new six-cylinder Alfa.

'You're definitely on the status ladder, my son,' she said, wondering if he would recognise some light irony. He paused, dropped his lids for a couple of seconds, and turned the conversation round to her again. She imagined a gear or a disk being changed behind the half-hooded eyes.

'You're not my idea of the average copper, you know. Can't be much of a job for a woman. You in the CID – fraud squad and all that?'

'Don't worry, Duncan,' she said; again he failed to pick up the irony, just like many of her colleagues. 'I did have a spell in the crime squad, working with the CID. But they're not that keen on women – it's a bit of a macho club, all hard drinking and legal procedure. No, I'm a home beat PC at the moment – that's something they will let us do. And it gets you closer to real people.'

'Oh, yes? But what do you actually do? Just walk round the streets, talk to people, that sort of thing?'

'That sort of thing. In a particular area, though, so you get to know it and the types who live there. My patch is the Chaucer Estate, just round the corner.'

'What, you mean you live round here as well? I live just down

13

the road at Greenland Dock – you could knock on my door sometime and I'll give you a cup of tea.'

Was he smiling or not? Judy gave an uncertain grin and told him briskly that he lived outside her patch, whose inhabitants tended to be more into petty thieving, injecting drugs, and selling their bodies than making long-term investments or juggling stocks and shares. She began to elaborate, but Duncan seemed to lose interest and stared sleepily round the bar until Clinton came back. Then he nodded at them, took his drink and strolled off to talk to a girl in tight black elasticated knee-length trousers who had just parked her notable rear on a bar stool.

'That guy's a jerk,' said Clinton tensely. 'A sodding smart-arse.' Judy leaned over to put her hand on his knee.

'I agree entirely – just in case you're worried,' she smiled – fully this time, her face taking on a new shape and exuberance. 'He seems to think the world exists just to provide an audience for him. I can't quite make him out, though – is he a cunning bugger, d'you think, or is he just harmless?'

'Neither – he's just a full-blown, first-rate plonker.' Clinton's face suddenly relaxed, and he broke into a gust of laughter which swept away the tension: he was back to his familiar self, and Judy dropped her head on his shoulder for half a minute as they giggled like children repeating a naughty word.

'That's the in-word with my colleagues at the moment as well,' said Judy, wiping her eyes.

'Your colleagues, eh?' grinned Clinton. 'Now there's a right bunch of plonkers.'

'Now, then, Clinton, I hold my colleagues in the highest respect and I can't have you taking the mick, OK?'

She was only half-joking, and Clinton coughed and looked away. They steered back to talking about the club as they finished their drinks, and Judy declared that she was ninety per cent ready to learn to play squash.

'I quite fancy dripping sweat on the carpet and talking about cross-court wrist lock and keeping it tight,' she said, narrowing her eyes at him.

Clinton squeezed her hand in response and set off for the reception desk to hand in his locker key. Judy was pulling on her jacket, peering through the window to gauge what the weather

14

was like, wher
voice close to

'By the wa
my promoti

She snap
focus on. '
obscure e
into her
but he v
the invi

'I, er
'Thi
ment
react
touc
Yet
for
bo
she n
and was strolling

For a moment she stoou
believe what had just happened. She n.
confused and excited by his cheek, but at the

CH

The afternoon sky
quarters moon,
of an aircraft,
back, drew a
trees of the
the late
nobod
beau
the

CHAPTER 2

was bright and serene, and in it hung a three-
ilky pale with shadowy patches. The vapour trail
in sharp near its hurtling source and puffy further
silent diagonal across the deep blue. On the ragged
Chaucer Estate, the odd yellow leaf hung glinting in
autumn sun, and the air had a chilly bite. There was
on the cracked pavements of the estate to disturb the
ty of the heavens – and then, suddenly, a familiar din split
e air.

Two police cars, their sirens switching between long slow wails
and startling wah-wahs, turned off the high road and sped along
the narrow roads between the shabby blocks, rolling and squealing
dangerously on the corners. Outside Miller's House, a ten-storey

fastened themselves upon him. 'Lucky they ain't after you for once, sambo.'

Winston kicked Wayne hard, fast and accurately in the calf, then cuffed him twice round the head. Other rituals of friendly abuse and retribution continued as they sauntered over to Miller's House to see what was up. Other spectators were trailing up from here and there for another act of local street theatre – a chance to witness the misfortune of others and shout a few insults at the coppers. There were a couple of pale-faced, lank-haired women in slippers, pulling on cigarettes, a group of snotty six-year-olds with a plastic football and a teenage girl with a baby on her hip. She had puce-coloured love bites on her neck and a dark bruise round one eye.

Wayne and Winston shouldered through the battered doors into the stained and chilly lobby, listening to the shouts and thumps echoing down the stairwell. They guessed it was the eighth floor, and sauntered into the pee-smelling metal-panelled lift. Among the riot of deformed hieroglyphics the only legible graffito, in yellow spray paint, declared: 'Sandra is a slag.' Wayne took out his keys and gouged absent-mindedly at the light on the control panel as the lift clattered and lurched its way upwards. They got out at the eighth, found they were one floor short, trod cautiously up the next flight of dirty concrete steps and positioned themselves discreetly at the top.

The police were taking it in turns to try to kick down the door of one of the flats with their great black shoes, but the door was studded with extra locks and fortified with a metal plate. The words 'Alamo – keep out' had been painted erratically on the door in white paint, and muffled shouts and screams came from behind it. The scream was a woman's, a terrified, trembling cry, and the shout, hoarse and shrill, was a man's.

'I kill her, I tell you, I kill her!'

Wayne looked laconically at Winston. 'Sumfing's upset 'im,' he said.

Winston shook his head and tutted: 'You're right, 'e's not 'appy.'

The officer who had failed to get his hat on his cropped head looked round at them balefully.

'Piss off, you two niggers,' he muttered. Wayne looked at Winston in wide-eyed mock outrage. Then the frantic door-kicking stopped and the four officers stood around panting and looking at each other, arms hanging indecisively at their sides.

'Shoot it open,' suggested Winston, pulling the brim of his baseball hat round to the side. 'You know – bang, bang.'

'I said piss off!' yelled crop-head, his face turning suddenly from pale to pink, his fists balling. Wayne and Winston retreated one step downwards.

'We'll have to go through that little window,' said another of the four, a smaller man whose dark, impassive face looked stone-hard. He fiddled at his belt to produce his truncheon from his trouser leg and pointed it at the glazed lantern, two feet by three, above the door.

'Come on,' he ordered. 'Lift me up.'

'You're totally out of your brain, Kevin,' said crop-head, sounding pleased.

He and one of the other officers squatted side by side, Kevin sat on their shoulders to be hoisted upwards, and the crash and clangour of glass breaking and falling under his truncheon was added to the howling from within. When the glass was clear, the others brought Kevin down and then somehow hoisted him feet first and dropped him through the aperture, as if they were posting a large and ungainly letter. Crop-head was then posted through by the other two and the screaming and banging from within was augmented by shouts and threats from the policemen.

The bedlam was at its height when the lift door banged open and WPC Judy Best appeared, out of breath and agitated. Dressed in her lumpy serge jacket and trousers, with her hat hiding most of her pale blond hair, she was not recognisable as the woman who had sat with Clinton in the Docklands Squash and Weights Club a few nights before. The two officers waiting outside the flat door greeted her with sheepish grins when she told them she was the home beat officer and knew the couple who lived inside.

'Call came from a neighbour – violent domestic,' explained one of them. 'Our mates are in there sorting him out.'

'Thanks, lads,' said Judy, flicking her eyes heavenwards in exasperation. 'But that's actually the last thing he needs. He throws a twister like this every couple of weeks – I can usually talk him down.'

'Sounds bloody dangerous to me,' said the fourth PC, a lanky youth with a pitted complexion and greasy black hair.

'Not really – he's a refugee, from Sri Lanka, in fact. Mr Maharasingham. He's a bit paranoid since they tortured him. He keeps thinking his wife's a police spy.'

'What they do to him?' asked the greasy PC greedily, eyes wide.

'Needles under nails, chilli powder in his prick and arse, if you must know,' said Judy roughly. The PC's eyes widened to saucer size and the noise inside reached a new pitch. This time it was one of the PCs screaming.

'He's stabbed me! The bastard's stabbed me!' It was crop-head's voice, high and quivering. There was a scrabbling sound just behind the door, and Judy and the two other officers crowded anxiously round it. Someone inside was scrabbling with keys. Winston chose this moment to make another contribution.

'Hi, Judykins,' he cooed, waving babyishly with his fingers.

Judy turned angrily. 'Oh bugger off, Winston, will you?' she shouted. Winston put on a sarcastic, sulky moue.

Just then the flat door was pulled open inwards and crop-head staggered out, clutching his bleeding right hand with his left. He was accompanied by the smell of ghee and spices, and closely followed by a small dark brown man in a brightly checked shirt who was being propelled forward with his arm up his back by the hard PC called Kevin. The man's face seemed almost covered by a luxuriant black moustache and his eyes were glowing like those of an animal in the dark. In the gloomy corridor behind them was another, vaguer figure, emitting more screams. The moustachioed man stumbled and fell with Kevin on top of him, and crop-head, steadily dripping blood, suddenly ran and kicked the slight, check-shirted figure in the ribs with a hollow thud. A groan echoed round the cold, bare landing.

''Ere – out of order!' jeered Wayne from under his dark track-suit hood. 'Get 'is number, Win.'

Judy pushed crop-head to a corner of the landing, found a clean handkerchief in his pocket, made a cutting remark about how well his mum looked after him, and bound up his hand. As she radioed the station to ask for an ambulance, Mrs Maharasingham, a frail figure in a soiled sari, wobbled out of the flat and collapsed against her. Kevin handcuffed the husband, who was now sobbing and shuddering, and pressed the button for the lift. They heard it, juddering and creaking its way up, and when the little metal

19

box arrived it spewed out half a dozen more officers with pale faces and scared eyes. Some had their truncheons drawn.

'Here comes the cavalry – late as usual,' remarked Kevin. 'You'd better look after that National Front supporter over there. And keep your effing hands off my prisoner.'

Half an hour later Judy was chatting to a few of the Maharasingham's neighbours at the foot of the block. Mrs Maharasingham had calmed down, her social worker was with her, crop-head had gone to hospital, the blood had been wiped up, the police cars and vans had disappeared into the chilly dusk, and the last remark about filth had been made by the handful of cheaply clad, blue-lipped spectators. It was an average sort of day on the Chaucer Estate, but she'd hoped for a better result. She half-watched a group of women, still young but ageing fast, as they shambled off in search of warmer places to loiter, some of them glancing suspiciously at her and returning a nod or muttered greeting. The flesh on their cold legs and faces was mottled pink and white in the patterns of honeycombs, their unwashed hair was dragged into fuzzy buns, and their heels flopped up and down in battered, ill-fitting shoes. She didn't like to look too closely at the defiance in their eyes, sensing it was just a film on the surface, and that beneath it were reservoirs of pain and confusion which she'd rather avoid.

'I've told you before, you really must ring the local station when this happens,' she said to a stooped old man with stained teeth who lived next door to the refugee couple. 'That way they can get on to me about it, or someone who knows the place a bit. Look, here's the number, pin it up next to the phone. If you ring 999, you see, the Yard puts it out to all cars and then suddenly it's like the Wild West.'

'But they was carryin' on worse than usual today – I thought he was killin' her.'

Judy heaved a sigh. 'All right, fair enough. But instead of a minor incident we've got an injured police officer and a charge of wounding with intent. Hello, you two, keeping out of trouble?'

The last sentence was addressed to Wayne and Winston, who'd suddenly materialised, leaning on the wall. Their eyes widened in theatrical offence.

'Wossat? Trouble? Leave it out, Jude,' said Winston.

'You're hurting our feelings,' said Wayne, his little predatory eyes following the old man as he shambled to the lift.

Wayne and Winston were a pair of minor villains, and she had once helped to arrest them on suspicion of handling stolen video recorders. When they were not in Tower Bridge magistrates' court or helping police with their inquiries, they spent their days hanging around in pubs or cruising the back streets and railway arches in Winston's ten-year-old silver BMW with its smoky exhaust and sagging suspension. She was aware that they were small fry, that they knew little about the darker deeds of low-life Bermondsey and Rotherhithe, and told her even less; but anything was better than nothing. They liked to think she thought they knew a great deal, which made them feel good, and they believed the snippets they passed to her from time to time impressed her and might one day keep her colleagues off their back; so it was a mutually convenient relationship.

Now, like the greasy-haired PC, they mainly wanted to hear more about Mr Maharasingham's ill-treatment by the Sri Lankan security forces. She told them what she'd heard from the woman at the refugee council, then switched to pumping them about a credit card fraud which the local detectives believed was being run from a flat somewhere on the estate. They agreed there was something of the kind going on somewhere, but insisted cagily they knew nothing about it.

'Anyway, whass all this about you goin' around wiv a black geezer?' asked Winston, eyeing her cheekily up and down.

'Fort it was against the rules, coppers gettin' a bit of black,' leered Wayne. 'You know what they say about black geezers.'

Judy felt her anger heating her face in the chilly air. She forced herself to laugh airily, but it sounded unconvincing. If these two knew, a lot of her colleagues probably did.

'That's my business, thanks, lads,' she said briskly. 'Anyway, I'd better get back to the station and sort out the paperwork from this little cock-up.'

'Cock-up's about right, from what I hear,' said Winston insinuatingly, under his breath.

Judy pretended not to hear, and walked briskly away from their sniggers, smacking one gloved fist into the opposite palm in a habit she'd learned unconsciously from her workmates. Overhead, the old vapour trail had faded and a new one was replacing it.

The cold blue of the sky had darkened, and two small clouds, bright and pink as smoked salmon in the setting sun, decorated its western edge. A huge, bow-legged youth in a combat jacket stamped past, studying her with vacant eyes; he had a dished face, a cluster of studs in one earlobe, and dull, bristling hair which reminded her of Frankenstein's monster. She shivered a little and thought without enthusiasm of the stewed canteen tea.

Behind her, Winston and Wayne, hands thrust in pockets, set off through the alleys and parking spaces of the estate in the bouncing and rolling gait of south London likely lads. They speculated about inflicting the sufferings Mr Maharasingham had endured on various enemies and acquaintances, then resumed an interrupted discussion from earlier in the afternoon.

Wayne had overheard a conversation during a recent visit to the launderette, made necessary by his mother's refusal to wash his clothes any more. As he'd sat half-hidden behind a bank of swishing machines, a woman who did the cleaning at some nearby sports club had been rambling on to the wheezy pensioner who minded the machines about how slack the place was: cash was kept there over the weekend, the security was rubbish . . . Wayne's ears had pricked up and tuned in.

'Yeah, but you ain't checked it out yet, 'ave you?' said Winston, impassively chewing his gum and gazing into the middle distance with sceptically narrowed eyes. 'I fink you better check the place out first.'

'Yeah, I'll check it out, don't worry. It's one of them old converted warehouses. All the yuppies go there for fitness an' that.'

'Fuckin' yuppies want sortin' out, that's a definite, man.'

'You interested, then?'

Winston cocked his head to one side and his gaze narrowed still further as he rolled lithely along. He had fantasies of being a serious player and his mannerisms were getting more businesslike these days.

'I'll give it serious consideration, Wayne,' he promised. 'You get back to me, an' I'll give it very serious consideration.'

CHAPTER 3

Judy's new flat was in a warren of culs-de-sac built on land reclaimed from the old Surrey Docks and described as 'Rotherhithe Village' on the black olde-worlde fingerposts erected here and there. The river was a quarter of a mile away, so the developers had dropped the grandiose architecture, left out the pretentious sales-talk about the therapeutic effect of water, and gone instead for packing the largest number of boxes into the available space. The result was a Legoland in different shades of brick with mock-Georgian frontages and paved parking spaces occupied by lightweight Japanese four-wheel-drives and smallest-model BMWs.

Judy lived in Dreadnought Close, which led up to Surrey Water, the only dock basin that had been preserved. It still had its cast-iron mooring bollards, each shaped like a pair of huge, pendulous breasts, and for good measure a couple of rusty anchors had been propped up on piles of chains. A tree-lined path led away from the basin towards some semi-landscaped waste ground called an 'ecological park', but many of the young trees had been snapped off, and weeds were sprouting among the coloured paving bricks and iron railings.

It was a windy, late autumn day. The walkways around the basin were deserted and a group of mallards swam aimlessly on the black and chilly water. From her second-floor window, Judy watched as dry leaves the size and colour of old pennies rolled along on their edges like children's hoops. It was her day off, and she was drinking coffee and yawning on her ill-padded pine-framed sofa. Like the curtains, the kitchen table, and the ugly brown-varnished chest of drawers in the bedroom, it had come from the attic or spare room of some relative back home in Reigate. Her family hadn't liked her becoming a policewoman,

23

and thought her even more foolhardy to buy her own flat in the big city like this. Only her grandmother, who'd had five years of independence working in munitions plants in Woolwich during the war, supported Judy. 'You don't want to depend on some man for your bread and butter,' she'd told her, drawing her aside last Christmas and breathing port fumes over her. 'Stand on your own two feet, then you can tell 'em where to go.'

She thought morosely about her parents. Her father, soon to retire now, resented his work as a salesman for a small engineering company and had come to blame his family for his fate. Her mother had escaped into piles of pulp romance from the library and daytime nips of cooking sherry, and Judy had lain awake at night listening to recriminations echoing up the stairs of their small Victorian villa. She'd taken the greater share of looking after her younger brother, blotting his grazed knees and supervising his school work, and played teenage peacekeeper in the conflicts between her parents. She had come to think she was the mooring point and that the rest of the family would drift away and founder without her. But finally, after one A-level and four years in a bank, she'd escaped to London, choosing law and order to offset the uncertainties so far.

Six years in the police had toughened her. She remembered her second road accident, where a sergeant had passed a severed hand out of the mangled car and said: ''Ere, put that in the fridge for us, Jude.' She'd learnt to deal with being called a 'plonk' by her colleagues and a stinking piece of filth by some of the public. She found she could accept the lawless passions and petty destructiveness of this part of London, much as she'd accepted the frustration and vindictiveness of her parents, but only if she kept her own life neat and tidy. She avoided the heavy drinking and gross parties, and went out running or to the cinema with her friend Beth. Beth, however, had recently got her face kicked in outside a pub and retreated to her home county of Hampshire.

Now Clinton, so cheery and undemanding, had filled the gap. She was meeting him tonight – a drink in the Mayflower, a laugh, a Chinese meal, a bit of grappling on the sofa, no more. Judy sighed and stared out at the darkening, fast-moving clouds. There was a vague desire for something new, something slightly less safe and predictable than the cautious cocoon she had built round herself. She turned round and found herself looking again at the little oblong card propped behind the candle on the mantelpiece.

She got up abruptly and stared out of the window at the building opposite, where a collection of Alice bands – blue velvet, tortoise-shell and white satin studded with beads – were clipped over the mirror of someone's dressing-table. The sight didn't distract her as it usually did, and she found herself walking across the room, picking up the card, and flexing it speculatively between her tidily manicured fingers. The name Duncan Stock was printed in harsh black capitals, with nothing left to doubt or ambiguity. Under-neath it were the words 'investment executive', altogether more nebulous in rococo italics, and the name of the company: Banks and Heritage, 19 Gracechurch Square. On the back was scrawled in felt-tip the details of the party. It was in the the Golden Vat wine bar in Pudding Lane from 6.30 'till late' the following Thurs-day: a different world.

Working in the fast-response cars the previous year, she'd often been involved in stopping young men in double-breasted suits speeding along Jamaica Road in their German cars. They were the first yuppie migrants to the Surrey docklands, and they exuded boorish self-confidence and the smell of money and wine. If they were arrested for being over the limit they sometimes earned themselves extra charges for swearing, struggling, or attempting to bribe a police officer. Then they'd turn up in court in their silk ties and loudly coloured braces and arrogantly sign cheques on the spot to cover their fines. They aroused a confusing mixture of contempt and envious curiosity in her, and here was one of them, a slicker, inviting her, a plonk, to a party. The women would be shoulder-padded and exotically perfumed. She remembered the cheeky, almost contemptuous arm round the waist: it must be some complicated wind-up, maybe a bet with his mates. On the other hand, maybe he liked her.

She looked at herself in the mirror above the mantelpiece, patting the pale blond hair into a more protective shape around her unmade-up cheeks. It was a round, small-featured, boyish face, which became less plain when she smiled, producing small dimples in her cheeks and a sparkle in her grey eyes. She tried the smile now, but quickly changed it to a grimace and put the card back behind the candle. Tomorrow she'd be back on duty, tramping round in the cold, attempting to substitute law and order

25

for the law of the jungle on the Chaucer Estate; so why was she daydreaming about some yuppie in the City where the law of the jungle – applied a little more politely – went unchallenged? The gloomy dusk was filling the room, and she walked over to switch on the light. Then she checked her watch, went into the bedroom to pick up her sports bag, and left the flat.

Discarded crisp packets whipped round her ankles and grit blew into her eyes as she came round the corner and saw the club ahead of her, an oasis of brightness in the gloomy riverside streets. On one side of it was an old four-storey council block, its long open landings dimly lit in spite of its recent face-lift, and on the other was the great bulk of New Falklands Wharf. There were a couple of cars in a chained-off parking bay, and one of them – a latest-model Audi – was propped at a nose-down angle on concrete blocks, its wheels missing. As she came closer to the building she heard a flapping noise, and peered up to see that a great banner had been hung on the flank of the half-empty building. The wind kept twisting and tangling it like washing on a line, but every so often allowed it to fall flat for a second or two. Judy made out the giant words: 'Live here for half price!' They'd be giving them away next.

The club was a rectangular two-storey building, solidly built in dark grey brick as administrative offices for the now-defunct wharves. Judy stepped into the pool of light thrown out by the brilliant neon sign and pushed through the swing doors to the little lobby where two or three bikes stood swathed in chains under the notice board. As she rang the bell and stood peering in through the glass door, Sharon Bunnie, phone to ear, looked up from the reception desk, recognised her, and pressed a hidden button. Judy pushed the door open and heard it click firmly shut behind her, propelled by its powerful spring.

'Hi, Judy. You got some coaching, right?' Sharon's little cockney voice was high and bouncy, her eyes were bright, and her thin jaws were grinding on a wad of gum. When Judy had first joined, the policewoman's part of her mind had immediately wondered what sort of pills this girl was on, but Clinton had told her she was too suspicious: Sharon was a fitness freak and could easily beat most men on the court.

'That's right. Six-thirty.'

Still talking on the phone, Sharon took her money, rang up the till, gave her change, passed over a key for a changing-room locker, and flashed her a smile in between grindings of the jaw. Judy turned round and went into the women's changing room, almost opposite the reception desk; the men's was further along, opposite the bar.

There were two other young women in there, giggling and hiding their bodies as they changed. One of them, a blonde in a tight lime-green top, was whispering something about sitting on someone's face, and the other, a brunette, was so convulsed in laughter she tripped over her blue leotard and fell against the lockers, eyes closed, mouth open, and breasts bouncing. Judy concentrated grimly on getting changed, then went out past the bar towards the courts. Robin, the coach, was waiting for her, smiling and lifting alternate feet to tap his racket against his shoes, like a nervous tennis player. She smiled back: he had a lithe body but a leaden personality.

As she passed the first court, there was a sudden explosion of metallic noise, like a car crash, followed by a sustained volley of foul language. Judy jumped and turned, realising it must be the bang of a ball hit with full power into the tin-covered strip at the bottom of the front wall. Through the glass door of the court she saw a tall, well-built young man with a long red face and curly hair stalking towards her, swishing his racket like a scythe and cursing freely. His enraged shouting was accompanied by flecks of spittle, some of them streaking his chin. His eyes met hers with no change in the expression of fury, and for a moment of instinctive fear she thought he was going to open the door and thrash her with his racket.

Then she noticed that the other person on the court was a smaller blond man with red shorts and white T-shirt: Duncan Stock. Cool and unflustered, he was standing on the red lines in the middle, studying his racket head with an undisguised expression of self-satisfaction and judiciously testing its strings with his fingers. She felt a tiny, unwished-for palpitation of excitement and prepared to greet him with a wave of her racket, but she was past the door before he saw her, and she wasn't going to go back. Her excitement was tempered immediately with annoyance at his self-absorbed smugness: no prizes for guessing

27

who's winning that game, she thought. She shook Robin's limp hand and stepped on to the brightly lit wooden floor.

As she stretched and reached and practised strokes under Robin's patient and tedious instruction, she was constantly aware of the violent sounds next door – the slamming of the ball, the cries of rage and frustration from the curly-headed man, and the score called out smoothly by Duncan. The tally was invariably in his favour, and it was only when his victory was complete and the storm died away that Judy could concentrate on her lesson. Robin was dissatisfied with her backhand: he seemed unable to realise that women couldn't do it as hard as men because of their breasts, and she felt unable to tell him.

At the end there was another handshake, moist as well as limp this time, and she pulled her track suit back on. As she walked towards the bar, her mind was divided between wondering nervously if she was going to bump into Duncan and thinking irritably that she had a long way to go as a squash player. She ordered half a pint of orange juice from Sharon and drank it slowly, staring out of the window into the sodium-coloured halo of the London night. She half-expected him to come in behind her and start touching her, in which case, she decided, she would hit him hard across the face; but he didn't, and she went back into the changing room for a shower, feeling strangely frustrated.

She had the place to herself and was sitting wrapped in her towel, disconsolately kneading the half-handful of spare flesh on the side of one thigh, when she heard a giggling noise behind her. She looked round, embarrassed, as if someone had caught her picking her nose. The two women who'd been changing earlier were coming down the spiral staircase, shoes squeaking on the metal steps, chatting as conspiratorially as before. Judy remembered that the staircase led upstairs to a sauna room, and that there was a door from the sauna room into the corridor outside the gym.

'I wouldn't mind,' said the blond one in the green top, gesturing widely with scarlet-tipped fingers. 'But he wasn't even wearing sports gear.'

'Unless you call cavalry twill trousers and tweed jackets sports gear,' said the dark one. 'I think he might have been staring at the machinery rather than us.'

'Don't you believe it, Chris,' said the blonde, pulling her hair

28

to the back of her head and tying it with a brightly coloured strap. 'He couldn't get his eyes off your tits when you were doing sit-ups.'

'D'you know, I'm sure he said something as we came out.'

'What was it?'

'I'm sure he said, my sport's swimming, or something like that. Daft sod.'

They pulled their clothes off, revealing all-over tans with a few paler triangles and the odd unexpected stretch mark, wrapped towels round themselves, and padded back up the stairs. The little wooden door of the sauna closed behind them, muffling their constant chatter, and Judy climbed into her jeans and sweat shirt. She'd have time for another drink here before going off to meet Clinton.

When she emerged from the changing room, slinging her bag on to her shoulder, she nearly collided with Duncan. He was standing talking to his squash partner, who had metamorphosed from the monster raging round the court into an ordinary human being with a normal-coloured face.

'Oh, Judy, hi,' said Duncan immediately, as if he'd been expecting her. 'Good coaching session?'

Judy started and stepped back, feeling a nervous lurch in her stomach. Duncan was wearing his charming smile, and her eye was caught by the dark cotton shirt and the soft, expensive, leather jacket he was wearing.

'Not bad,' she said defensively. 'How did you know I'd had coaching?'

His eyelids dropped lazily for a second, and he looked away at the other man. 'Oh, we watched you a bit from the gallery upstairs – didn't you see us?'

'No, I certainly didn't.' She felt spied on, like the women in the gym, and stared at him defiantly. His short blond hair had a touch of russet in it and reminded her of teddy bears. He ploughed smoothly on.

'Judy, I want you to meet a friend of mine, Eddie Nutting. Eddie, this is my policewoman friend I was telling you about.'

Eddie stepped forward and shook hands, smiling a sycophantic, insincere-looking smile and bobbing his head up and down like an ill-controlled puppet. His handshake was unnecessarily long and powerful, and Judy noticed that the curls were thinning and the long face was pock-marked. He was a full head taller than her.

She wanted to ask Duncan why Eddie could have a surname and she only had a Christian name, like the waitresses in American-style eating places wearing badges offering them intimately to the world as Debbie or Trixie. She also wanted to ask what he'd been saying to his friends about her after their one brief meeting. If she'd been on duty dealing with a member of the public, she'd have no difficulty putting such questions, but instead she asked meekly who'd won their game.

'Oh, Dunc did,' said Ed, head bobbing and smiling despite an edge of sarcasm in his voice. 'I couldn't win – he'd sack me.'

Dunc's eyelids fell modestly, but his lips held an enigmatic, self-satisfied grin.

'Come on, Eddie – it was very close,' he murmured. He told her how he was going to show Ed and another friend from work round his new apartment before going on a crawl of the riverside pubs: Mayflower, Famous Angel, Cook and Monkey.

'I see, slumming it, eh?' she said.

'Now, now,' said Duncan. 'Why not come along and slum it with us? Jeremy has got his old Fiat outside, plenty of room in the back.'

'Sorry,' said Judy, hitching her bag decisively up her shoulder again. 'I'm meeting Clinton.'

'Oh yes, Clinton.'

She couldn't decipher the undercurrent in his voice, but he leant towards her and took her elbow gently.

'Look, you won't forget next Thursday, will you? It'll be lovely to see you.'

'I'll think about it.'

'Cheerio then.'

'Bye.'

She pulled her arm away and walked towards the bar, sidestepping a big young man in a tweed jacket coming out of the men's changing room in a hurry. He had a little smile on his face and a self-absorbed look in his eyes, but he threw her an apologetic nod as he passed. She looked round to see him joining Duncan and Eddie, and realised he must be both the third friend and the spectator at the gym. She found herself grinning confusedly as she ordered her orange juice.

'Whassa marra wiv you?' asked Sharon Bunnie as she filled the glass.

'I dunno,' said Judy, shaking her head. 'These city types. I suppose I'm not used to being treated like that – you know, nice handshakes, charming smiles. But underneath, I've got this feeling they're a bunch of head-bangers.'

'Yeah,' said Sharon, wrinkling her nose in agreement. 'Too right. Wanna watch that lot.'

CHAPTER 4

The passengers on the East London Line of the Underground were as charmless as ever. A rhythmic fizzing sound was leaking from earphones clamped round the head of the youth slumped in the corner seat, beneath a defaced notice asking people to keep their personal stereos personal. It was as if some clockwork snake, in time with the background drumming, was sticking its head out of a basket every couple of seconds – dum-dum *hiss*, dum-dum *hiss* – and spitting malevolently round the carriage. Judy stared irritably at the vacant eyes, the slack red mouth, the training shoes spattered with coloured bands and insignia, with huge tongues projecting upwards like shin pads. The train clattered and rumbled through the stained brick vaults of Shadwell and Wapping stations, and Judy got out at Whitechapel to change trains. A pigeon was flying hazardously up and down at head height, and when it landed it skidded on the shiny platform, ending up with one mutilated foot in the air.

The more cheerful, modern carriages of the District Line made little difference to the clientele. A fat man next to her, wheezing heavily, had his elbow on the arm rest between them and his *Evening Standard* half in front of her face. She tried to avoid looking at his hand, which was bulbous and red-mottled like a pound of pork sausages, or breathing the wisps of a sour, decaying smell which seemed to escape from the folds of his clothing. She wanted to push his newspaper away and tell him to have a bath. But she restrained herself and tried instead to stimulate more charitable feelings by smiling sympathetically at a thin old lady with long yellow teeth whose face bore an expression of profound tragedy. But the old dear stared blankly through her, and Judy was distracted by slurred shouting from the other end of the carriage.

32

A swaying man with a flapping, greasy overcoat and an unkempt ginger beard was clutching a lager can and telling anyone who looked at him that he was from fucking Scotland and he'd fucking well had enough. His neighbours studied the floor or their newspapers impassively, but a well-built, well-groomed young man in a camel-hair coat was eyeing the drunk coldly and fingering the handle of his umbrella, as if he was tempted to use its metal point to skewer him to the wall of the carriage like some bizarre shaggy beetle. The only consolation to this journey was that Judy was travelling against the rush-hour traffic so there was at least somewhere to sit.

The smart young man got off at Tower Hill, heels clicking as he strode away down the platform. He took the stairs two at a time, ignoring a scruffy young woman with green hair and a dejected-looking dog who was crouching at the bottom with a cardboard notice reading 'homeless and hungry'. Judy reflected that Duncan and his friends probably never descended into this bright noisy subterranean world of overheated carriages and cold gritty winds, where London's poor rubbed shoulders with shoals of tired, impatient commuters. She suddenly forgot her depressing surroundings and a thrill of nervousness ran through her stomach at the thought of where she was going. She pulled out the card to check the address of the wine bar for the tenth time.

She emerged at Monument, breathed in the fresh, damp air with relief and walked two hundred yards along Eastcheap before turning right into Pudding Lane. There it was, halfway down, unmistakable with its illuminated sign in fat gilt letters: the Golden Vat. She slowed down a little to listen to a small internal voice telling her she could still just turn round and go home. She could ring up Clinton, say she was sorry, arrange to meet him instead, fall back on the comfortable and familiar.

But then she remembered his behaviour when he'd come round unexpectedly two nights ago and confronted her: Sharon Bunnie had overheard Duncan repeating his invitation to her at the club, and had fecklessly asked Clinton on his next visit where the do was going to be. Either she'd assumed innocently that Judy and Clinton were going as a couple, or she was deliberately stirring it. Clinton's unusual anger and querulousness had awakened a streak of defiance in Judy: no man was going to tell her what to do. Clinton had called her a rotten cow, she'd reminded him she

33

wasn't his property, and they had parted on bad terms, with a slammed door. She tried to push the scene out of her mind as she clumped down the wooden steps to go underground again, this time into a very different atmosphere.

The warm, hazy air of the cellar was saturated with the mingled smells of smoke, food, beer, wine, perfume, sweat and the saw-dust on the floor. At first all Judy could see were eyes and mouths, the eyes flashing and glinting and the mouths spewing out a babble of cacophonous noise. People stood in groups, with cigarettes and slopping drinks in carelessly gesticulating hands, or sat around upturned barrels packed with glasses and dirty ashtrays. She edged into the mêlée, disorientated, wondering if this was the party, and after half a minute of looking round vainly for Duncan she asked a blond girl whose carmine lipstick was gradually being transferred from her mouth to the rim of her tumbler of gin.

The girl tossed a curtain of hair back from her face and switched her blurred eyes from a man in a chalk-stripe suit to Judy.

"Course it's not the party,' she said unkindly in a Roedean voice. 'The privileged few have taken over the side room – why d'you think it's so bloody crowded in here?'

The man in the chalk-stripe bellowed with laughter, revealing a powerful set of tobacco-stained teeth, as if the blonde had just made a riotously funny joke. Judy gave him a cold stare as she moved away. She pressed on through the hideous bodies and found the side room, which was just as crowded as the main bar, but still could not see Duncan. Most of the people in the room seemed to be rowdy men in suits, but there was a scattering of young women in scanty, expensive-looking dresses, with a lot of gold on their necks, wrists and ears. Her eyes were starting to sting from the smoke, she could feel beads of perspiration forming in the small of her back, and she began to feel helpless and lost. If she'd been in uniform instead of her black dress, and was here to shut the buggers up and get them to go home, she'd have known what to do. As it was, she didn't know where to begin and wished she'd stayed where she belonged.

Drink was the first answer, she decided. But as she pushed her way towards the bar a large, noisy man suddenly sprang in front of her, holding up his arms, pressed together at the wrist, like a praying mantis.

34

'Snap 'em on, Judy!' he shouted. 'It's a fair cop! I'm a bad boy! Treat me rough!'

Hovering between relief at making contact with someone and irritation at the hackneyed joke, Judy pushed the hands aside and recognised Eddie, Duncan's curly-topped colleague from the squash club. He was panting and grinning maniacally.

'Sorry, Eddie,' she said mildly. 'I don't do correction when I'm not on duty. You could get me a drink, though – and tell me where Duncan is.'

'Absolutely,' shouted Eddie. 'What's it to be? Should be some champers left.'

'That'll do,' said Judy, trying not to sound surprised. Eddie moved away, nodding and bobbing. Then a strong hand closed insidiously round her elbow from behind, and she heard Duncan's non-committal tones, intimately close to her ear.

'Lovely to see you, Judy. Glad you could make it – I thought you'd come in the end. Don't take any notice of my so-called friends.'

She laughed nervously and turned to him. Their faces were only a foot apart, and she noticed for the first time the colour of his eyes – grey, like hers, but cooler and paler, all calculation and no fire. The lids dropped for a moment and he began peeling her coat from her shoulders without asking permission. She shrugged it off completely with a brusque gesture, stepping away to avoid any trailing hand. Eddie appeared again and put a cold glass of wine in her hand, complimenting her fulsomely on her dress while staring into her cleavage. Then someone yanked him away from behind and he disappeared suddenly into the mêlée, like a jack going back into its box.

The champagne bubbles sent tingling sensations up her nostrils and fizzed finely into extinction around her mouth. After only two swallows Judy felt unreal and light-headed. She looked around the room, scarcely registering what Duncan was saying to her. One man stood out because he was nearly a head taller than everyone else, and she recognised him as Duncan's other friend at the club. Apart from Duncan himself, all these toffs seemed so well fed, so physically big – bigger than most coppers, even. This one seemed to be grimacing slightly most of the time, or moving his eyes strangely – or was it just the effects of the drink on her – or him? She found herself giggling untypically.

35

'How was the pub crawl the other night?' she asked Duncan, trying to take control of her nerves.

'Oh, good fun,' he drawled. 'I was just showing the other chaps the geography. They didn't believe anything exists south of the river apart from hostile natives. Eddie's got a place down in Wapping, but Jeremy's still in traditional territory over in Chelsea.'

'Jeremy's the big one, head nearly touching the ceiling?'

'That's the one. Surname Heritage, as in our firm.'

'Oh, yes? He one of the directors, or something?'

'Not exactly.' The eyelids dropped as Duncan took a sip from his glass of red wine; Judy thought he seemed a good deal less drunk than the rest of them. All around her, people were swilling alcohol down their necks as if it was free. Perhaps it was, with Duncan paying.

'By the way,' he said. 'Your Clinton's a bit upset with me.'

'Why, what's the matter?' Judy suddenly felt sober again.

'Oh, nothing too important. He rang me up last night, you see, and we had a frank exchange of views, as they say.'

'What did you tell him? About tonight, I mean?'

'Only that it was a large, non-intimate social occasion and you were a free agent.'

This was largely what Judy had told Clinton herself, not entirely believing it. Duncan was smiling handsomely at her again, and she smiled back, accepted a refill of champagne from a bottle which had appeared in his hand as if by a conjuring trick, and found herself being introduced to a couple of people near them. The shouted conversation switched to Duncan's promotion, which was quite obviously the envy of all his colleagues. It meant that he would, he said, be 'dealing with more important clients, handling larger portfolios and making strategic investment decisions'. The others jabbered boisterously about medium-term buying opportunities and the timing of base rate reductions, and Judy let it wash over her head, glad that no one was making silly remarks about bang to rights and coming quietly.

An orange-haired, freckled-faced woman called Grania seemed to conceive a keen interest in her and started talking so rapidly that Judy was reminded of the squeaky gabbling of a tape on fast forward. She gradually worked out that Grania was an investment adviser and her interest stemmed from the fact that she had been

Duncan's girlfriend until recently. She was evidently trying to work out whether Judy was the next candidate, but seemed less worried about the possibility when she heard what Judy's job was. Judy felt suddenly resentful at the implication that you needed a cut-glass voice and a job with money before a man could find you interesting. Before Duncan, Grania confided, she'd also gone out with Eddie; Judy said acidly that it all sounded, well, a bit incestuous.

'Mm, yah,' said Grania, looking around the room rather sadly. 'Awful lot of shagging goes on sometimes.'

'Yes, well,' said Judy, awkwardly. 'Everyone does seem to be enjoying themselves.'

'You mean this bash tonight?' Grania's mouth showed a sudden bitter smile. 'Nobody knows if they'll have a job tomorrow, the way things are in the City these days. Orgy before the slaughter, if you ask me. Eat, drink and be merry, and all that.'

Judy escaped by heading for the ladies', and realised despite her own tipsiness that the level of drunkenness had climbed significantly. She noticed with a shock that a young man with a red face had pinned a girl into a wood-panelled corner, pulled up her dress at the back and stuck a hand down her knickers: she was wriggling and simpering as the hand kneaded her, and he was staring at the ceiling with glazed eyes, occasionally puckering up his features like a masseur encountering something unusual in his daily work. At a nearby table someone else was roaring and protesting as his face was forced slowly and inexorably forward into an ashtray by the tall man standing behind him, who was shouting something about bloody little squits, or possibly shits, or gits. Judy turned away, feeling the profound disorientation which goes with entering a strange country for the first time, and stepped gratefully through the door of the ladies', into familiar territory with universal rules.

It was a sudden haven of softly lit peace, and a comfortable-looking woman of about forty-five who was adjusting her make-up at the mirror turned to her with a smile.

'Hello, dear,' she said. 'Haven't met you before – you one of Duncan's?'

'You make it sound like a harem,' said Judy, looking in the mirror and seeing the hectic flush on her cheeks. 'He invited me, if that's what you mean.'

'Oh, I didn't mean anything, dear, no offence,' said the woman pleasantly, snapping shut her compact and pulling her dress straight round her matronly bust. 'It's just that I know that lot inside out. That's a nice little black dress, dear, lovely figure, too. No, there's nothing they could do to shock me any more.'

'It's certainly getting a bit torrid out there.' Judy tried a pout in the mirror, then remembered Clinton's remark about tropical fish and decided her lips were too thin.

The woman looked at her archly, struggling now with the belt on her skirt. 'You haven't seen nothing yet, my dear. They'll be like wild animals later on. Wild, oof, drunken, oof, beasts – and that's just the secretaries. No, I'm only joking, dear, really. But I'll be on my way home shortly, leave you young things to enjoy yourselves.'

For the first time that evening Judy felt she was with someone who talked the same dialect and shared some assumptions about life, and they continued chatting while Judy went into one of the cubicles, washed her hands and put on new lipstick. The woman was called Lynne and had been at the firm for fifteen years as receptionist and switchboard operator. She'd lived through the Big Bang, the era of golden hellos and canary-coloured Porsches, and then watched the blood and tears flow during Black Monday and the first round of shakeouts which followed. She knew all about Eddie and Grania and Grania and Duncan, and little seemed to escape her notice.

'I don't want to be indiscreet, dear,' she said, putting a hand inside her dress to struggle with the thick shoulder-straps on her bra. 'But that Duncan, you mark my words, he's going places. They may not be very nice places, but he's definitely going there. That's what this new job's all about. This used to be a nice traditional firm, gentlemen dealing with gentlemen. But when this Swiss lot took over all that went out of the window and the go-getters were brought in. Put a few of the old-style noses out of joint, I can tell you. Like poor old Mr Heritage, he soon got put out to grass. Come on, dear, you'd better get back to the fray.'

'I'm not sure how much more I can take – it's a menagerie out there.'

'Now, now, mustn't give in. And anyway, Duncan will be waiting for you. No, he's not as noisy as the rest, smooth is more the word, I'd say, but that boy's destined for higher things. He doesn't care what anyone thinks of him, see, so he doesn't mind what he does to them.'

'Fatal flaw, if you ask me.'

'Oh no, dear, that's the way to the top. D'you know, I think I've had a bit too much to drink. Anyway, there's nothing much going to stop him, I'm afraid.'

Two hours later, Lynne's words, made muzzy by alcohol, were echoing hazily inside Judy's head as she struggled and fought to get Duncan's hands off her body. One moment he'd been politely escorting her through a City alleyway he'd described as a short cut, the next he'd pushed her into a doorway, clamped his mouth on her neck like a vampire and started groping ferociously under her unbuttoned coat. He shoved one hand into the opening of her dress at the back, pulling off, one of the buttons, and was fiddling violently with the fastening of her bra. One of his knees was insistently trying to lever her legs apart, and although he wasn't as big as his friends he was wiry and strong. For a moment he raised his mouth from her neck, and she saw that his eyes were clamped shut, as if in pain.

'C'mahn,' he grunted urgently through gritted teeth, like someone trying to start a reluctant motor. 'C'mahn, c'mahn.'

'Duncan,' she gasped back. 'Get your bloody hands off me – what d'you think you're doing?'

'What am I doing?' he grunted, opening his eyes in surprise. 'Bonking a copper, that's what I'm doing. Pity you're not wearing your uniform.'

The crudeness and absurdity of it swept through Judy, and she started to giggle. Part of her felt this wasn't really happening, that if she just submitted to the groping, it would stop: he was now squeezing one of her breasts rhythmically, and a faint gargling noise was coming from his throat. But the stronger, more sober part of herself was outraged and humiliated. Other people were passing through the alley, craning their necks to see what was going on in the doorway.

'Look, just you get off me,' she said firmly, the source of the giggling suddenly dried up. 'Get off me or I'll, I'll . . .'

He pulled his head back from her, leaving his hand on her breast, and in the strange monochrome of the street lighting she focused hard and from close range on the bland face and pale eyes. His lips looked thin and livid, his breath was hot and sour, and she wondered why she'd ever thought she liked him.

'You'll what?' he said expressionlessly, and grinned, his mouth a wine-blackened crevice. 'Call the police? Kick me in the balls?'

Feeling his grip relaxing, she allowed herself to smile back. 'Both – only don't get too excited about it. Go on, let go.'

She gave him a shove and he half-staggered backwards into the narrow roadway, where he stood panting lightly and watching her, like a wary dog. Once she'd pulled her bra and dress into place, thinking sympathetically of Lynne's mighty adjustments and bucklings in the ladies', she buttoned her coat protectively up to the chin and stepped out of the doorway. Duncan immediately took her arm, confidently and possessively.

'OK,' he said, his smooth voice slightly slurred. 'We'll drive back to your place instead.'

She pulled her arm brusquely away from him. 'I've already told you, you're in no state to drive. And I haven't invited you to my place.'

'OK, we'll take a taxi to my place and do it there.'

Judy stopped suddenly in the middle of the alley and squared up to him. The intoxication and all trace of amusement had been fading rapidly inside her, and she was suddenly possessed by fury, tired but clear. This arrogant, hooded-eyed yuppie had taken her for a silly little tart, tried to fuck her against a wall, and now he thought he was going to continue the seduction elsewhere.

'Get lost!' she shouted, ignoring the ill-concealed grins on the faces of a passing couple. 'You go that way, Duncan' – she pointed the way they'd been going, as if she was directing traffic – 'and I'll go the other way. And don't you dare come near me again, you hear, or I'll bloody well kill you.'

She heard the threat echo from the tall, dark buildings and felt shocked by it as she turned and hurried away, heels tapping fast on the asphalt. Uttering threats to kill – a criminal offence: she knew it, but she didn't care. She luxuriated in feelings she could not remember having before – a murderous rage, which she knew took part of its force from disappointment. She heard Duncan call cheerily – mockingly? – that he'd see her at the club on Sunday night, and the rate surged into her throat and threatened to choke her. As she emerged at a near-run from the alley she bumped into a tall figure in a black coat who turned and protested poshly. She headed for Monument station, but as she came round a corner into Eastcheap a cab was passing with its yellow light on. The prospect of another dose of staggering and leering on the late-night Underground was too much for her, so she hailed the taxi and collapsed, panting, into a black-upholstered corner.

'Cheer up, sweetheart,' said the fat middle-aged cabbie kindly above the revving acceleration. 'Got boyfriend trouble?'

If a woman was upset, it had to be because of a man: the same old knee-jerk. The galling thing was that, this time, it was true. Judy wanted to snarl something sarcastic, but the hunched round back and flat cap of the driver reminded her of her dad and softened her.

'Not so much a boyfriend,' she muttered. 'More a total shit.'

'That right? Plenty more where he came from, darlin'.'

'I bloody well hope not.'

Judy clasped her hands together so her arms formed a loop inside her coat sleeves, giving her a feeling of safe enclosure and self-sufficiency. She sank back and listened to the comforting rattle of the diesel engine, watching the shapes and shadows of night-time London slip past outside the window. They moved out on to London Bridge, emerging from the huddled busyness of the City into the cooling space and open views offered by the river. She sat forward alertly to absorb the wider sky and the bright reflections of the riverside buildings on the dark water. But as they passed over the bridge's gentle hump, her sense of relief and escape was broken by a group of young people yelling and waving bottles. As she glanced back at them, wondering if they'd been at the party, she suddenly saw, downriver, above the warehouses of Wapping, the tower of Canary Wharf shafting dimly upwards through the gloom, topped by a lighted pyramid: the phallic symbol of Docklands.

She snorted with renewed disgust, remembering something hard pressing on her stomach as Duncan had forced her back into the doorway. Why had she ignored her instinct that his world was alien and unsavoury and allowed herself be taken in by him, by the handsome smile, the seductive manners, the smell of excitement, money, success? It was her feeling of shame, she suddenly realised, which would stop her playing it by the book – calling the police, making a complaint, seeing him charged with attempted rape. It would mean having to face the scorn behind her colleagues' sympathy, scorn that she'd been deceived by the glitter, failed to keep her feet on the ground. The police prided themselves, above all, on being nobody's fool, and she'd been well and truly taken in.

As they came off the bridge into the cluttered buildings and road junctions of Southwark, she tried to clear her mind by reading the advert on the back of the driver's compartment. 'You're a special client,' it told her. 'Demanding – discerning. You deserve the best, and that's what we plan to give you.' There was a picture of some posh tart with a Dallas hairdo and a snotty expression, and Judy suddenly understood why the kids on the Chaucer Estate kicked in the adverts at bus stops and ran screwdrivers along the sides of expensive cars.

CHAPTER 5

Daisy Clutter hurried dangerously down the stairs, like some teetering, stiff-legged bird, her face the colour of junket and her eyes rolling in panic. On the half-landing she stopped suddenly, clutched the metal banister, and vomited a little yellow puddle of breakfast on to the hairy brown carpet tiles. She hung on to the rail with both hands for a few seconds, panting, then wiped her mouth on the sleeve of her nylon housecoat and staggered down the next flight to the ground floor of the club. She had to stop again, soiling the blue nylon fur on her slippers, before she managed to lift the hinged flap in the reception counter, pass into the office, lift the telephone and dial 999. She didn't notice that the bottom drawer of the desk was hanging open.

A voice asked her which service she required. 'I want the bleeding coppers, what d'you think?' she gasped stickily. 'There's a geezer 'ere been done in.'

It was the Monday morning following the party in the Golden Vat, and Daisy had hoovered the bar and poked around the showers with a mop before encountering the scene in the gym. When the police car pulled up outside, wailing and flashing, she just managed to click open the security door for the two young policemen before slumping back on to a little wooden chair, sucking weakly at her untipped fag.

''S upstairs,' she whispered weakly, flapping her bony hand towards the interior of the building. 'In the bleedin' whatsit.'

The officers looked at each other, one of them lifting his eyes to heaven. The other bent over Daisy with his big-knuckled hands on his knees and managed, by asking loud and simple questions, to cajole her into revealing exactly where the whatsit was. The two of them charged along the ground floor and stamped up the stairs.

They pushed open the door of the gym, walked a few paces inside, and came to a stunned stop in front of a pool of black-red blood nearly the size of a bedsheet. In the middle of it, on his front, lay a man in shorts and a pink T-shirt, his head smashed flat under a stack of black metal weights in a machine which looked like a children's climbing frame embellished with wire ropes, pulleys and little padded seats. Bits of bone, brain and tufts of fair hair lay around the base of the stack and the shoulders of the dead man's T-shirt, which had soaked up some of the blood on the wooden floor like a wick. The message on the back of the shirt, in a flowing light blue script, read 'ciao Roma'. The shorts were red – the bright orangey red found on life jackets, which clashed sickeningly with the gluey liver-coloured blood. The two stood silently, like strangers in an empty church, and stared at the dreadful sight for half a minute.

'Well, go on, Mike,' said the one who'd raised his eyes to heaven. 'Feel his pulse.'

'Nah,' said the other, straining to stay equally impassive. 'I think he's dead already.'

'Couldn't have been an accident, could it?'

'Nah, someone topped him. Bit like a guillotine, only blunt.'

Detective Inspector Ron Slicer was equally impressed by the method of murder when he arrived at the club forty minutes later. While the scenes of crime team struggled into their green overalls and plastic gloves in the corridor outside, he walked into the gym as gingerly as into a baby's bedroom and stood looking at the corpse for several minutes, giving quiet little whistles and shakes of the head, like a builder inspecting a job before giving an estimate. A large foot wearing a shoe with a complicated sole pattern of stripes and roundels had trodden in the glutinous blood near the edge of the pool, and left one clear and one faint print on the blond wood between the body and the door. Near the mangled head, half in and half out of the blood, lay a three-foot long piece of metal about half an inch in diameter.

'Looks like a bit of that stuff they use on building sites,' he said to the sergeant who'd entered the gym behind him. 'Re-inforcing rod, or whatever.'

Detective Sergeant Stone leaned forward with difficulty and peered at the object. He had a round, bald head, a puddingy face, and a voice which emerged tired and flat from the thickness of his neck.

'I dunno,' he said. 'Looks a bit like a stair rod to me.'

Slicer fixed him contemptuously with his little black eyes. Stone's fondness for do-it-yourself was the office joke: he was known to have a model railway in his loft and several remote-controlled fountains, lit with coloured lights, in his garden.

'Well,' said Slicer. 'I've no doubt forensic will tell us in due course. Better leave it there till the pathologist has seen it. Who's coming down?'

'Prof. Binder.'

Slicer rolled his eyes like a punch-drunk boxer.

'Christ. I hope he was off the sauce last night. And who's the Super coming down from the Area Major Investigation Team?'

'Manningbird.'

A grin seemed to crawl out from under Slicer's sleek black moustache.

'That's better,' he said smugly. 'Pushover.'

The scenes of crime men came in, looking like a team of surgeons about to perform an operation. Slicer gave them a few instructions while a photographer began taking shots of the body from unalluring angles. Then he strolled off into the recesses of the gym with the smile still playing round his crooked mouth, studying the other blue- or orange-painted machines which stood around like contraptions in some high-technology torture chamber. He tapped the weight stacks with his foot, pressed the little padded seats with his fingertips, and tweaked the various metal cables as if he were testing the tension of a fanbelt.

Each weight stack consisted of up to twenty rectangular blocks of metal an inch thick, each with three round holes in it. The two outer holes allowed the weights to slide up and down two vertical chrome bars, which were each welded to the top and base of the machine's frame. The lifting mechanism was a wire rope, one end of which ran upwards and then downwards over pulleys to various handles of complicated shapes. The other end of the cable was attached to a two-foot chrome plunger with holes in it, fixed at its top end to the highest weight in the stack, and extending downwards through the central hole in all the lower weights. So if you pulled a handle down or raised a bar or pushed a padded panel, at least one weight in the stack would slide up and down

45

the guide bars, pulled by the cable, and the plunger would glide in and out of the hole in the lower weights without moving them. If you slotted a six-inch metal rod through little grooves between the weights and through the matching hole in the central plunger, all the weights above that point would be raised. And once you had about two-thirds of the weights in a stack attached to the plunger in this way, and pulled them a couple of feet up the guide bars, a potentially lethal space was created between them and the remaining weights beneath. It was a space eight inches wide and a foot high, just the right size for a human head – provided that a human was foolish enough to put his head there.

'Here, Ron,' called Stone, who was peering closely at a gleaming black-and-silver contraption garnished with round pads, like huge rolled bandages. 'Listen to this: "Warning: you assume a risk of injury using this type of equipment," blah blah blah. "To reduce chance of injury, keep head and limbs clear of weights and moving parts at all times. Don't be careless, stay alert. Maintain at least a three-inch clearance between head and weight stacks in bench work." '

'Does it really say that, Jim?' murmured Slicer noncommittally. 'Sure it's not a stair rod?'

'Yeah. This poor sod had a bad attack of not staying alert, I reckon. Shows what happens when you don't follow the rules, eh?'

Slicer glanced at him with distaste.

'Come over here a sec, would you, Jim?' he murmured, sitting down on a kind of chair with a back which moved away and downwards, lifting a stack of weights, when you pressed your spine against it.

Stone shambled over, hands deep in the pockets of his oatmeal-coloured overcoat, and stood next to the machine as Slicer heaved backwards, lifting most of the weights in the stack and holding them nearly two feet off the ground, his face going dark with the effort. With a forefinger, he gestured hurriedly at the hole in the stack.

'Go on, Jim, stick yer bonce in there,' he gasped breathlessly. Stone threw him a sceptical glance.

'Not bloody likely,' he muttered.

'Well watch how it's done, then.'

Slicer jack-knifed forward suddenly, his face nearly hitting his knees, and the weights crashed downwards with a noise like a car accident, shaking the floor and bringing nervous shouts of protest from everyone in the gym.

'Even your skull wouldn't take too kindly to that, now, would it?' asked Slicer, ignoring the complaints and trying to control his heavy breathing.

'You want to watch it, man of your age,' said Stone, his little porcine eyes fixed cannily on Spicer. 'Give yourself a hernia, ruin a promising career.'

Slicer's career was a matter of some ill-feeling in the CID in Surrey Docks division. At the age of forty-two, he'd just come from one of the Home Counties forces and walked into a job coveted by many home-grown Metropolitan Police detectives. The promotion was largely the result of his successful handling of a couple of sensational and well-publicised rapes just before his move, but word had it he'd fouled up on a case about ten years ago when a disgruntled former pupil had tried to blow up some minor public school. He and his senior officer had apparently spent a lot of time barking up the wrong tree, and DS Stone had discreetly asked one of his detective constables to dig up the details, just in case they came in useful some time.

'Nonsense,' said Slicer airily, standing up and running his hands over his neatly cut black hair. 'Perfect condition, me.'

'There's only one problem,' said Stone.

'Oh, yeah? What's that?'

'If your murderer's busting a gut like you were, holding up one of those stacks of weights, there's no way he can shove the victim's head in the hole. He'd have had to prop 'em up with something like that stair rod. Or whatever it is. And it would still be hard to get his head in the hole.'

'Good point, Jim, good point,' said Slicer with a patronising grimace which revealed a rodential set of incisors. 'But there might be more than one murderer. Two, for instance, or three. Or the murderer might have used the reinforcing rod to bash him over the nut before feeding him into the machine, so to speak. Then chocks away, and the sky turns red.'

'Yeah, all this bleedin' blood around,' muttered Stone, looking over at the corpse, which now had three green-overalled men kneeling around it like worshippers. 'The bloke must have been covered in it.'

47

'This is something we just might be looking for in a suspect,' said Slicer sarcastically. 'Ah, here's Binder. Let's see what he has to say.'

An unkempt-looking man with a slight stoop and a chaotic shock of white hair had just walked into the gym carrying a well-used brown leather case. The scenes of crime officers got to their feet and backed off in a respectful group, folding their hands, as the Professor advanced hesitantly towards the body. He paused occasionally to stoop and peer at it interrogatively, as if making sure that a skittish pet was not going to take fright and scamper off.

'Morning, Professor,' said Slicer heartily, as if they were meeting on a golf course. 'And how are you today?'

Binder looked at Slicer and shook the proffered hand without enthusiasm. His eyes were pale and mournful from gazing into the livid depths of too many eviscerated bodies, and his hand, though trembling slightly, was unexpectedly dry and robust, like a carpenter's.

'Well, Inspector,' he said gloomily. 'This seems to be a most unusual cause of death. What you chaps might call a bit of a sickener, eh? But you seem to have a fair bit of evidence, at least.'

He nodded towards the two gory footprints around which the scenes of crime officers had drawn large squares in chalk. Slicer gave a flippant little jerk of the head.

'Knowing our luck they probably belong to the two plods who got in here first,' he said. 'Anyway, what d'you make of it, eh? Very nasty the way that eye's jumped out of his skull like that.'

Binder walked slowly round the body and the machine in a wide circumference, the men in green overalls shuffling back to give him room. He was wearing strong brown shoes, crumpled grey flannels, a tweed jacket with frayed edges and leather elbows, and a blotched khaki tie with which he played as he walked, occasionally whirling the end of it round like a tassel. Finally he moved in close to the machine and peered at the little red numbers on the stack of weights, the tip of the tie swinging like a pendulum just above the mangled skull. Then he took hold of the body's upper arm between thumb and forefinger, testing its movement. The dead fingers dragged an inch or two through the blood, leaving a trail like some crawling creature. Slicer, hands in pockets, rocked impatiently on his heels.

'Well,' said Binder eventually, signalling the scenes of crime men back to the job as he walked back to Slicer, shaking his head dolefully. 'It's a new one on me. Human ingenuity in devising the means of death never ceases to amaze. Rivalled only by ingenious means of procuring sexual satisfaction.'

'Yes, well, we won't go into that just now,' said Slicer, his moustache twitching. 'What d'you reckon went on in here?'

Binder cocked his snowy head on one side and screwed up his sad eyes.

'Well, dead about twelve hours, I reckon. No obvious signs of struggle, either on the body or in the surrounding area. But somehow a fit and strong young man has been forced under a column of weights which would have needed considerable strength to hold up.'

'Yeah, that's why we thought that metal bar had been used to stun him first, or to hold up the weights while he was forced underneath.'

'Mmm.' Binder looked over his shoulder at the sprawled body again. 'I'd incline to the former. There's sixty kilograms in that stack of weights, and the rod is what, about three feet long. I think the weights must have fallen from the very top position – a drop of about four feet – for that sort of weight to crush the skull. As you'll remember from schoolboy physics, force equals half the product of mass times the square of velocity.'

'Come again, Prof?'

Binder gave Slicer a mildly reproving look.

'You don't remember? What it means is, the velocity of approach, which increases with the height of fall, is the crucial aspect in causing damage. Or, to illustrate it in a more familiar way, the further the boot swings before it hits the face, the more damage it does.'

'I know that, thanks, Prof. But surely that sort of weight would crush the skull falling from just a couple of feet?'

Binder held up a trembling stubby finger and cocked his head.

'Ah, Inspector, the human body is always more resilient than you think. All sorts of things have been known to just bounce off it – buses, bullets, the lot. Nobody could quote you exact facts and figures because it's rather difficult, not to say against the law,

49

to do realistic experiments on live humans. But if you don't believe me, try dropping a few weights on an inverted twelve-inch flowerpot in your back garden – it'll take more than you think to break it.'

Slicer, who didn't have, and didn't want, either a flowerpot or a back garden, looked at the pathologist as if he'd just suggested child abuse or necrophilia. Binder smiled mildly back, his mouth emitting the faintest after-odour of whisky.

'We'll do the PM at Tennis Street in the morning,' he continued. 'I don't think there's much doubt about the cause of death, but there might be some marks or bruising to indicate what went on beforehand. Or some interesting organic conditions, or illegal substances floating around in the blood. You never know.'

'Indeed you don't, with the so-called modern generation,' said Slicer with feeling. 'OK, Prof. I'll leave it in your capable hands for now, then, and see you at the PM. All that liver and bacon, eh? I'd better go and see if the owner of this place has arrived yet – dozy bugger.'

CHAPTER 6

Judy had spent a dismal weekend trying to stop dwelling on the episode with Duncan. She'd contacted Clinton on Saturday, and he'd reluctantly agreed to meet her in the afternoon. They sat under the harsh strip lights in a hamburger place near his home, surrounded by shouting teenagers and whingeing children, while she told him briefly about the party and swore she'd never be seeing Duncan again. She left out the attack in the alley, partly through shame and partly because she didn't want him getting too angry; but he only grunted noncommittally, refused to look her in the eye, and stalked out without any arrangement to meet again. It wasn't like him, and it was what she'd always feared. She'd watched TV, numbing herself, from six until midnight on Saturday.

She'd hoped that coming to work would snap her out of it with some sort of action or interest, but there was nothing very exciting mentioned on early morning parade. Then, when she had been on duty for nearly an hour, she heard the first traffic on her personal radio about a murder in Rotherhithe. She reported in and offered to help, but the harassed communications officer said they had everyone they needed and would she kindly get off the air so he could deal with more important messages. She stopped at a call box on the corner of Jamaica Road to ring the home beat office for more news of the killing, and as she waited for an answer Winston's battered brown BMW, with its twin-eared bunny logo on the back and Winston and Wayne inside it, lurched out of a side road and headed towards Tower Bridge, making a noise like a tractor and producing coils of blue smoke. She made a mental note to check Winston's MOT certificate at the next opportunity, and wondered why a pair who kept such late hours should be up and about so early on a Monday morning.

It was the languid voice of Fred Beans, known for his idleness and occasional shafts of wit, which eventually came on the line and told her that the murder was at the Docklands Squash and Weights Club and the lethal weapon was a pile of weights on a machine in the gym. He didn't spare her the details, and for a moment Judy was silent with shock.

'Christ, are you sure?' she said weakly. 'I'm a member of that place, believe it or not. Any idea who the victim is?'

'No positive ID yet, apparently. Just white male, twenties or early thirties, medium height, athletic build.'

'God, that could be anyone, Fred – about half the membership is young, white and fit.'

'Yeah? Well this one's what you might call dead fit.'

'Give it a rest, will you?' said Judy, leaning her cheek against the cold window of the phone booth to dispel the hot feeling of nausea which had invaded her. 'It might be someone I know.'

'Sorry, Judy. Anyway, they don't need any of us lot, apparently, because the Territorial Support Group are out there tidying up and helping the CID.'

'And insulting the public as usual, I expect.'

'Which is no more than the public deserves. Bye, Judy. Hope you keep your breakfast down.'

Judy tried to keep her mind off the mental picture of a head mangled in a stack of weights as she made her way shakily to her next appointment, wondering if she'd been right to give up her ambitions to join the CID. A murder at the club, in the very gym where she'd stood and watched people as they sweated and grimaced and admired themselves in the mirrors, and here she was flat-footing it around one of the toughest estates in inner London, trying to pretend she was some kind of village bobby. She tried to think positive thoughts about community relations and bridge-building as she headed for her meeting with the Revd Simon Bird, an unsmiling young man with a blond beard who wanted some 'police input' for the youth club in his church hall. He meant someone to stop the little buggers throwing pool balls through the windows and pulling the washbasins off the walls.

Within an hour of Daisy's grisly discovery at eight thirty that Monday morning, the club had been taken over by the police and their paraphenalia. Large officers from the TSG were looping

52

tapes between lampposts to keep people away, and every few minutes saw the arrival of another white van with opaque windows or another unmarked car full of slightly overweight men wearing sharpish suits and ties. An ambulance stood outside the club in the watery sunshine with its rear doors open, exposing its stretchers, oxygen cylinders and piles of red blankets like bad omens; but the body was still lying in its blood being studied by the pathologist and the forensic team, and there was nothing for the ambulance crew to do except beat their way through the cloud of cigarette smoke and vomit fumes and comfort Daisy in her state of shock.

As Slicer came down into the main lobby of the club a wiry, harassed-looking man was hurrying towards him. It was the owner, John Whale, looking highly agitated. He'd had to go through three leaden interrogations by suspicious PCs before being allowed into his own premises, and hadn't been told anything in return about what was going on. When Slicer described the nasty murder committed under his roof, he put his head in his hands, gripping it hard as if testing a melon for ripeness, and groaned. Slicer looked impatiently at the tufts of grey hair sticking through Whale's fingers as he squeezed his skull.

'We'll need to identify him, but there's not much left of his face,' said Slicer, with breezy vindictiveness. Whale groaned harder and staggered sideways into the bar area, where he collapsed into one of the blue-covered seats. Slicer followed him, still talking.

'At a guess he'd be about thirty, medium height, well built, short blond hair, wearing bright red shorts, poncy pink T-shirt and trainers. Any ideas?'

Whale raised a face drained of blood but filling with disgust, and looked sideways at Slicer, slowly smacking his lips and swallowing ominously.

'That's a description of about a third of the members. Jesus, I feel sick.'

Slicer sighed impatiently and stared out of the window as Whale staggered off into the men's changing rooms. Stone had already trodden in one of Daisy's puddles. This guy hadn't even seen the corpse and he was heaving. Through the window Slicer saw Bill Gibbons, the bespectacled crime reporter from the *South London Press*, skirting the police tape like a crab, squinting at the building, notebook in hand. Slicer was already familiar with Gibbons's fast response time and suspected that he listened in to police radio.

'There's a key in the door of one of the lockers in there,' said Whale weakly, returning from the changing rooms and crumpling into a chair again. 'Must be his, I suppose.'

Slicer left Whale to regain control of his insides, walked over to the changing room, pushed through the door and stood looking around. It was a room about forty feet by twenty, with yellow metal lockers round the walls, wooden benches running down the middle, and some high frosted-glass windows. At the far end was a metal spiral staircase leading upwards, and through an alcove on the right were the white-tiled showers and washbasins. A sour, acidic smell drifted from it, and Slicer wrinkled his nose, snapping on the strip lights.

The single key in the line of lockers stood out like a fingerpost. Slicer walked over, eyeing the locker warily as if it might contain another piece of crushed anatomy. He levered the door open with a fingertip, and the large number tag attached to the key swung and scraped against the metal.

On the shelf of the locker there were a pair of black Levis, some red underpants, and a dark blue sweatshirt with Columbia State University printed on the front in white. One pocket of the pair of jeans contained some small change, the other was empty. There was no coat or jacket, and no wallet or bunch of keys. A black sports bag with 'Head' on the side in gold letters lay on the floor of the locker, and beneath it was a pair of expensive loafers with blue woollen socks tucked inside them. As Slicer pulled out the bag and put it on the bench to go through it, there was a clanking noise from the spiral staircase and a little man in overalls and plastic gloves came down it. He had protruding eyes and a receding chin.

'I hope you're not disturbing things too much, Inspector,' he said in a squeaky voice. Slicer recognised him as one of the scientists from the Forensic Science Laboratory, gave him a withering look and grunted a greeting. Normally the scientists stayed safely in their lab where they couldn't get in the way, but everyone seemed to be moving in on the act today. Slicer continued laying the contents of the bag on the bench: a white towel, a plastic bottle of herbal shampoo, some talcum powder, a deodorant stick, a plastic soap container, a tablet of rose-coloured soap, and a crumpled copy of an out-of-date *Times* Business News.

'Sod all,' he declared grumpily. Bug-eyes bent over the bag, discovered an inside pocket, came up with a packet of condoms and a couple of scuffed business cards, and gave Slicer a withering look in return.

'Clearly a man who goes equipped,' he said.

'Or comes prepared,' muttered Slicer, taking the packet and opening it. 'Only two left – I wonder which young lady had the benefit of the other one – or gent, for that matter. Oh well, he won't be needing those any more.'

He tossed the packet back into the bag and read aloud from the card: ' "Duncan Stock, investment executive, Banks and Heritage, 19 Gracechurch Square." A member of the yuppie classes, it would seem. You wouldn't have guessed from the clobber, except for that pair of fancy shoes. I'll just show this to the proprietor, if you don't mind.'

Outside in the bar, Whale grimaced when Slicer showed him the card. 'Christ, is that who it is?'

'Know him?'

Whale nodded. 'Joined about a year ago – lives in one of the new blocks a bit further downriver. Some sort of job in the City. Nice enough bloke, from the little I knew of him. Had this funny way of blinking his eyes. Christ, who'd want to do him in?'

Slicer leaned closer and talked fast and intensely at the shrinking proprietor, jabbing a forefinger at various parts of his thorax.

'It seems pretty strange to me, Mr Whale, that anyone had the opportunity to do him in in a place like this. This must have happened during opening hours, with other people in the building and the place lit up like a football pitch. There must have been a struggle and a fair bit of noise before a strong young man like that submitted to having his head shoved into a stack of weights, but nobody seems to have noticed anything until the next morning. So perhaps you could explain the set-up here a bit. Or, in plain English, what the bloody hell's going on?'

Whale looked at Slicer and blinked anxiously. There was a strand of what looked like Shredded Wheat in the grey corner of his mouth.

'Well, yesterday was Sunday. The place closes at nine thirty and there aren't usually many people in. It's always the quietest night of the week and we only have one member of staff here. Duncan could have been in the gym by himself for a long time, and that upstairs corridor is really quite cut off from the rest of the building.'

Slicer leaned backwards to take himself out of the range of Whale's polluted breath.

'D'you keep some kind of record of everyone who comes in and out – members and guests? Computer system, anything like that?'

Whale shook his head.

'So who can tell me who else was in here last night?'

'Sharon – Sharon Bunnie. She was on duty last night. I'll get you her address and phone number from the office.'

'Yes, and get me Mr Stock's home address while you're there. Someone might have been visiting him before or after he became indisposed.'

Stone appeared at Slicer's side, looking excited and breathing noisily after a quick descent of the stairs.

'Window's been forced at the end of that upstairs corridor, Ron,' he reported. 'At the far end, past the viewing gallery for the squash courts. Someone just stuck in a jemmy and broke the lock on it. They're trying to get some prints off it now.'

'See anything outside the window?'

'No, but it must be pretty quiet at night down that end of the building – well away from the road, up against the riverside path. And the window's not as high as you'd think – you could stand on someone's shoulders and reach it.'

'Mm,' said Slicer, showing him Duncan's card. 'And there was no jacket or wallet in young Dunky's locker – just this and a packet of rubbers. My guess is that a City type like this wouldn't go far without something well padded in his pocket.'

Stone reflected for a moment, his little eyes narrowing. 'Yeah,' he said eventually. 'But you don't go around sticking someone's head in a weights machine when you're nicking a wallet with a few quid in it, do you? The villains round here are as thick as pig shit, but they're not that thick.'

'I dunno, Jim. I dunno. You've seen the headlines, you've worked on the cases: "Mugger threatens baby with knife". Happens every couple of weeks in this city. Don't underestimate those scumbags out there – you should know that, you're a local lad. Anything else from upstairs?'

Stone gave him a resentful look and sniffed.

'They've just bagged up that rod. Iron bar, or whatever. It's got some sharp edges on it so I've asked forensic to check for a second source of blood.'

Slicer gave him a hard stare.

'Look, if anyone had cut themselves on it there'd be drops of blood on the floor or the door handle or whatever. Any sign of that?'

'Not so far,' said Stone sulkily, like an eager schoolboy who'd been slapped down. 'But they're working on it.'

Slicer relented.

'All right, Jim. Worth a try, I suppose. I dunno, you and your bleeding stair rod. What's the problem now, Mr Whale, someone pinched your Dinky toys?'

Whale was striding back from the office, looking less pale and more angry, holding out a slip of paper with Sharon's name and address on it.

'We've been robbed as well,' he declared indignantly. 'Someone's broken open the drawer in the office and had the whole weekend's takings. Three nights. Hundreds of pounds, probably. And d'you think people are going to come back here after all this? Are they hell. I'm ruined, you know that? This place is finished.'

'You should have had it alarmed, then, shouldn't you?' said Slicer indifferently, glancing at the paper and turning to Stone with a sly smile. Whale opened and closed his mouth helplessly.

'You see, Jim? It's not just a few quid from a wallet after all. Let's have a quick look. Then I think we'd better go and talk to Miss Bunnie Rabbit about all this, don't you?'

Judy promised the Revd Bird that she'd put up a notice at the station asking if there was any officer who was interested in coming down and supervising the basketball and table tennis. She omitted to tell him that there was a fat chance of getting any response because most of her colleagues were too eager to get back to leafy Streatham or into the boozer after their hard day's work. They talked for a minute about the murder, which he'd just heard about on the news and described as 'rather exotic'.

57

'Apparently he worked in the City and was called Stock,' said the clergyman as he gave her a hard little farewell handshake.

'What?' she stared at him, feeling suddenly winded.

'Yes . . . rather appropriate, in a tragic sort of way, of course. *Sic transit* . . . I say, are you all right?'

Unable to speak, Judy made a vague gesture at him and stumbled out into the street and away, suddenly finding it a strange effort to draw each breath into her lungs. Once round the corner, she stopped and leant against some rusty railings to try to absorb the shock, but for a while she seemed to lose her capacity to think or feel. A couple of young men with hands thrust deep into the pockets of their bomber jackets walked past, looking at her warily as if she were a beggar or a tramp.

She took a slow detour to the riverside and sat on a wooden bench in front of some half-built houses, staring at the maroon-painted warehouses over in Wapping, the first foothold of the yuppies in docklands. The Thames looked like a bright ribbon of molten metal, bouncing the sunlight painfully into her eyes, and the seagulls were screaming and swooping over a chain of rubbish barges on their way down to Rainham. She thought of the case where they'd searched the tips down there until they found the various bits of a chopped-up body.

She'd last spoken to Duncan two days earlier, on Saturday morning. He'd phoned her to apologise for the events of Thursday night, saying it was the first time for years that he'd been so drunk; but his tone had been so cocky that she'd immediately seen red and put the phone down on him. Deep within her now, she became aware of an atavistic sense of satisfaction: the would-be rapist had got what he deserved. A simple Old Testament justice had been applied. She remembered how, for half an hour last Thursday night, she'd have happily done it herself. Now the thought crossed her mind that some other victim of Duncan's gropings, or a husband or boyfriend, had killed Duncan. That ginger-haired woman at the party, perhaps?

But swamping any sense of satisfaction was a growing feeling of dread: someone she knew, someone whose warm body she had watched, touched and fought with a few days ago, was actually dead. This was a normal day, she was sitting by the Thames, the pubs were just opening, aeroplanes were passing overhead, a workman was laughing on the building site behind her, but

Duncan was a piece of meat with a flat head in a mortuary somewhere. She felt as if she was trying to swallow a great cold stone. She was familiar with hot-blooded, usually drunken, hatred and violence among the people she dealt with professionally – the bottlings in pubs, the stabbings in street fights and robberies, and the punching-in of women's faces in cold, crumbling council flats. But Duncan was a paid-up member of the white professional middle classes, cautious, prosperous, protected, insulated by thick layers of money from the raw, volatile world of violent criminality. Such things didn't happen to people like him – until, like now, out of the blue, they did.

What made it worse was the deliberate, almost mocking dimension to the murder. Sticking someone's head in one of those stacks of weights had a ritual quality, as if he'd offended against the code of some secret society and been punished according to a bizarre formula. She thought of the oaths of the Masons and the little black attaché cases she'd seen senior officers carrying out of the station on Lodge nights. She thought of the Italian banker who'd been found hanged under Blackfriars Bridge ten years ago.

She began to feel faint, and leant forward with her head between her knees for a few minutes, drawing steady breaths and trying to empty her mind of conspiracy and mutilation. Then she forced herself to get up and set off for her appointment with Mr Pendry, chairman of the local Neighbourhood Watch committee, recently retired from cleaning carpets. He was a former Navy man with bristly black hair, wild eyes and tattooed forearms, and he was always up to date with local atrocities and brimming with simple responses and violent solutions. Judy wondered grimly what he'd make of this one, which by Rotherhithe standards was just a shade out of the ordinary.

CHAPTER 7

It was nearly noon, and Slicer and Stone were driving along Creek Road towards Greenwich in their unmarked red Cavalier. Twenty detectives were on the case now, and an incident room was being set up at Surrey Docks police station. One team was interviewing people who lived or worked near the club, three men had gone to Duncan's office, two more had gone round to his flat, and one was trying to trace his parents and family. Slicer had told young Gibbons and a local radio reporter that he was keeping an open mind at this stage but it was almost certainly a murder inquiry linked with the robbery. He'd kept Duncan's identity and some of the gory details back, but the news bulletins were already calling it 'savage and motiveless'.

They passed a bridge where an inscription of 'Tories Out' had resisted several attempts at erasure, and stopped at the traffic lights at Deptford Church Street. A couple of black youths on the pavement, one with a huge tam on his head in Rastafarian colours, grinned and waved at them facetiously. The two detectives moved nothing but their eyes.

'Friends of yours?' murmured Slicer from the passenger seat.

Stone shook his globular head. 'Bleedin' toe-rags, can't tell one from another. Probably felt their filthy collars for them, some time or another.'

Stone's blotchy complexion darkened and his mouth was compressed for a moment. A little later a smell like rotting meat spread through the car.

'Christ, Jim, that you?' As Slicer screwed up his face, the sharp front teeth appeared for a moment beneath his sleek moustache.

'Sorry, guv,' murmured Stone smugly, gazing impassively through the windscreen. 'Tandoori nights, if you know what I mean. Up to the right here, then fourth left, wasn't it?'

'It was, and for Christ's sake control yourself while we're talking to this girl. Lives with her parents – respectable family.'

The address was in a ten-year-old council development, where the houses were built traditionally in brick, with pitched roofs in imitation slate and proper lead flashing. They were eccentrically arranged, joined to each other in unlikely places, and surrounded by little alleyways, dead ends and unexpected flights of steps. Stone pressed the bell, his little eyes running with enthusiasm over the imitation lead-mullioned windows, and the panelled and varnished front door with brass hinges and a spy hole.

'Right to buy,' he murmured. 'Good old Mrs T.'

The heavy wooden door was opened by a slim woman with thin, fluffy hair and slippers. Slicer flashed his warrant card and did the introductions, and she led them anxiously into the front room to await her daughter. No, it wasn't anything her Sharon had done, they reassured her.

When Sharon came in, Slicer was sitting on the sofa looking with wary distaste at the bulky hindquarters of Stone, who was bending over to study some Capo di Monte ornaments in a glass display cabinet. Her short brown hair was tousled, and she was wearing a cocky expression and a dark blue shell suit, which rustled as she moved. When she heard there'd been someone killed at the gym her face seemed to collapse and she sat down suddenly in an armchair.

'Duncan Stock, his name is – you know him?' asked Slicer.

Sharon nodded and her blue eyes grew wider: ''Course I do, dunn I? 'E was in there last night. Bleedin' 'eck. I don't believe this – what on erf 'appened?'

'His head was crushed in a stack of weights.'

Sharon looked at him disbelievingly, her mouth hanging open to reveal tiny, perfect teeth. Then she shook her head, as if to dislodge a bad dream.

'I've told John those bleedin' things are dangerous. Which one was it – which stack?'

'Er, it was the one with a wide handle dangling down from the other end of the cable, on one side of that machine with lots of doo-dahs on it. Forget the name.'

Sharon was still shaking her head as she unwrapped some gum. 'Yeah, I know the one. Lat pulls. Nasty.'

'What pulls?'

'Lats – latissimi dorsi, sort of muscles in yer back,' said Sharon, chewing hard now, and giving Slicer's body a look which suggested his lats weren't up to much. 'I always fort that stack was dodgy – it's easy to get too close to it, and the weights go up higher than most. It makes like a sort of 'atchway you could stick your foot in – or your 'ead, I suppose. You reckon someone did it to 'im, or did 'e do it to 'imself?'

'Why, did you think he was suicidal?'

''Im? Nah, never. Finks too much of 'imself. Fort, I should say. Quietish, not as noisy as some, but a right big 'ead. You could tell. Some people come and keep fit and work out 'cos they love the sport, know what I mean? But wiv 'im, it was like vanity. I reckon, anyway.'

'So we've found his first enemy already.' Slicer flashed a clever little smile.

'Who, me? Can't say I liked 'im much. There's plenty much worse than 'im, though. Rude, arrogant, treat yer like a skivvy. Was the place all full of blood, then, or wot?'

'Fair amount. Got a strong stomach, have you? The rest of the staff have been puking up at the very mention.'

'Me? Nah, I worked down the 'ospital one year. Auxiliary. See it all down in casualty. Legs off, the lot. Poor old Duncan, eh? Not that bad a bloke, really. Shouldn't speak ill.'

Stone was still studying the pictures and ornaments, inclining his head from time to time like a quizzical terrier, and seemed unaware that anyone else was in the room. Slicer took out his notebook, cleared his throat, and started questioning Sharon about the previous night.

There'd been hardly anyone in after about seven thirty: Clinton Pink and Sean Patrick had come in for a game, Christine and Alexis were in for a sauna around the same time, and then there was Duncan, who came in most Sunday nights for a quick session in the gym. If there'd been anyone else, she'd have known, because they couldn't have got in without ringing the bell and waiting for her to press the button which opened the security door. Sean had changed straight after the game and had a drink, and she'd chatted to him at the bar. Then she'd been called over to the reception desk by the two women, who gave in their locker keys and towels and left. Clinton had come down later in his squash gear and joined Sean in the bar for a drink. Then Sean had left as well and Clinton had gone in to change. By the time everyone had gone it was nearly 9.30, so she'd cashed up, put the takings in the bottom drawer of the office, switched the lights out, locked up and left.

'Didn't you hear anything? Those weights must have made a hell of a crash, even if Duncan's head was acting as a shock absorber.'

'There's always loads of bangin' an' crashin' up there, but downstairs is too far away to 'ear it. 'Sides, there's the music in there, too, really loud.'

Slicer nodded, narrowing his eyes and watching her closely.

'I see,' he said. 'Well, let's trying something else. Someone got in through an upstairs window, broke the drawer open and legged it with the takings. Know anything about that?'

Sharon gawped again; the wad of grey gum could be seen, stuck to her molars like a multiple filling. 'Wot, you reckon whoever nicked the cash did Duncan in as well? Bleedin' 'eck, nuffin's safe round 'ere, is it? They get in frew that window at the end, above the courts?'

Stone suddenly turned from studying the carriage clock on the mantelpiece. The strain of his bending and peering had left his face with pale and dark patches, like the surface of a quiche.

'You haven't been telling any of your mates about where the cash goes at the weekend, have you?' he said aggressively. Sharon did a shocked double-take, and blinked; Slicer closed his eyes in martyrdom.

'Don't take any notice of my colleague,' he said wearily. 'He's in a hurry to solve the crime, that's all. Respectable citizen, horrible murder, everyone a bit edgy, eh? Now, then, let's get a bit more about the victim's precise movements.'

He'd arrived about quarter to nine, said Sharon, carrying his black bag and wearing an expensive-looking brown leather jacket. He'd produced his membership card from his wallet (Slicer made a note about the jacket and wallet, smiling privately) and handed it to Sharon in return for a locker key. She'd warned him that she was closing in three quarters of an hour, and he'd said he was just having a quick work-out and wouldn't be long.

'So where were the other two blokes when Duncan arrived?'

Sharon studied the marmalade-coloured carpet before replying. She was tighter and more sullen since Stone's intervention.

'Sean was in the bar, and Clinton – well, 'e must've been in the gym or sumfing 'cos he didn't come for a drink till a bit later. That's wot a lot of players do – well, good ones like Clint, anyway. They 'ave a quick session on a bike or sumfing, after a game.'

'So Clinton and Duncan would have been in the gym at the same time?'

'Well, yeah, I s'pose so, could've been. Depends 'ow long it took Duncan to change and get in there.'

'Did they know each other?'

'Yeah, I fink they 'ad the odd game together.'

'Good relationship?'

Sharon hesitated a moment, then shrugged warily. ''Ow would I know?'

Slicer paused and exchanged impassive but significant looks with Stone, whose round face was clenched in concentration.

'All right then, how did Clinton seem when he came down from the gym for a drink with Sean? What was he wearing?'

''E was wearin' 'is red track suit – I remember seein' 'im pullin' it on as 'e came down the stairs. 'E was a bit quiet, bit pissed off, to be honest. Don't fink it meant anyfing, but normally 'e's a lovely bloke, always cheerful.'

'And this Mr Clinton Pink, would I be right in thinking that he's a coloured gentleman?' Slicer asked the mock-polite question in a light, noncommittal voice, looking at Stone with one eyebrow slightly raised.

Sharon nodded: 'Yeah, black geezer. 'Ere, you trying to put a frame round Clinton, or wot?'

'We'll ask the questions, thank you, Miss Bunnie. Only a few more.'

'Charmin',' said Sharon, bridling and blinking.

'Cut the clever remarks,' said Stone. 'Come on, when did the women leave?'

She told them sulkily that Christine and Alexis must have left a few minutes before Clinton came down from the gym. They'd handed in their keys and gone home without staying for a drink, complaining they'd have to be up early next day. Then Sean must have gone about a quarter past nine, and Clinton ten minutes later, still looking surly and hardly saying goodbye. She'd taken keys from both of them and handed them back their membership cards.

64

'So where did you think Duncan had got to?'

'I s'pose I thought 'e'd gone a bit earlier.'

'What, after Sean but before Clinton?'

'Er, yeah, suppose so.'

'What made you think he'd gone?'

'I asked Clinton when 'e went if anyone was still in the changin' room, and 'e said no, 'e was the last.'

'Yes, but Duncan could still have been in the gym.'

'Yeah, well, that's what I fort. But when I went up to see, the lights were all out.'

'You went up? How far?'

'Just to the 'alf landin', that's all, where I could see the lights were out.'

'But you didn't actually look inside the gym, and you assumed he'd gone even though you didn't actually see him go?'

'Listen, I was on me own, I can't keep tabs on everyone all the time. If I'm in the bar servin' or cleanin' up or sumfing, or if I'm in the office, I can't see the door, see? People can't get in wivout me pressin' the buzzer, but they can let themself out. I was told 'e'd gone, and the lights were off in the gym, that was good enough for me. And 'e wasn't in the changin' room – I could see it was dark through that bit of frosted glass in the door.'

'But he hadn't handed his key back, had he? Don't people have to do that before they go?'

Sharon snorted, her grinding jaws pausing a moment while she popped a fresh piece of gum between the pearly molars. 'They're meant to, aren't they? Got notices everywhere about it. But lots of 'em just take 'em 'ome and give 'em back next time. If they're in an 'urry to go and there's no one on reception, there's nuffing to stop 'em walkin' out wiv' em. Anyway, I can't see what difference it makes now. It's daft accusin' me of not seein' 'im go when 'e never even went.'

Slicer sighed and rubbed his face, his fingers leaving white lines down the pale pink of his cheeks.

'You've got a point there,' he said grudgingly. 'But if only you'd found him last night, we might have started on all this about ten hours earlier, that's all. And for all we know you're just making excuses for not checking the place out properly before you closed up.'

Sharon jumped to her feet and strode athletically up and down the room, shell suit rustling. Her face was going dark and her eyes brightening as if someone were twisting a dimmer switch.

'You coppers don't 'ang about, do you,' she shouted. 'Poor 'ole Duncan's only been dead five minutes and you've got Clinton lined up as the 'omicidal maniac. Then you accuse me of settin' up a robbery and not doin' my job properly. Well, fanks a lot, I can do wivout it.'

Slicer also stood up, carefully straightening his trouser creases, and she faced him angrily, hands on hips.

'Don't get too excited, young lady,' he said smoothly, putting up his hands in a placatory gesture and widening his crooked mouth in an ersatz smile which lasted a bare second. 'We'll be off now, if you don't mind. Work to do. Someone will be along later to get a full statement.'

Sharon continued to glare at him as he moved towards the door, but he was now talking to Stone.

'We'll just drop down to the club and get the whereabouts of Sean and these two bints' – he consulted his notebook while Sharon gave an indignant snort in the background – 'that's right, Christine and Alexis. They might be able to throw a little light on the subject. Thanks, Miss Bunnie – we'll let ourselves out.'

As he opened the front door, Sharon's mother appeared from the kitchen, almost hidden behind a large tray of coffee and biscuits. Slicer reached out uninvited and took a couple of ginger nuts.

'Thanks, Mrs B,' he said. 'No time for coffee, I'm afraid. Lovely daughter you've got there – nice personality. Very mature. Bit of a tomboy, though, eh?'

With a little help from his employers, who were alarmed to hear the police wanted to talk to him, Slicer and Stone found Clinton at about four in the afternoon. A bright day had turned to drizzle, and he was working in a telecommunications manhole on the pavement in the Old Kent Road, enclosed in a little red and white striped tent.

'Is that Mr Pink inside there?' asked Slicer pompously from underneath the brown trilby hat which had recently become part of his get-up.

'Yeah, who wants him?' came a friendly, muffled voice from within.

66

'Police officers, that's who. Pack your stuff up, Mr Pink, you're coming down the station with us.'

CHAPTER 8

Detective Constable Ahmed walked up the long granite-paved ramp and through the high, imposing archway into Gracechurch Square, looking warily about him like a cat entering a strange garden. Great cliffs of polished stone and glass, their shapes and colours and angles all in conflict, rose up on four sides, and he felt a twinge of giddiness as he looked up and saw a cloud glide rapidly past the top of a tower faced in pink marble. He focused instead on the splashing of water from a fountain in the sunken centre of the square, where several office workers in suits sat eating late lunchtime sandwiches among raised flowerbeds containing a few thorny shrubs with bright orange berries.

'Come on, Gunga Din,' called one of his colleagues from one of the grand glass doorways. 'It's not a sightseeing trip.'

Gunga Din, Gandhi, dhobi-wallah, even Paki – Ahmed hardly noticed the names any more. At first he'd been hurt and insulted, and when he complained, senior officers had tried to tell him soothingly that it was no more malicious than nicknames like Nobby Clark, Chalky White, Jock or Taffy. He knew, and he believed they knew, that this was a shabby evasion and another example in itself of the racist attitudes at large in the force. But he had learned not to worry about it, and concentrate on the job. At least his colleagues knew and accepted that he was a good detective, patient, and with a knack of getting people to talk to him without threats and blows. He'd passed his sergeant's exam and was due to be promoted shortly.

He walked briskly over to the door, which one of the others was holding open for him. There was a security desk – marble again – where a wiry, blue-uniformed man with bright eyes and tattooed hands told them which floor they needed and looked Ahmed insultingly up and down. The lift was a cage of glass and chrome which rose silently and fast up the middle of the atrium, past successive open-plan office floors like the busy layers in a beehive. Under the soft fluorescent lights, every desk had a screen and keyboard and every neatly dressed young person looked the same. A kind of catwalk took them from the lift door to the eighth floor; Ahmed looked down and saw the man at reception, insect-like now, still craning his head to watch them.

The reception area for Banks and Heritage was wood-panelled and deep-carpeted, and a young woman in black with a gash of red lipstick nodded impassively when they explained their business. She spoke inaudibly into a phone for a moment or two, then asked their names and tapped them into a little machine which instantly produced name cards to be inserted in plastic tags and clipped to their lapels. All three big policemen complied silently with the ritual like overawed schoolboys, and she motioned them to a black leather sofa.

'Someone will call you when a conference room is free,' she said indifferently, and then turned away to stare into space as if they no longer existed.

They waited silently, hardly daring to clear their throats, until a worried-looking young man in a light-grey double-breasted suit opened a tall wooden door and called them through.

'The managing director and the head of the investments section are waiting to see you,' he said over his shoulder as he bustled down the corridor. 'They're very busy, so I hope this won't take too long.'

The three policemen exchanged long-suffering glances and said nothing. They turned a corner and their guide showed them into a large square room with a dark wooden table the size of a small lawn. Beyond it, two more men in double-breasted suits, one thin and balding and the other chubby and pink, were talking quietly with conspiratorial looks on their faces and gleaming white coffee cups in their hands.

Ahmed, as planned, did the introductions. The thin one, who turned out to be the managing director, raised his eyebrows slightly and looked quizzically back and forth from Ahmed to the others, as if expecting one of the white men to take over the talking and restore normality. Ahmed kept his dark brown eyes firmly levelled on him. There were no handshakes and no offers of coffee.

'You may know why we're here from listening to the news,' said Ahmed as they settled into chairs, each camp on opposing sides of the table.

'Er, yes, awful, shocking business,' said the managing director, flapping a hand and glancing uneasily at his colleague. 'We saw it on the wires a couple of hours ago. Everyone here is deeply upset – he was a most valued colleague.'

'Yes, I'm sure,' said Ahmed. 'You have our deepest sympathy – it's an extremely nasty business and we're determined to solve it as soon as we can— '

'Yes,' cut in the managing director, leaning forward and beginning to drum his fingers lightly on the table. 'Haven't you any idea yet who might be responsible? I'm sure you'll appreciate that the longer the whole thing drags on, the worse the effect it'll have on the firm. Wasn't there something about a robbery?'

Ahmed leaned back, his eyes hardening a little. 'Well, sir, it's early days yet, but we've got a large team working on it and we should be making progress very quickly. As for the effect on the firm, well, we can't help that . . .'

'But what about this robbery? I mean, presumably they're the ones who did it?'

'We just don't know yet. We have to consider every possibility. That's why we'd like to talk to everyone here, especially the people who worked closely with Mr Stock or knew him at all.'

'What, everybody?' Again, the quick look passed between the two City men.

'More or less,' said Ahmed slowly, looking from one to the other. 'But before we begin, is there anything you can tell us? I get the impression you might already have some information we don't know about.'

It was the turn of the investments head, whose name was Wacker, to clear his throat and speak. His chubby cheeks twitched a little with reluctance and awkwardness.

'Well, yes, it may be pure coincidence, of course, but on the other hand . . . You see, there's been a bit of break-in here, actually. Nothing dramatic, of course, but none the less, very embarrassing . . .'

The three policemen shifted and shared interested glances.

'Oh, yes?' said Ahmed. 'So much for that shower down in the lobby, then. Do you know what's missing?'

70

'Not really. We know that several desks have been broken into, all in my department, actually, but apart from that nothing major seems to have been taken. I mean, they could have had PCs, equipment . . .' He waved a hand vaguely at the opulence around them.

'Whose desks were they?'

'Well, er, one of them was Mr Stock's desk, actually. And the others belonged to, er, Miss Grania Forbes and Mr Jeremy Heritage.'

The other two policemen were now twitching impatiently and making little eager noises, like animals about to be let out of a cage.

'I see,' said Ahmed. 'And have you called the police?'

'Er, no, not yet . . . but you're here now, aren't you?'

'Yes, well, we are, but I'm afraid an offence committed in this part of town will have to be looked into by the City of London Police. We're the Metropolitan Police.'

Wacker gave a long-suffering smile, as if he was being obliged to put up with the foibles of an eccentric client.

'Ah, yes, of course, these traditions and demarcations . . . all gone these days, of course, in our sphere of things . . .'

It was Ahmed's turn to cut in sharply.

'But all the same, Mr Wacker, I'd like you to show me these desks while my colleagues run through a list of employees with the managing director and work out who we need to talk to.'

Duncan's office was a little glass enclosure with a grey metal desk, complete with screen and keyboard, at one end of the open-plan investment department. Wacker said the sparseness of books and papers on the shelves showed how little time the poor chap had been in his new job – but people kept most things on computer these days, didn't they? Ahmed stood by the glass wall and looked out on to the floor like a guard over a prison wing, fiddling with the bright tie which was part of CID identity these days. A few people were sitting behind desks studying multi-coloured information on banks of screens, but most were standing in knots, looking subdued, talking quietly, and occasionally glancing over at the glass office. He noticed a tall man with curly hair, leaning against a filing cabinet and talking volubly to a woman in a green shoulder-padded jacket.

Wacker explained gloomily that they'd concluded, after talking to the security company, that it had to be an inside job. There was no sign of breaking and entering, and the building was securely locked at the weekend. But someone with a swipe card – anyone above the level of secretaries, switchboard operators and post-room staff – must have used it to get in the main door while the security guard was away from the desk. Then he – or she – must have gone up in the lift or by the emergency stairs, and used a second card to get through the door into the offices of Banks and Heritage. A simple kick had exploded the flimsy lock on the door of Duncan's office. It could have happened any time between Friday night and Monday morning.

'Duff security, between you and me,' said Wacker, shaking his head and wiping the palms of his hands nervously down the front of his suit. 'The freeholders were too mean to install the up-to-date card system, which gives you a print-out of which card has been used at what time, and so, I'm afraid, were we. The idea is you rely instead on the so-called humans on the front desk. But all that sort of gear's a lot cheaper than it was a few years ago, and we're going to put it in now, I can tell you. Apparently you can have one which doesn't only print out – you can program it to refuse certain card numbers at certain times. Magic stuff.'

Ahmed was looking at the mark on the desk top made by whatever strong metal lever had been used to spring open the drawers immediately beneath. Again, the locking device was flimsy and easily broken. The top two drawers contained Sello-tape, pens with chewed ends, business cards, a card-index of names and phone numbers; the bottom one was full of files under headings like Personal Equity Plans and Correspondence. Wacker said that with Duncan gone there'd be no way of knowing what had disappeared.

'What about the others – Forbes and, what was it, Heritage?'

'Yes, well their desks are out on the floor – God knows why they were selected and no one else. Grania's the one out there with the red hair, by the way. She reckons she's lost a bit of cash she had in there and some gold studs for her ears. Women do seem to have the most bizarre things in their drawers and handbags.'

'I'm not married, Mr Wacker,' said Ahmed neutrally. 'And Heritage?'

'He went up to Yorkshire at the weekend to see a client there first thing Monday. He's away for a couple more days, but I

72

suppose we could get him back if you wanted. He's not working on anything vital.'

'Does he know what's happened to his desk?'

'Yes, we got him on the phone earlier and he didn't seem all that bothered. He said there was nothing of any value in it, and the drawers certainly don't look as if they've been disturbed very much.'

'We can wait to see him, I should think – we'll see how it goes with the others. Meanwhile I think we can leave the fingerprinting and all the rest to the City police and get on with taking statements relating to the murder – you first, then Miss Forbes, perhaps.'

Ahmed straightened up from peering in the drawers and gave his upper lip a reflective stroke, watching a well-built middle-aged woman walk past outside the glass, sneaking an anxious glance at him.

'What's she worried about?' he asked casually.

'Oh, that's Lynne – old retainer of the company. Very cheerful lady, normally, but takes the weight of the world on her shoulders sometimes. It's a bit, well, creepy, knowing that one of your colleagues could be a burglar, as it were. We want whoever it is weeded out as quickly as possible.'

'Well, you've got to remember somebody could have lost their swipe cards, or had them stolen by someone who knew they could use them to get into this building. But even that would imply someone with a close knowledge of the place.'

Wacker, with his portly little stride, was leading the way along the corridor now and turned into a smaller version of the big conference room they'd been in earlier, with a walnut-topped table the size of a double bed.

'We've set this room aside for you to do your work, Mr, er,' he said, sitting down with a grateful little grunt and folding his short-fingered hands on the polished wood. 'I do hope this isn't going to take too long, though – I've got an awful lot of work to do. Busy day on the markets.'

CHAPTER 9

Judy was sitting in the home beat office, trying to fill in forms in triplicate about various minor incidents of the previous week. But she found herself, much of the time, staring through the dirty windows as the drizzle ran down them and the light drained gloomily out of the afternoon sky. She kept thinking about Duncan's hooded eyes and the repulsive, half-remembered feel of his winey mouth on her neck, and then imagining the scene in the gym with that teddy-bear head smashed and bloodied by the weights. She couldn't decide whether to go along to the incident room at the back of the station to tell them she knew the victim. She hardly knew him at all, after all, and they must be speaking to plenty of people who knew him far better. Besides, the latest word was that the murder might have been connected with a £900 robbery at the club, and that they were also bringing in some bloke with a grudge against the victim. The incident room would be far too busy for interruptions from her.

She was packing papers away, about to go home, when the phone rang. It was Clinton's mother Ketura, whom she'd met half a dozen times at their little terrace house in Peckham. Clinton saw nothing wrong with living with his mother at the age of twenty-six, especially since she did his washing without complaint, supplied beautifully cooked meals on demand, put no restrictions on his comings and goings, and charged a cheaper rent than any other local landlord. Judy had berated him about exploitation, but he had just smiled and shrugged and said his mum was happier with him there than she would be without him. His mum's voice was now distorted with anxiety.

'Judy? Sorry to disturb you, darlin', but I got big trouble. My Clinton been arrested by the police.'

'How do you know, Ketura?' she said, trying to keep her voice calm.

'One of his mates call me from Telecom. The police was asking where he was and picked him up on the street. And two officers just been here and taken away his clothes.'

'Clothes? What clothes?'

'His track suit. Sports bag and that.'

'Do you know why?'

'I got no idea. You know what Clinton like, he always stay well clear of trouble. He got no quarrel with anyone. Someone makin' a big mistake.'

'Yes, I'm sure they are, Ketura. Listen, do you want me to try and find out what's going on?'

'Oh yes please, darlin', yes please.' Mrs Pink sounded as if her troubles were suddenly over, and Judy didn't feel like explaining that they were probably only just beginning.

'OK, Ketura, I'll ring you back later.'

She put the receiver back gently. What was it Duncan had said? That was it – 'Your Clinton's a bit upset with me . . . a frank exchange of views.'

The incident room contained half a dozen men with their jackets off, sitting on desks clutching plastic cups of tea or talking on the phone. Near the door a detective constable Judy knew slightly was sitting in front of a computer terminal, jabbing irritably at the keyboard and mouthing swear words. She asked him if Detective Inspector Slicer was in, and he jerked a thumb towards the sleek-haired figure standing by a filing cabinet at the end of the office. Her hands were sticky with nervousness as she walked towards him, nodding and trying to grin at another detective she knew.

'Excuse me, sir.'

Slicer turned and focused his sharp, dark eyes on her. She noticed how his neat little ears lay close and tidy on his skull, and she was reminded of swift creatures that lived down holes and killed for pleasure.

'I'm WPC Best, home beat officer on the Chaucer Estate. It's just that I'm a member of the club and I know a couple of the people involved, so I thought I'd better come and talk to you.'

Slicer raised his eyebrows sceptically, then pursed his lips and slid the drawer of the filing cabinet home with a clunk. Judy remembered a psychology lecturer at the Hendon training college talking about negative body language.

'Right,' he said sarcastically. 'Always got time for a fellow police officer. Let's go round to an interview room.'

As they walked along the corridor he asked her if she was the one who'd been in the crime squad for a while. She said she was, and he smiled at her derisively as he flicked on the light and closed the door of the small, bare room. Judy felt rattled as they settled in plastic chairs on opposite sides of a cheap desk, its plastic veneer peeling off the wood-chip. She told Slicer that she'd met Duncan a few times but didn't know him very well.

'And?'

'Well, I also know Clinton Pink. He's, well, quite a good friend.'

'And?' Despite the noncommittal phrase, Slicer was interested now, and leant forward over the desk.

'Well, the word's going round that Clinton's being questioned, and I wondered if I could help.'

'I see. Listen, your first name's not Judy, is it, by any chance?'

'Yes, it is.'

Slicer's face fired up.

'Well, I'm very pleased you've come to see me, WPC Judy Best. Because sooner or later I'd have been looking for you. There's more than meets the eye in your part in all this.'

Slicer got up, walked round the table and stood close to her, just behind her shoulder, with his hands in his pockets. Judy felt cold inside and looked down at the floor. Slicer was wearing a pair of highly polished black slip-on shoes decorated with a couple of little leather tassels.

'What do you mean, sir?' she asked.

'What do I mean? Well, we've been talking today to two young ladies who were in the club last night. Taking a sauna, they were. Know them, do you? Christine Bottomley and Alexis Topping? One's a beautician, one's a catering manageress. Very tasty, the pair of them.'

Judy shook her head, guessing it might be the two glamour-pusses she'd seen at the club the second time she'd met Duncan.

'No? Well, they were just coming out of the sauna at about nine o'clock last night when they heard a bit of an argument. It was a quiet night, not many people in, so they put their head round the door to see what was going on. The door from the women's sauna into that upstairs corridor, d'you know it?'

Judy nodded. She was sure that Slicer was staring down scornfully at specks of dandruff he'd discovered in her hair, and she ran her hand nervously over her head.

'So they put their pretty little faces round the door, and what do they see but Mr Stock and Mr Pink having a bit of a ding-dong in the gymnasium. Hard words being spoken. And next morning Mr Stock is found with his head in a bit of a mess. What do you make of that?'

'Surely you don't suspect Clinton, sir? He'd never do a thing like that.' Judy wanted to moan and put her face in her hands, but managed to stay impassive and keep her voice even.

'Wouldn't he now? Well, isn't that what they all say? And just what was your relationship with Mr Pink?' He emphasised the word 'mister' sarcastically, making it into an insult.

'I've been going out with him for a few months.'

'Yes,' said Slicer, hissing the word slowly through his teeth. 'That's also what we've been hearing from my two girls, although they only knew you as Judy and had no idea you were a police officer. Same goes for me, in fact, until you so kindly walked in here. Most convenient. I was going to trace you through the club.'

'Well, I'm not trying to hide anything, sir. Only I'm sure there'll be a different explanation. What about this robbery, sir?'

'The robbery, eh? Well, we're working on it, thanks very much, and I've no doubt we'll get a result there as well. But you see, my two popsies tell me they'd heard from young Sharon on the reception desk that Duncan was asking someone called Judy to go out with him and Clinton didn't like it. Young Sharon omitted to tell us that detail herself this morning, for which she's going to find herself in hot water. But that's another story – I'm interested in you and your black and white magic.'

Judy suddenly pushed her chair back and sideways so that Slicer was no longer looming behind her and she could look up into his face. His nose was shining greasily in the harsh light, and his crooked mouth was wearing a leering expression of distaste.

'I'm surprised to hear that bloody little busybody didn't tell you the lot, sir,' she snapped. 'Because it seems she doesn't know how to keep her mouth shut.'

77

'Maybe she was trying to protect Mr Pink as well,' said Slicer coldly. 'Maybe he's giving her a big one as well.'

Judy looked at him in astonishment for a second, then turned away, shaking her head disbelievingly. She reminded herself carefully that she was speaking to a senior officer, and waited until she had got her anger under control. The strip light above them was buzzing like a trapped bluebottle.

'Look, sir. Duncan did ask me out, and Sharon must've heard him doing it, because she told Clinton and Clinton and I had a row about it. And she told everyone else, by the sound of it, nosy little cow. Anyway, it didn't really amount to asking me out because it was only to a party at some wine bar in the City, last Thursday. I went to it, there were loads of other people there, I had no plans to see him again, Clinton and I are going to patch things up, end of story. It's not the sort of thing which produces a murder, sir, honestly it's not.'

'You would think that, wouldn't you? I say a jury might think differently.'

Slicer walked slowly back to his chair, sat down and suddenly looked at her hard, a new gleam in his eyes and his nose wrinkled up.

'Tell me,' he said, his voice thick with feeling. 'What's a policewoman doing humping a nigger?'

Judy clasped her hands on her lap and watched them trembling slightly. This was exactly why she'd not wanted her colleagues to know about Clinton. This time she tried to forget she was being interviewed by a senior officer and to say what she'd say to a member of the public. Her voice wavered.

'I'm not answering that question, sir, because I find it offensive and racially prejudiced.'

Slicer bellowed with humourless laughter and rocked about in his chair. Judy chose a small blemish on the wall behind him where the pink plaster was showing through the grey paint, and stared at it hard.

'You're a card, Judy, you really are,' he said, taking out a freshly ironed handkerchief and blowing his nose precisely. 'You'd better come back into the office and I'll find someone to take a statement off you.'

'Sir, where's Clinton?'

'In the cells cooling off a bit, where d'you think? We'll be talking to him later on.'

'Can I see him?'

'You certainly cannot,' said Slicer indignantly, as if she'd suggested posting a turd to the Queen. 'At least, not until I've had a little conversation with him. Who knows, he might want to cough. Oh, and by the way, there's something Mr Pink probably hasn't told you in his pillow-talk.'

'What's that?' Judy stood up, steeling herself.

'He's got a record – actual bodily harm.'

Slicer smiled vindictively, pushed past her and strolled back to the interview room, whistling Rule Britannia quietly through his teeth and folding the handkerchief carefully back into his pocket.

On her way out of the station half an hour later, Judy went to the charge-room to speak to the custody officer. He was a thin, middle-aged sergeant with a pale face and a stomach ulcer, and he'd always been friendly and helpful to her. He was sitting with his feet up on the desk, suppressing a constant series of burps; every so often his abdomen jumped, his lips pursed, his cheeks inflated, and he issued a little puffing sound, like a toy steam-engine.

'Phil, have you got someone in the cells called Clinton Pink?'

'Hello, Judy, how are you getting on, all right? The answer is, well, yes and no.'

Judy's face clenched in irritation. 'What d'you mean, Phil? Sorry to sound a bit short, but I've got a load on my mind just now.'

'That's OK, love, quite understand. No, he's sitting in a cell waiting to be interviewed, but he hasn't been arrested so he's not actually in custody. No custody record – door's not locked or anything.'

'But that means he's free to go any time?'

'Yeah, but he doesn't know that, does he?' said Phil, emitting another puff through a grim little smile. 'And if he tried to, he'd just be nicked. You know the set-up – pretend there's nowhere else for him to wait, let him sweat a bit.'

Judy clenched her fists angrily. 'That Slicer's a right bastard,' she said.

'Don't tell anyone I said so, but you just might be right.'

Outside, the street was clogged with traffic and the chilly air was stained with exhaust fumes. Two streets away from the station, she called Clinton's mother from a phone box to tell her where he was and why the police had taken him in. She promised to get him a lawyer and said he'd be out by the end of the evening. Then, surprised at her own calmness and efficiency, she rang Deptford Law Centre and asked to speak to David Righter.

Righter was a defence solicitor she'd met several times at the magistrates' courts, a committed lawyer with a bony, earnest face, the type who was bound to be working late. He had a ferociously accurate knowledge of the Police and Criminal Evidence Act and specialised in demonstrating exactly how officers neglected to follow the rules. In the past Judy, like her colleagues, had groaned and protested theatrically whenever his name was mentioned. Now she needed him.

'David Righter speaking.' He gabbled so fast that Judy had to think for a couple of seconds to work out what he'd said. His mind was always speeding ahead of his speech.

'Listen, I'm a police officer and I've met you before. I've got some information for you, but I don't want to give you my name – is that all right?'

'Has to be, I suppose. But I won't necessarily believe what you tell me.'

'No, fair enough. But I'm calling on behalf of Mrs Keturah Pink, whose son is in Surrey Docks police station. They're going to interview him in connection with this murder this morning, but they haven't actually arrested him. He's not the sort of guy who knows his rights and he ought to have a solicitor.'

Righter suddenly sounded more alert and less sceptical. 'OK,' he said. 'Clinton Pink, did you say? He ought to be in gay cabaret with a name like that. Black, I assume? Yes, thought he would be. Telephone engineer. Address? Phone number? OK, got it. Well, as it happens I'm the duty solicitor tonight so I'll give the station a ring straight away. Who's in charge of the case? Oh, no, not Slicer, that really is bad news, I'm afraid. He'll probably give us the run-around all night. OK, I'll do my best, Judy.'

'What? How d'you know my name?'

'Just remember your voice from talking to you at court. Don't worry, I won't tell Big Brother. Bye for now.'

CHAPTER 10

When Judy was woken from a deep sleep by loud hammering on her door, her first panicky thought was that it was the police: Slicer and his team had decided to make her their latest suspect and were doing the 5 a.m. routine with sledgehammers and handguns. But when she switched the bedside light on and realized it was only half-past midnight, she sat up and began to think more steadily. She shivered and gritted her teeth as she swung her legs out of bed and fumbled for slippers and her red towelling dressing-gown.

'Who is it?' she called, leaning wearily against the front door.

'It's Clinton.' His voice was taut and nervous, almost a squeak.

She pulled back the bolts and undid the lock to let him in. A cold gust of misty air blew into the room with him from the open landing outside. She stared at him as he stood dumbly just inside the room, trembling slightly, hands thrust into the pockets of his blue denim jacket, looking like a frightened child in trouble at school. Her first impulse was to hug and console him, but there was an unfamiliar hint of reproach and accusation in his eyes, and a new sense of suspicion and reserve held her back. She took his hand and led him silently through to the kitchen.

'Sit there and I'll make you some tea. I know where you've been, you must have had a horrible time. Have you told your mum you're out?'

He shook his head. Judy put the kettle on, then refastened her dressing-gown around her before bending down to switch on the electric heater and get the milk out of the fridge.

'Well, ring her now. She's been very worried about you. That's how I found out where you were, when she phoned me at the station. Go on, you know where the phone is. She's probably waiting up, I told her you might well be out tonight.'

81

Silent until now, Clinton suddenly began to talk. He was too full of what had happened to him at the police station to think about his mother. They'd refused to tell him if he was under arrest or not, made him wait for four hours in a cell with no heating, given him nothing to eat or drink. Then they accused him of killing Duncan, called him a black bastard, and interrogated him for two hours. After that they'd put him back in the cell for another hour and warned him before letting him go that they'd be wanting to talk to him again. His forehead was clenched into deep furrows, and every so often he shuddered.

'Christ, Jude,' he said, looking at her as if it was her decision. 'They're not going to do me for it, are they? I'd no idea it was Duncan till they got me in that room and started getting heavy.'

'They couldn't do you without any evidence, Clinton, you know that.'

Clinton turned on her bitterly. 'Oh couldn't they? They fucking well could, Jude. You ought to know that – you're one of 'em. And I know they could, that's for sure, because they've done it to me before.'

'You mean, your record?' Judy blurted it out unthinkingly, immediately wishing she hadn't.

'You know, eh? I was never going to tell you, but your stinking colleagues have already obliged, obviously.'

'Sorry, Clinton,' said Judy, her pale hair falling round her face as she looked wearily at the floor. 'It was only this afternoon that I heard.'

'Heard what?'

'Nothing – just that. No, a bit more – ABH.'

Clinton snorted angrily and hit the edge of the table with the palm of his hand. Judy had never seen him like this, and covered the unease it caused her by getting up to make the tea.

'It sounds like I done a murder or something, doesn't it? It was nothing, it was something that happened while I was a kid of eighteen, but they've hung that label round my neck for the rest of my life. You probably wouldn't believe it because you're not black. And you're an effing copper.'

'Try me,' said Judy through the steam of the water she was pouring into the pot.

'The usual story. Group of us were coming back from a dance and these cops in a van were cruising past, winding us up and calling us nigger boys. And when we answered back they jumped on us, gave us a good hiding and did us for assaulting a policeman.'

Judy gave him an arch look, instinctively sceptical. 'You sure it was that simple?'

Clinton got to his feet angrily. 'See what I mean? Forget it, Judy, you're not black. God knows why I'm here. God knows why I ever went out with you. I should have walked away as soon as I heard you were a copper, but I thought things had moved on a bit.'

Judy reached out, grabbed his hand and slowly pulled him back to his seat again. 'I'm sorry, Clinton. All this is such a shock, I just don't know who or what to believe at the moment. But listen, didn't a lawyer come to the station to see you? He should have been in the interview with you, bloke called David Righter. I told him you were there, asked him to come down and help.'

Clinton laughed grimly, pulling his hand away from her but staying on the chair. 'Oh yeah, I saw him. But only at the end, when they put me back in the cell. They told him the interview wouldn't begin till ten, which was actually when it ended. Lying bastards – they kept him hanging around like a spare prick for about three hours. And don't give me that bullshit again about am I sure it's that simple. I hope something like this happens to you one day, then you'll bloody believe it.'

'Don't worry, I was put through the wringer as well this afternoon. Nasty piece of work called Detective Inspector Slicer had a go at me about what was my relationship with Duncan and why did a nice girl like me have a black boyfriend?'

'Slicer – that's the man.' Clinton laughed bitterly, shook his head and relaxed a little. He began telling her about the interview and sipping the tea she put in front of him. Slicer had done most of the questioning, but a fat superintendent was there as well, leaning against a table in the corner and not saying much. There'd also been a junior officer writing things down.

'Slicer kept going on about me being in the gym and having a row with Duncan about you. I told him it wasn't really about you – it was about the bloody bike. There's only one exercise bike working, and I was on it when Dunc arrived. He started the argument with some sarky remark about hope you're not going to be on that thing all night. I said no I wasn't, all polite, but I asked him if he'd had a nice time last Thursday. I suppose I was trying to needle him a bit, especially about what you told me on Saturday, you know, that you wouldn't go out with him again and all that. But I never expected him to go over the top, you know how cool he is all the time. And he just yelled at me, told me I was welcome, that you were . . . well, he said some pretty nasty things about you.'

'A frigid cow, prick teaser, all the usual stuff?'

Clinton smiled and nodded apologetically. 'Yeah, 'fraid so. I'd nearly finished on the bike anyway, and I just walked out in the end. But those bloody coppers wouldn't believe me. They were trying to say I was so jealous I somehow got him down on the floor, lifted one of the weight stacks and dropped it on his head. Can you imagine it? Really ridiculous, like I was Superman or something – Duncan's a strong guy. Was a strong guy, I should say, poor sod. You'd have to hold him down with one hand, lift the stack with the other, and then stuff his head in the gap. Crazy. So then they said I hit him on the head first, knocked him out, then dropped the stack on his head to try to make it look like an accident. Jesus, Judy, you don't think I'm a murderer as well, do you?'

Judy smiled reassuringly and shook her head. As she drank her tea, she wondered why he seemed to be staring in distaste at her mug, forgetting that it had found its way into the flat from the station canteen and was decorated with the crown and badge of the Metropolitan Police. He had an open, innocent face, without malice, a mouth whose natural shape was two thirds of the way to a smile. But who could be sure? His eyes were troubled, she couldn't read them now as she usually could. Given the right circumstances, even the Pope was capable of murder. She felt glad now that she'd held back from telling him the previous Saturday about what Duncan had tried to do in the alleyway – that would have given him a far stronger motive. Suddenly she felt a deep internal thrill at the idea of Clinton killing Duncan because of her. At the same time she was sure he hadn't. He sighed violently and continued.

'I kept saying, look, if I'd done him in, I'd hardly have gone straight downstairs and told Sharon and Sean that I'd had a row with him, would I?'

'What did they say to that?'

'That I was cunning enough, basically – that I'd do that to cover

84

my tracks. Then they went on about how Duncan's jacket and wallet were missing.'

'What, they reckon you took them?'

'Too right they did. You know what he said, that bastard Slicer? That it was a typical West Indian crime. He's a racist pig, that guy, I tell you.'

'But it doesn't make sense – one minute you're meant to be killing someone out of jealousy, the next moment you're just interested in robbery.'

'They reckon that once I'd killed him, I sort of calmly looked around and thought things over and took his key from his pocket or wherever and had a snoop round his locker, see if I could lift something. I decided I might as well be hung for a sheep as a lamb, that's what they said. Can you imagine it? A guy who's just knocked someone off, calmly strolling around looking for something to nick and telling his mates he's just had a row with the guy he's killed?'

'Didn't they say anything about the burglary?'

Clinton's eyebrows rose hopefully. 'What? What burglary?'

'You can't have heard about it on the news or anything before they took you in. No, someone broke into the club as well last night, came in through an upstairs window and took nearly a thousand quid from the office – whole weekend's takings.'

'What? Why didn't those bastards tell me?' Clinton shook his head and snorted with relief, spreading his arms and sagging back in his chair. 'Well, that's it, isn't it, has to be? He got in their way, probably. That must be it, they did it and put his head in the weights to try to make it look like an accident. Then they took his jacket and wallet as well. Bloody hell, Jude, why are they giving me a hard time if they've got that sort of lead to follow?'

Judy shrugged, her mind carefully turning over what he'd just said. After her interview with Slicer in the afternoon, she'd also been assuming that the robbers should be the main suspects, but would it actually fit the timetable? If the place closed at nine thirty, Duncan must have been planning to leave the gym by about nine fifteen or nine twenty. That meant that if the robbers had killed him, they would have had to break in while the club was still open, all lit up and with people inside, visible through the windows. Surely they'd come in and robbed the place later, unaware that there was a body lying in the gym in a pool of blood?

She kept these thoughts to herself and was about to tell Clinton to go home to his mum when he looked up from the floor and wagged a finger at her.

'Yeah, that must be it, you know?' His voice was the melodramatic stage whisper of someone who'd just painstakingly solved a mystery. 'I told those coppers that I'd heard someone in the changing room when I went back in after having a drink in the bar. They reckoned I was making it up, of course, pretending someone else was there who could have done it. But I did hear a noise on that staircase that leads up to the sauna. I mean, I didn't think anything about it at the time, I thought it must be Duncan on the way out . . .'

'Yes, but why would anyone go out of the changing room through the upstairs, instead of through the downstairs door into the lobby?'

Judy's tone was urgent, her tone almost accusatory. Clinton looked at her in surprise for a moment, then shrugged.

'I suppose I thought he'd left something up in the gym, his track-suit top or something. I thought he was going back to get it, and would go down the main stairs outside. That's why I told Sharon I thought he'd gone, see? Slicer tried to make a lot of that, of course – another piece of nigger cunning. According to him, I was trying to make sure she didn't go up there and discover my victim. But I was wrong, the noise must have been the guys who'd broken in. They must have done him in, then waited till everyone had gone and robbed the place.'

Judy finished her tea and pushed back her hair with a forced grin.

'Come on, Sherlock Holmes, you're not going to solve the case at this time of night. I know they can be bastards, but the CID are working on it, don't worry. They'll sort it out in the end, Clint, they just had to eliminate you from their inquiries.'

'But they said they wanted me in again.'

'We'll see. If there is a next time we'll make damn sure you have a solicitor with you.'

'Yeah, I've arranged to go down and see your guy tomorrow. Listen, Judy, can I stay?'

This was a far cry from the rejecting, impassive Clinton of the previous Saturday, the one who wouldn't even have a drink with her in the evening and insisted on meeting her in a grubby café, as if she were a stranger. Judy gave him a regretful smile and shook her head. This defeated-looking, child-like creature was not the real Clinton either, and the last thing she wanted was a sleepless night rebuilding his self-confidence. He gave in without argument, and she took him by the shoulders and steered him out into the living-room, picking up her car keys from the table and pressing them into his hand.

'It would only make things more difficult at the moment,' she said gently, putting a sterile kiss on his cheek. 'Just take my Metro and get on home to your mum. Make an old woman happy.'

'I'd rather make a young woman happy,' he replied, setting off down the stairs. This flash of Clinton's old spirit kept her watching at the door with a tired smile on her face until she heard the car start. She felt wearily, in her bones, that she was going to be pulled still further into this affair, if only to get Clinton in the clear. She went back to bed and lay with her hands behind her head, staring at the bluish gleam of the street lights on the curtains and listening to the eternal hum which lay just beneath the silence of London.

CHAPTER 11

The radio was saying next morning, as Judy wearily crunched her way through her cornflakes, that no arrests were imminent in the 'yuppie Docklands gym murder', but police were talking to a number of men to eliminate them from their inquiries. There was a brief interview with Detective Superintendent Manningbird, who had come in from area headquarters to run the case. His voice was plump and rotund, and the proportion of inappropriate h's in his speech increased as the interview went on. 'Natchurally we are hendeavouring to bring this hextremely hunpleasant matter to a satisfactory conclusion as, as, er, as hexpeditiously as possible,' he intoned. Pompous prat, thought Judy, rinsing out her bowl so vigorously that a spurt of water rose out of it and shot up her sleeve like an icy snake. She tried to calm her temper with the thought that Manningbird might put a brake on the worst antics of Slicer.

At the station several people looked at her oddly during the brief parade, and she suspected that Slicer had been putting in a bad word for her here and there. Everyone who did speak to her had a new rumour about the murder: Duncan's flat had or hadn't been broken into, his car had or hadn't disappeared, there was or wasn't a letter saying he was depressed. When she reached the home beat office Fred Beans, feet on table, was finishing off a joke about identifying Duncan by his circumcision scar and moving on to the news that Manningbird was bringing in some trick-cyclist from Watford University to do a 'psychological profile' of the killer. It was all the rage at the Yard, he said, ever since this bloke had helped to find the Railway Rapist.

'Apparently this guy looks at the MO and the time and place and all that, and any skin or blood or sperm or shit he leaves behind, then he works out that the suspect is a twenty-five-year-

88

old Londoner with a wart on his left buttock and a chip on his shoulder because his mum didn't breast-feed him. Then they send me round the streets asking all twenty-five-year-old men to show me their arse and you, Jude, round all the hospitals finding out who was breast-fed from birth and who wasn't. Then you spend weeks putting it all on a computer to narrow it down to twenty thousand people, and meanwhile the poor bloody taxpayer shells out a thousand quid for this guy's services. Brilliant, isn't it? What's wrong with good old-fashioned coppering, that's what I want to know.'

His eyebrows had risen so high that they almost disappeared into his hairline as his sarcastic indignation reached its crescendo. He looked round as if for applause, but everyone else had lost interest and was getting on with work.

'You're overdue for retirement, Fred,' said Judy, giving him a mirthless grin as she closed the door behind her and set out for the Chaucer Estate.

The weather was raw and grey and a V-formation of Canada geese was flying low over Southwark Park, honking laryngeally and heading south. She pulled on her gloves and hat and crossed the road by a hardware shop where someone had wound tinsel round the handles of the spades and hammers in the window. The lampposts were festooned with coloured signs, another local version of early Christmas decorations, directing lorries to Docklands building sites with names like Scott's Wharf and Duke and Duchess Point. Judy headed briskly into the park where the huge scabby-trunked plane trees tried to hide the back of the derelict hospital, its windows broken and its two brick towers dark against the sky. It had been on the market for years, but the developers were too busy trying to save their riverside schemes to bother with a crumbling pile like this. Five minutes later, feeling short of sleep and spiritless, she dodged through the speeding vans on the main road and entered the estate, where yet more satellite dishes, like some technological fungus, seemed to have sprouted overnight on the pebble dash cladding.

There was no one about apart from a few pensioners plodding stoically off to the Post Office and one or two women with pinched faces and inadequate coats heading for the corner shops; the few men who had jobs round here had gone to them by now, and those who didn't would still be grunting and scratching in bed.

She had an appointment to see the man from the borough housing office, who worked at the bottom of Monk's House in a little office fortified with metal grilles and unbreakable windows like a Belfast police station. Today the wall by the end window bore a new smoke stain above the twisted remains of some milk crates, and the sickly smell of melted plastic hung in the air.

As she turned the corner at the bottom of Reeve's House, she heard someone rapping urgently on glass. The noise was coming from one of the ground-floor flats, where she could dimly see a bespectacled face and a gesticulating hand among the shadows and reflections in the window. She turned up the little pathway towards the block, walked through a door half-hanging off its hinges, and found herself in a ground-floor replica of the landing where Mr Maharasingham, with his blazing mad eyes, had been dragged out of his flat in the adjoining block a couple of weeks ago. Illegible multi-coloured spirals and zig-zags decorated the walls and the wet patches on the bare cement floor gave out a vivid smell of urine. The frantic barking of a small dog erupted behind one of the flimsy green doors, which opened to reveal a tiny grey wisp of a man in outsize carpet slippers with a Yorkshire terrier struggling and yapping in his arms.

''Ere, officer, I got sumfink for yer. Shuddup, will yer, Binkie, or yer goin' in yer basket, you 'ear? Come inside a sec, will yer?'

Judy braced herself for the stifling smell of dirty dog and unwashed body and followed him into the narrow corridor. The man was barely as tall as her chin and the grubby sinews on the back of his emaciated neck stood out like tree roots. He wore a tattered grey pullover and the top of his collar was greasy and frayed. Binkie glared at her balefully over his bony shoulder, and when she made a placatory kissing sound she was rewarded with another hysterical spasm of eye-rolling and ear-splitting yaps. She could smell its meaty halitosis a yard away.

'Right, yer little bugger, that's yer lot. In yer bleedin' basket. Wait 'ere, will yer, miss? Back in a sec.'

Judy walked into the front room and looked round. There was a gas fire on low, its orange-and-blue flames waving and bending, an uncomfortable-looking armchair with wooden arms, and a packet of rolling tobacco and the *Daily Express* on the little table.

'Sorry,' she said, as the little man came back from the kitchen, breathing heavily and brushing Binkie's long moulting hairs from his pullover. 'I think that little outburst was my fault.'

'Nah, little bleeder's always shootin' 'is mahf off. Look, I got this for yer – Binkie picked it up behind them railin's dahn the end of the estate.'

He opened a little bureau stuffed with allowance books and red-printed final reminders and pulled out a wallet. It was large, beautifully stitched, in rich brown leather, and it looked as out of place in these poverty-line surroundings as a Dior dress in a street market. She knew before he handed it over whose it was, and sure enough the initials DBS were stamped on one corner, next to four or five deep scratches. She looked through it and slipped her fingers into its many folds and pockets, feeling like a pick-pocket.

'Nah, I was takin' that little bugger for a walk, just before dark, and 'e always 'as a widdle on that patch o' grass just before you get to the main road, know where I mean? Behind them green railin's. And 'e picked it up, like. Sorry 'baht them teef marks – little so-an'-so didn't want to let go.'

The wallet was empty apart from a few receipts tucked into the deepest pocket at the back. Any cash would have been converted into white powder or brown liquid by now, and the plastic had probably been used several times yesterday morning and dropped through a grating in the street. One of the receipts was for £485 from the Golden Vat, Pudding Lane, and another showed that Duncan took out £150 from the National Westminster cash machine at Surrey Quays at lunchtime on Sunday December 2. So the wallet would have been much thicker when it was lifted.

'Thanks very much for handing it in,' she said to the man. 'Lots of people wouldn't have bothered, and this one's really important.'

He gave her a boyish grin marred only by the off-putting gap between his grey-looking gums and the pink-and-white plastic of his dentures.

'Nah, the kids just chuck 'em over the fence after they've nicked 'em. There's 'andbags and all sorts lying around this estate, like bleedin' confetti after a weddin'. But I always 'and 'em in if I find 'em. Someone might want 'em back, sentimental value or sumfink.'

'Well, I just wish we could give you some reward,' Judy said, scrawling his name and address in her notebook. On her way out she heard Binkie being released from the kitchen in a fusillade of barking and scratching. Then she buttoned the wallet into the front pocket of her tunic and walked rapidly back to the station. As she'd predicted, she was getting involved.

In the incident room, Detective Sergeant Stone was sitting by himself, leafing through the morning papers. Judy knew him from several cases he'd dealt with on the Chaucer Estate, and had usually managed to get on well with him. She didn't like his unsavoury personal traits and his brutal methods, although she accepted they sometimes got results. It was still early in the day, so his temper was reasonably good.

''Ere, look at this, Jude,' he said affably, showing her a double-page spread in the *Daily Star*. 'They're really getting their rocks off on this one. Diagram of how the weights machine works, artist's impression of murder scene – very nasty, pools of blood – and an interview with the *Star* psychologist: "This is the crime of a sadistic psychopath." What's the matter with you, then? You're all pink and panting – looks like you've just had a close encounter of some kind.'

Judy tossed the wallet on to the newspaper in front of him and pulled up a chair.

'It's his – it belongs to Duncan Stock. Look at the initials. An old geezer found it on the Chaucer Estate last night. Or rather, his pooch did. So it's ten to one that one of our local experts did the robbery. Maybe more than the robbery. Where is everyone?'

Stone picked up the wallet and stroked the scars in the leather with his thick, lumpy fingers.

'Manningbird's called a conference to review the case so far,' he said. 'They've all gone up to the Chief Super's office, so I'm minding the fort. How d'you know this is his? Must be hundreds of people with the initials DBS.'

'Bit of a coincidence, though, isn't it? And anyway, there's a receipt inside showing payment for a party he had last week. I know about it because I was there – you've probably heard that I knew this guy?'

Stone's little eyes flashed her a sly look as he was opening the wallet. 'Yeah, that's right,' he said, noncommittally. 'And I did hear you've been mentioned at his firm by some of his mates.

What d'you reckon then? This thing would've been full of plastic a short time ago, wouldn't it?'

'I'm thinking, maybe Ollie Ford could point us in the right direction.'

'Me too. Watch out, here come the lads.'

A dozen men, most of them wearing dark suits, colourful ties and highly polished black shoes, clattered into the room, followed by Slicer and Manningbird, a large, bulging man with grey skin and pale, peering eyes, like a mole's. As Judy's eyes met Slicer's, his face immediately fired up and he pointed an accusing finger at her.

'I want to talk to you, Best,' he shouted across the room. Judy looked at Stone, who stared back with no trace of sympathy. All the officers who'd been at the conference were now standing silently, looking at her. Feeling as if she had two heads or a nasty growth, she walked out through the door Slicer was holding open. Manningbird followed them into the interview room and lowered his big body gingerly on to one of the small plastic chairs. Here we are again, she thought, her mind suddenly fuzzy and her heart kicking.

Slicer paced theatrically up and down with his hands in his pockets for half a minute before speaking. His face was still red and his dark little eyes were gleaming.

'Didn't you get a message to come and see me first thing?' he asked angrily. Judy looked blank, and he turned away to talk in a different tone to Manningbird.

'I tell you, Bryan, this station would have to burn down before the uniform side took any notice of anything. Sodding plods.'

Manningbird shrugged, his upper body heaving like an animal in a sack, and Slicer turned back to Judy with renewed vehemence.

'Do the words "If you ever touch me again, I'll kill you", ring a bell?' His voice was sarcastic and insinuating. Judy's stomach lurched and her mouth opened, but she couldn't think of what to say.

'Because we have an impeccable witness who tells us that these were your last words to the murder victim in an alleyway in the City of London last Thursday night.'

Judy remembered the few shadowy figures, half a dozen maybe, who'd passed by while she was fighting off Duncan in the doorway.

She'd only been dimly aware of them, and certainly hadn't recognised any of them.

'Who told you that?' she said stickily, her mouth drying up with the sudden anxiety.

'Never mind who,' snapped Slicer. 'Let's just say we've been interviewing all his colleagues very carefully, and one of them had an interesting little episode to tell my men. Why didn't you tell me about it yesterday, Best?'

'Well, I didn't think it mattered, it was private, I wanted to forget it . . .'

She must have met six or eight people at the party who knew who she was, she thought; and suddenly she remembered Grania, the orange-haired airhead who'd been out with Duncan and seemed over-curious about her, perhaps a bit jealous. Then Slicer hit the desk with the flat of his hand, making a noise like a gunshot.

'You're in trouble here, Best,' he shouted, a fleck of white spittle landing on the desk between them. 'Withholding information on a murder inquiry. Issuing threats to kill. You realise this makes you a suspect, don't you?'

'But surely, you can't think . . . Listen, he'd just pushed me into a doorway and tried to, well . . . Look, that's just the sort of thing anyone would say if they were being treated like that. I didn't mean it literally, I'd had something to drink, this guy was attacking me . . .'

'Yes, I've heard you've got a nasty temper,' said Slicer with his twisted smile, suddenly calm. 'I've heard the odd story from your fellow officers about your little outbursts. Where exactly were you on Sunday night?'

Judy glanced over at Manningbird in the corner, but he was busy scratching at a gravy stain on his tie with his fingernail, a frown on his forehead.

'I was at home, watching TV.'

'Got someone who can confirm that, have you? Another of your boyfriends, perhaps?'

'Yes . . . I don't know. I was by myself, but I had a couple of phone calls from people. Listen, surely you don't think I killed him, do you?'

'Why not? And if you didn't fancy the job yourself, there's all your mates from the Chaucer Estate. One or two of them are open to commissions, I hear.'

Judy's stomach felt full of ice and her throat was now painfully dry. 'But villains like that would just use a knife or a lump of concrete in an alleyway and dump the body in the river . . . this was so deliberate, it must have been carefully planned.'

'Stranger things have happened, Best.'

'But you haven't got any evidence.'

'We've got a motive, which is a pretty good start. The forensic will be through before long.'

'I want to speak to a solicitor,' Judy said slowly, trying to control the unsteadiness of her voice.

'Ah, yes, a solicitor,' said Slicer with a renewed access of sarcasm, pacing rapidly up and down the room again like a ferret in a cage. 'Perhaps I could recommend a certain Mr David Righter, a long-haired commie from the law centre? Does that name ring a little bell, perhaps?'

'Well . . .'

'Because I've got good reason to believe that you sent that little prat down here last night to interfere with our interviews with your other boyfriend – I'm talking about the black one this time. Whose side are you bloody well on, you lousy little plonk? Are you a fucking police officer or not?'

Judy sat looking back at him dumbly, like a rabbit in the headlights. There was gentle throat-clearing from the corner and Manningbird spoke, this time with hardly any h's at all. His voice seemed to come through a mouthful of wet gravel.

'Sorry, Judy, but we've talked to the Chief Superintendent, and 'e agrees. Wouldn't look too good if the press or someone got 'old of it that you were involved and you were still working. You'd better go off duty till all this is sorted out.'

'You mean I'm suspended? But you can't, I'm working on the case, I'm helping, I just brought in Duncan's wallet, an old guy found it on the Chaucer Estate.' Judy flapped her arms aimlessly, like the wings of a grounded bird. The two men exchanged a doubtful glance.

'Is that what you were telling Stone about?' asked Slicer, his voice suddenly civil and unsure. She nodded.

'You handed it over and told him what you know?' She nodded again.

'Don't worry, then, we'll take care of that,' said Manningbird. 'You'd better go up and see the Chief Super so 'e can formally sign you off, and then take yourself off 'ome. And don't go away – we might want to interview you again.'

Stone put his head through the door of the Victory and looked around. There were three workmen in woolly hats and boots spattered with paint, playing cards and drinking pints of lager by the door. A couple of old women were sitting silently under a picture of a man-o'-war in full sail, their glasses of stout half-full in front of them and little moustaches of brownish froth above their toothless mouths. At the bar, a slack-faced man in a baggy suit was slumped over a small but well-filled glass, blowing cigarette smoke over a plastic display case containing rolls with thick lumps of cheese and onion sticking out of them.

Stone flashed an artificial, glint-eyed smile at them all and was about to turn and leave when his eyes fell on a small freckled man with bushy ginger hair, tucked on a stool at the far end of the bar, next to a partition of carved wood and engraved glass. He was slowly lifting his evening paper high enough to cover his face, but Stone squeezed past the tables and slipped on to the stool next to him. He ordered a half of lager from the barman, a pale, paunchy youth with dead eyes and a slash scar on one cheek.

'Afternoon, Ollie,' said Stone unpleasantly. 'Can I get you one?' Ollie Ford grunted and continued reading his paper.

'You're getting hard to find, Ollie. I've been in three boozers already looking for you. I need a word, it's urgent.'

'I can't talk to you in here, you prat,' hissed Ollie through his full raspberry-coloured lips, casting a furtive look round the bar. The man in the baggy suit was rubbing his face wearily, but appeared to be watching them through his fingers.

'OK, we'll see you round the corner outside the Post Office in fifteen minutes,' said Stone quietly. 'Red Cavalier. And don't start pissing us around or I'll arrange for you to spend Christmas somewhere nice and cosy, like Wandsworth nick.'

Ollie looked up from the racing pages, eyes frightened and malevolent. 'You won't go far wrong with Running Dog in the three thirty,' he said loudly. 'Going well at the moment, 'e is.'

Stone gave a laugh that ended in a convulsive cough and finished his drink in one long pull, winking at the fish-eyed barman. Ollie's racing recommendations, like his information on local villains, were usually worth a bet. His life was a dangerous balance between providing enough information to avoid prosecution for dealing in stolen credit cards, and avoiding the suspicion and retribution of those he informed on.

When he slipped into the back of the Cavalier next to Stone, his little blue eyes were fizzing with fear and anger. The constable driving the car eased away for a slow tour of Rotherhithe.

'What the fuck you bastards trying to do?' spat Ollie. 'Word gets around I'm grassing, I'm a dead man. Can't you bleedin' wait till I phone in?'

'Not this time, Ollie,' said Stone indifferently, withdrawing his index finger from one nostril and examining it like a man checking a car dipstick. 'This one's a bit urgent. And it's your choice, you know that – you can go down for the cards, or you can give us a steer now and then.'

Ollie sank into the corner of the seat and pulled the collar of his greasy suede jacket up round the ginger curls on his neck. He was suddenly flat and defeated, the anger gone.

'Yeah,' he said bitterly. 'Over a bleedin' barrel with a poker pointing at me bum. I got a family to look after, you know that?'

'Don't make me cry,' yawned Stone. 'Anyway, this one's worth fifty nicker to you, you come up with the goods.'

'Spit it out, then.'

'There's been this murder at the weights club – you know that, don't you, Ollie?'

Ollie looked at Stone like a bullock at the man with the humane killer. 'Nah, nah, I don't wanna know about that,' he stuttered. 'Can't help you on that one, guv.'

Stone put a podgy hand on his arm. 'Wait a minute, Ollie, you haven't heard it yet. Someone nicked the victim's credit cards, and the wallet was found on the Chaucer Estate. Your patch, I'd say – wouldn't you?'

'I'm saying nothing.' Ollie folded his arms protectively and retreated further into his corner. Stone lurched across the back seat, rocking the car so that the driver had to correct the steering, and grasped Ollie's jaw like a butcher picking up a couple of pork chops. Ollie's eyes rolled back and his mouth pouted redly.

'Listen, you little toe-rag. If you want to come down the station and we'll throw the book at you, that's fine with me. We've got

97

it all on file. Or you can think back to Sunday night and tell me if you bought any cards off anyone. In particular any cards with the name Stock on them. As in stocks and shares.'

Ollie pulled Stone's paw off his face and massaged his chin sulkily. 'OK, I did move a couple Monday night. But I shifted 'em straight away, like. You won't find 'em now, they'll be long gone down the drain.'

'Thanks, Ollie, we know how it works. What we want is names – who brought them to you.'

'Well, the geezers who brought them to me aren't the ones what nicked them, necessarily. Can't jump to no conclusions in this game. You goin' to do 'em for the murder, or what?'

'We'll worry about that, Ollie. Just give us the NAMES!'

On the final word, Stone's voice rose from a conversational level to a pop-eyed roar, and he loomed above Ollie, raising a fist the size and colour of small oven-ready chicken. Ollie looked at the fist for a moment, then swallowed heavily and began to talk.

CHAPTER 12

It was half an hour after dark when the two Cavaliers, each containing four men, drove slowly on to the Chaucer Estate by different routes, parked near the foot of Friar's House, and switched their lights off. A short distance away, a brown BMW with a sagging exhaust pipe was parked with two wheels on the pavement. Five minutes later a white police van full of the dark shapes of uniformed officers drove up, lurching heavily over the lumps in the road designed to slow the traffic. A couple of head-scarved women, hunched into their thin coats and carrying plastic bags, passed by without curiosity.

Slicer got out of the red car, his breath clouding in the chilly air, and carefully put on his brown trilby. He grinned and rubbed his hands together as he walked back to talk to the inspector in charge of the van. Then he tapped on the roof of the car and opened the boot, lifting out two sledgehammers. He handed them to two big men who got out of the other car, and walked rapidly over to the entrance of the block. Five detectives followed him into the lift where he pressed the button for the sixth floor. As they lurched upwards, the electric motor clicking and whining, he pulled a mugshot of a young black man from his overcoat pocket and showed it around silently in the dirty yellow light. The others nodded. The lift stopped with a bump and they filed out on to the bare landing.

Slicer rang one of the bells and motioned the other officers to stay out of the line of sight of the glass panel in the flimsy door. It was opened within ten seconds by a tired-looking black woman in slippers who jumped backwards, eyes widening, as Slicer pushed past her, banging the door against the corridor wall. Winston was getting to his feet, mouth open and a cigarette paper in one hand, as Slicer, Stone and an officer in jeans walked fast into the living-room, grabbed him, pushed him face down on the table in front of the window, told him he was nicked, and snapped some handcuffs on him. Then the shouting started.

Winston's mother shouted that they didn't have a search-warrant and what did they think they were doing kicking their way into people's houses. One of the officers calmly put down his sledge-hammer in a corner, as if he were a guest depositing his umbrella, and pulled a piece of paper out of his pocket. He held it in front of her frightened face for a few seconds, then advised her roughly to go into the kitchen and shut up. Winston shouted that he hadn't done anything, and they couldn't go round nicking people for just nothing. Stone pushed him so he fell awkwardly on to the sofa with his hands pinioned behind his back, and Slicer picked up a dark little nugget from a piece of silver paper on the coffee-table and sniffed it slowly, fixing Winston with a sarcastic smile.

Winston yelled that he wasn't dealing, it was just for his personal use, man. Slicer told him he could tell that to the magistrate, along with the fancy excuses he had for breaking into the Docklands Squash and Weights Club two nights before. Winston stared at him defiantly, swore he'd never been near the place, and said he wasn't saying a word until he saw his brief.

'You there, sir?' It was Ahmed's voice, hissing from the radio in Slicer's pocket. Slicer pulled it out and said he was there.

'Second suspect approaching the block, sir.'

'Right, let's hope he doesn't see the van and change his mind.'

Three minutes later the bell of the flat rang again. The officer in jeans opened it and made a grab for Wayne, who hurled himself backwards, eyes wide with alarm in his spotty face, shook himself free, and ran for the stairs. The officer cursed and tripped over the doormat, banging his knee hard on the edge of the door, as he tried to follow the fleeing figure. Three other officers who'd been searching the living-room realised what had happened and tried to run out of the flat in pursuit, but the first of them fell over the bulky body which was already struggling and swearing on the hall floor. It was nearly half a minute before anyone disentangled himself and set off down the stairs after Wayne.

In the front room, Slicer was speaking into the radio again: 'Little bastard's on his way down again, on the stairs. Get the lads out of the van and get him at the bottom. Shut up, you, unless you want a fat lip.'

The final sentence was addressed to Winston, who was rolling and hooting derisively on the sofa, his knees drawn up to his chest in feigned mirth. Stone, who was standing behind the sofa, slapped him resoundingly round the ear. The laughter stopped suddenly, and Winston screwed his head round to tell Stone resentfully that he knew what an assault was and he'd be pressing charges. Stone told him to shut his gob.

Ahmed was waiting at the bottom of the stairs, but Wayne came down fast and ran into him at full speed, his forearms crossed protectively in front of his chest. Wayne was smaller and lighter than Ahmed, but his desperate aggression and the element of surprise made up for it: the policeman found himself sprawled on the dirty concrete as Wayne shoulder-charged the swing doors, banging them back on their hinges, and disappeared through them.

Outside, he was faced by two helmetless uniformed officers charging up the short path from the parking area with several others following behind. When they saw him the first two stretched their arms wide, like athletes breasting the tape, as if he was going to run happily into their embrace. Instead he turned like a hare, his rubber trainers squeaking on the stained flagstones, and sprinted off away from them. He was past the rubbish chutes and the blue Cavalier before the detective inside it, who'd been left without a radio, had managed to clamber out of the driver's seat.

His arms pumping frantically, Wayne ran on down the potholed road. He seemed not to see a little grey-coated figure coming towards him, and ran into the lead linking the old man to a tiny dog beside him. The dog yapped and yelled, rolling over and over like a hairy football, and the old man went down heavily in the gravel. Wayne tripped and staggered, spinning round, but he kept on his feet and veered off across the unkempt grass towards a group of brightly lit buildings two hundred yards away.

It was a vision beyond Wayne's reach, a council estate tarted up by the Docklands Development Corporation to improve the view from the upmarket private development on the other side. Newly painted red and green railings beckoned him from the landings, and a grandiose broken pediment, fixed on the roof of each block and lit from below, looked down on his efforts.

Wayne's pursuers, twenty yards behind him and gaining slightly, yelled like hunting dogs as they saw he was running towards an eight-foot tall wire mesh fence which quarantined the Chaucer Estate. But their quarry veered to the right, one arm windmilling, and hurled himself at the wall of a seven-foot flat-roofed building, part of an electricity sub-station, which offered a bridge over the fence.

'Don't do it, you'll 'lectrocute yourself!' panted the leading officer expectantly as Wayne thrashed and struggled to swing his body up on the roof. He'd got one knee over the edge and was pulling up his trailing leg when the policeman made a desperate jump and got one hand on his ankle. Wayne kicked and squealed like an animal in a snare, but his pursuer hung on grimly and managed to get the other hand on his thin leg. There was nothing on the roof for Wayne to hold on to, and the officer lifted his knees to his chest and put all his weight on the leg, like a man trying to climb a rope. Wayne slid smoothly off the roof and landed on the officer with flailing limbs just as the others pounded up, slithered to a halt on the wet grass and pitched in.

Grunts and curses flew up from the mêlée, climaxing in a shrill scream from Wayne as one of the officers applied a wristlock and jolted his arm nearly up to the nape of his neck. As the handcuffs were snapped on him, his panting pursuers stood back, grinning and brushing the mud from their clothes. Wayne's spotty cheek was bleeding as they pulled him upright and propelled him, limping and crying, back to their van. Two of them stopped to help the tiny old man, who was sitting on the ground with staring eyes, holding and stroking his trembling Yorkshire terrier.

'Very nice arrest, lads,' said Slicer smoothly, standing at the front of Friar's House, arms crossed across his chest like Pharoah. 'Let's have a look at him – I say, that's a nice-looking leather jacket. Bit out of your price range, though. No rewards for guessing where you got that from, eh, you little scumbag?'

Wayne looked back at him, sobbing and bleeding like a child beaten up in the playground. Winston, head high and walking jauntily, was brought out of the block of flats by Stone. He nodded cheekily at the dozen people who had been tempted out into the cold by the sounds of running and shouting.

'Don't tell 'em fuck all, you hear?' he shouted sternly at Wayne. Stone cuffed him from behind and pushed him on towards the van.

'Fucking harassment,' shouted a young black man with a table-top haircut. 'Fucking pigs are at it again.'

Two more youths ran up from an adjoining block and stood threateningly behind the police van, as if to prevent the doors being opened. Slicer talked hurriedly with the uniformed inspector, looking round to gauge how many more people were arriving. Wayne and Winston were hustled quickly in the other direction and manhandled into one of the unmarked cars. As they were driven rapidly away, the youth with the table-top banged on the roof of the red Cavalier.

'Fucking racist pigs! Let him go!'

A uniformed officer grabbed his shoulder, spinning him round, and raised an index finger under his nose.

'Move along or you're nicked,' he threatened. The youth spat thickly on the ground and stayed put, tense and ready. The inspector sidled up, motioned with his head for the constable to come with him back to the van, and directed a sickly, artificial smile at the youth, who glared back, unmoving.

Shifty-eyed and edgy, the uniformed officers gathered round the inspector as the group of youths stared and muttered twenty yards away. Several lank-haired women had gathered, alternately gnawing at their lower lips and dragging on cigarettes held in cupped hands.

'All right, you lot,' said the inspector, his voice flat and over-controlled. 'We're staying put until they've finished searching the flat. There's reinforcements standing by on the main road, just in case it gets nasty.'

'Shall we get the shields out, sir?' asked an officer with a flushed face and a wispy moustache.

'Don't be a twerp. Get your coats and helmets on, all of you, three outside the flat, three at the bottom of the stairs, the rest of you in front of the van. If they give you some verbal and call you a piggy-wig, just smile and say nothing. If they ask you a reasonable question, answer it politely and suggest they go home. Anyone throws anything, don't try to arrest him unless you're quite sure he's the one. There's no call for hysterics, not yet anyway.'

A few more people had drifted up and several were hanging out of windows, watching sullenly as the police deployed themselves. A siren started up on the main road, and a flashing blue light came closer, bounced like a strobe from shabby buildings and leafless branches. Some of the youths dodged off behind the rubbish chute, bending to look for bricks and cans. But instead of a police van, an ambulance lurched up and stopped.

'Some old geezer been knocked over?' called the fat, blue-sweatered woman attendant who climbed out of the side door and waddled round to the rear. 'Blimey, what's this, Billy Smart's circus?'

The old man was limping painfully towards the ambulance on the arm of a woman neighbour. The youths behind the chute dropped the few tin cans they'd collected and came out to watch. Wayne and Winston seemed to have been forgotten.

'What d'you do to the old guy, then?'

Table-top directed the question aggressively to the officers by the van as the patient was put in a chair and lifted into the ambulance. The midget dog performed a near-vertical leap, trying to join its owner in the vehicle, but was arrested in mid-air by the neighbour jerking on the lead, and fell heavily to the ground with a strangled squawk.

'We didn't touch him,' said one of the uniforms. 'It was the bloke we were chasing who ran over him.'

'Why were you chasing him, then?'

'He's suspected of a serious offence, sir, that's why.'

The truculent conversation continued spasmodically as the plain-clothes men came down from the flat with several bulky plastic bags which they loaded in the van. One by one the bystanders were growing cold, losing interest and drifting away. Eventually the police all returned to the van and it ground away out the estate, adding the cloud of its exhaust to the traces of cold mist which seemed to be creeping up from the river.

An hour later Wayne and Winston, their clothes sent to the forensic lab, were sitting in paper overalls staring silently at the dull brick walls of their cells, and the CID men were standing in the garish, brightly lit saloon bar of the Trident, laughing loudly and knocking back large Scotches.

'I'm saying nothing,' said Wayne sullenly for the tenth time, his eyes fixed on the table in front of him, one finger picking at the ring on the zip of his overalls. 'I want to make a phone call.'

A dressing the size of a small envelope covered his right cheek and there was a plum-coloured bruise rising beneath the acne of his left cheekbone. Slicer looked down at him coldly.

'Look, you poxy little creep, you don't seem to realise you're in big trouble here. There's been a murder committed and we've got good reason to believe that it was done by you and that jungle-bunny mate of yours in the course of a robbery. You were arrested wearing a leather jacket which was taken from the dead man's locker. And we've got a witness who saw you in there. You're going to have to talk about it sooner or later, so you might as well start now.'

Slicer's consonants were slightly blurred. Wayne looked fearfully up for a moment into his dark little eyes, then shook his head and looked down again. 'I want to see my brief,' he mumbled.

Slicer threw himself back into his seat with an exasperated grunt and looked over at Stone, who was sitting in the corner making notes. There was silence for a few seconds.

'He doesn't seem impressed with our witness, so shall I tell him about his prints?' Slicer asked Stone in a light, speculative voice. Stone's brow, already clenched from the effort of writing, tightened further. Wayne looked up furtively.

'Whassat?' he muttered.

'Oh, we're interested now, are we?' said Slicer sarcastically, turning back to him. 'I thought you might take a bit of notice of that. Fact is, pal, your dabs are all over the place in that club – so are your mate's. So why don't you tell us about it and save everyone a lot of trouble?'

Wayne looked round at Stone, overalls rustling, then back at Slicer. For a moment his mouth twisted and he looked as if he was about to talk, but a sudden shadow seemed to cross his face and the hesitation disappeared.

'Nah, he'll fuckin' skin me,' he muttered. 'I told you, I wanna phone my brief.'

Slicer heaved a still more exasperated sigh and ran a hand heavily down over his face, pulling down his lower eyelids for a second and revealing the inside of them, pale and watery like the contents of an oyster. He looked over at Stone, addressing him as if Wayne was suddenly no longer in the room.

'This little bleeder's got ideas above his station, Jim. I reckon he needs a few more hours banged up to think it over, don't you?' he said.

'That's right, Ron,' said Stone, using a kindergarten voice. 'He seems a bit too impressed by what his mate's going to say. So maybe it's time we had a word with this big, important mate of his.'

'You reckon it's all right, guv, I mean saying about the witness and the dabs and that? Probably won't get much from forensic before the end of the week.' There were dark, moist furrows across Stone's wax-coloured forehead, like the lines round a parsnip. Slicer laughed, surprised.

'Don't you worry your head about it, Jim,' he said jovially, clapping Stone on his ox-like shoulder. 'You've got to pull the odd fast one on little shits like this, you know that. We'll get it out of them one way or the other. They reckon they're hard nuts, but we know different.'

The door opened and Winston, his wrists handcuffed in front of him, was guided into the room by a uniformed officer with a hand on his elbow. He took Wayne's place on the hard plastic chair, wriggled his muscular shoulders beneath the thick white paper, and gave each of the two officers a defiant, three-second stare as his handcuffs were unlocked. Slicer looked back impassively.

'OK, Leggit, let's not beat about the bush. We've got a witness who saw you in there, we've got your prints all over the shop, and your mate's chirping away like a little cock sparrow. So why not tell us the full story, and my colleague over there will write it down?'

Winston glared at Slicer and loudly hawked a lump of phlegm up from his throat. Slicer stiffened and leaned back as if to move out of range, but Wayne swallowed the lump and gave him a wicked little smile instead.

'You're lying,' he said calmly. 'I can always tell when a copper ain't got no evidence. I'm saying nuffin till I see my lawyer, so you're wasting your time.'

Slicer's cheeks turned red and he suddenly leaned over the table so his neat little pink nose was only inches away from Wayne's big untidy black one.

'Don't piss me about, you little turd,' he hissed. 'I'm going to do you for this one, you hear? We'll have all the evidence we need by the time I'm finished.'

106

Winston stared impassively back. His face gave nothing away, but he started picking rhythmically at a large, soiled plaster stuck round his left forefinger.

'That's what they call a fit-up,' he said calmly. 'I don't think a jury would be very impressed. And you've been drinking, officer. I can smell it on your breath.'

He shook his head and tutted sarcastically. Slicer was non-plussed for a moment, then banged the table abruptly and stood up.

'OK,' he said briskly to Stone. 'Holding charges for the pair of them: resisting arrest, assaulting police and possession of drugs. We'll ask for bail in police custody pending further inquiries, and' – he turned to Winston and raised his voice to a sudden shout – 'we'll see how you like that, dickhead!'

CHAPTER 13

Judy stood at the lock gates of Greenland Dock in bright December sunshine and watched two windsurfers plying up and down the dark water of the basin. They came smartly towards her, their rubber-suited bodies leaning out sideways and flexing slightly as the boards bounced over the slight chop created by the brisk wind. Just when it seemed certain they would crash into the stone side, they changed course slightly, let go of the brightly coloured sails so the wind whipped them round, and were suddenly charging back the way they had come, a splash of cold spray blowing off their wake. Up and down they went, as if on rails, a couple of hundred yards each way, under the blank eyes of the half-empty apartment blocks. This was the future which the advertisements said was about to begin – waterside living in Docklands, expensive, near-deserted, and only half a mile from the vandalised, rubbish-strewn estates of Bermondsey and Deptford. Perhaps Duncan had been a windsurfer.

As she'd left the station the previous afternoon, angrily clutching a box of belongings from her desk and not looking where she was going, she bumped into Ahmed on the ramp leading out into the rear yard. He grabbed her firmly by one arm to prevent either of them falling over, and as they apologised and backed off Judy – used already to colleagues deliberately avoiding her eye – caught a look of sympathy on his face. She was surprised, because word had got around that it was he who had done the interviews at Banks and Heritage which had brought out the incident in the alleyway, including the threats she'd made which led to her suspension. She already knew him from one or two cases on the estate, so she looked a second time, cautiously; perhaps he had reasons, unlike many other police officers, to take the side of the rejected ones. He smiled awkwardly, pushing his hands deep in his anorak pockets.

'You off, then?' he said.

''Fraid so,' said Judy. 'Not my idea, I can tell you. Done any more interesting interviews?'

He took the question as an accusation, winced, and shrugged: 'Yeah, sorry about that, Judy. It won't come to anything, they're just covering their backs, suspending you. Sounds to me you handled that guy just about right.'

'Thanks, Ahmed.' It was the first approving thing anyone had said about it.

'You know we just brought in Leggit and White?'

'Yeah, through the wallet I brought in.'

Ahmed grinned. 'You should be on the case, not off it.'

'Reckon it's them?'

He screwed up his face sceptically.

'Long way to go,' he said, sidling towards the door. 'Must go, Judy. Anything I can do, you let me know.'

The longer she thought about it now, the more she felt convinced that the only way Wayne and Winston would get involved in a murder would be by some freakish accident – and Duncan's murder looked far from accidental. They wouldn't deliberately jeopardise a career of moderately profitable petty crime by getting involved in serious violence. They might be stupid, but they were smart enough to know that dead bodies meant a lot more police attention than the two of them usually got. But then, if they didn't do it, who did? The only other suspects so far were Clinton – and, of course, herself.

After she'd watched the windsurfers for ten minutes, neither of them had hit the quay or fallen off their board, and Judy turned round to watch the river instead. The tide was running out heavily against the easterly wind, and swirls and humps of muddy brown water bucked and plunged treacherously across Limehouse Reach, as if some mighty underwater creature was rolling and writhing beneath the surface. A police launch was ploughing upstream, wallowing occasionally or cutting into a heavy wave with a high burst of spray. But that, too, avoided mishap and disappeared round the corner, near the great silver tower of Canary Wharf, totem of the developers and property men. Judy tried to cool her resentment of everything she saw by closing her eyes and turning her face into the wind, letting it blow back her hair and freeze her forehead.

Further along the riverfront a removal van was parked outside one of the luxury blocks, being filled with expensive-looking furniture. Would it be too soon for Duncan's place to be emptied like that? After all, respect for the dead wouldn't cut much ice if there was no one left to pay the mortgage. She wished vehemently that she had never met him, that his reptilian grey eyes had never looked through the glass wall of that gymnasium and fallen on her. But it was her own fault for letting herself be titillated by his world of money and self-interest, and for going to that party full of drunken Ruperts and Fenellas who, according to that Grania woman, all 'shagged' each other.

She walked on, hands in the pockets of her anorak, wondering if she had a future in the police force. Even if the murder was solved and her suspension ended, it would stay on her record and make it harder for her to get promotion. And now everyone knew about her relationship with Clinton, which would make everything even more difficult. She wished she'd never met him either, with his cheerful, seductive charm and easy-going ways.

When she'd got home the previous evening, she'd found he'd left her car and put the keys through the letterbox, without any message. She had immediately phoned him to tell him she'd been suspended and to seek some sympathy. Keturah had answered the phone, and thanked her warmly for getting David Righter to help Clinton. But when Clinton came on he was cagey and distant and said they ought to 'cool it' for a while.

'It's not just me who says so, Righter reckons so too. Said I should keep a low profile for a bit.'

'So you don't want to see me?'

There was a brief silence. 'I'll give you a call in a couple of days.'

'That's great, Clinton, when you've been hauled in by the police and you want a shoulder to cry on, you can bang on my door at midnight. When I get suspended and want a bit of support, you don't want to get involved. Thanks a lot.'

'Sorry, Jude, I've got enough trouble with the police already.'

She felt some satisfaction now that she hadn't told him that Wayne and Winston had been arrested and were probably the main suspects now: he could sweat a bit longer and hear it on the news. And anyway, the spotlight might come back to Clinton before long. Maybe he had done it after all; maybe that was why he wouldn't see her, because he thought she was on to him. Clinton Pink, the mild-mannered murderer. Secret life of the telecom charmer. Killer who sweet-talked a cop.

Judy's pace slowed as she came nearer to the Docklands Squash and Weights Club. Her mind was running through a lurid, slow-motion scene of two men, one black and one white, fighting like dogs on the floor of the gym, with her standing shouting in the corridor outside, beating unheard on the glass partition. She came to a stop in front of a massive new apartment block, its two projecting wings enclosing a sparkling glass building like a giant conservatory, and found herself watching a scene which seemed to merge with and replace the scene in her mind. She moved a few steps closer, shading her eyes from the sunlight which knifed back and forth between the river, the glass, and the cream-coloured façade. She felt faint and unreal.

In spite of the brilliance all around, the interior of the glass structure was lit with powerful lights. Men in gaudy shirts moved back and forth like parrots between palm trees and pieces of equipment. A girl in a black one-piece swimming costume was reclining, legs crossed, on a white towel spread across a big fan-backed cane chair. Her dark hair was cut short and her expression was sulky and irritable. A bearded man in white shoes was talking rapidly to her, making placatory little hand movements. Eventually the girl uncrossed her legs, stood up and strode lithely to the edge of the pool, where she stood without moving as the crew of parrots fussed and fiddled with their equipment. Then, at a signal from the bearded man, the girl in the black costume dived into the pool, her ankles and feet pressed tightly together as they disappeared into the turquoise water. She heard nothing of the splash or the clapping from the bearded man and his parrots, as if the plunge had taken place in another world. It *was* another world round here, divorced from the real life of London. Judy turned away suddenly and walked off briskly towards the club.

It was just before noon when she rang the bell and Sharon's pixie-like head looked up from the reception desk. A shadow of anxiety seemed to cross her features as she saw who it was, and she hesitated a moment before reaching over to the buzzer to let Judy in.

'Hi, Judy,' she said breezily, fiddling with things on the reception desk and keeping her eyes averted. She was wearing an electric-blue shell suit which seemed to vibrate under the strip light. The place was hushed and deserted, but Judy restrained herself from saying it was like a morgue.

'Hi, Sharon. Surprised you're even open after all the drama this week.'

'Yeah, so'm I really. Opened again lunchtime yesterday, believe it or not. Still got the upstairs all closed off, various coppers coming an' going. But John reckoned we should act normal, business as usual an' all that.'

'Anyone much been in, then?'

Sharon turned the corners of her mouth down and shook her head. 'Nah, not many. You're the first today. Too creepy for most people, I suppose. I'm not too keen, I can tell yer.'

There was an awkward silence before Judy took the plunge.

'Listen, Sharon, I want to have a talk with you,' she said in her best home beat manner, matey but firm, leaning on the counter. 'You know I'm a police officer, don't you?'

Sharon stopped fiddling and looked up to hold Judy's eye for the first time. 'Yeah, Clinton told me. 'E was in last night, see, about eight, just before I went off. Told me what's been 'appening.'

'Did he just. You probably know I've got a bone to pick with you, then? Mainly about him?'

'Yeah, sort of. I'm sorry if I got yer into trouble, Judy, I know I shoot me mahf off sometimes. Listen, John'll be back in a minute and I'll come round to the bar and we'll 'ave it out properly, right?'

Sharon's blue eyes were screwed up with honest anxiety and some of Judy's vindictive feelings began to seep out of her. She walked slowly along the brown carpet tiles into the main part of the club, looking at the layout of the place with new attention and wondering for the hundredth time about the movements of Wayne and Winston, or Clinton, or whoever it was who had killed Duncan.

The little reception area contained a till, a telephone, a board hung with numbered locker keys, and the booking sheets and light switches for the courts. If you went under the hatch into the reception area and turned left, you'd be in the office, which seemed to have no windows – only an opaque panel in the door. If you turned right, you'd pass along a narrow corridor cluttered with boxes of squash balls, stationery and T-shirts bearing the club's name. This would lead you into the serving area of the bar.

On the right as you entered the club was the door to the women's changing room, opposite reception. A bit further along was the door to the men's changing room. Both changing rooms, she remembered, had internal staircases leading to their respective saunas and jacuzzis on the first floor, and doors from there led into the upstairs corridor opposite the gym. Beyond the men's changing-rooms on the ground floor was the main staircase, at the top of which was the door to the gym. Beyond the bar and main staircase were the squash courts. The viewing galleries from the courts formed a continuation of the upstairs corridor.

It struck Judy as she sat down on one of the blue-padded seats in the bar how difficult it would be for any one person working at the club to know what was going on in the building. If you were in the office, you couldn't see a thing, except perhaps the outline of anyone standing at the reception desk, or just in front of it. If you were behind the reception desk, you could see the entrance door and anyone standing in the little lobby outside it, the door to the women's changing room, and the narrow corridor into the back of the bar. If you were behind the bar, you could see the whole area in front of you with its chairs and tables, part of the corridor leading to the doors to the squash courts, the lower half of the main staircase and – if you leant out across the bar – the door to the men's changing room. Wherever you were, events in the changing rooms and on the first floor were entirely closed to you. They ought to get a few internal observation cameras installed.

Sharon came and sat down next to her carrying two half-pints of lager. It was a peace offering, but Judy never touched alcohol during the day. And what was a fitness freak like Sharon doing drinking at all? Sharon gave her an imperative nod.

'Go on,' she ordered. 'Do you good – it's been a bleedin' awful week. Clinton told me you aren't on duty for a bit, like.'

Judy found herself lifting the glass and laughing.

'How old are you, Sharon?'

'Me? Nineteen. Why?'

113

'I don't know. You're a bit young to be telling people what's good for them.'

'I grew up at an early age,' said Sharon grimly. 'I'll tell you about it sometime. So what's this bone you want to pick?'

The prickly bubbles of the lager made Judy's eyes water and her head swim after only a couple of swallows, and the complaints about Sharon, nursed sleeplessly in the small hours, flowed easily out of her. If Sharon hadn't eavesdropped on Duncan asking her out, it would have saved everyone a lot of trouble. If she hadn't added insult to injury by asking Clinton about Duncan's invitation to her, Clinton would never have known and wouldn't have challenged her, Judy, about it. If he had never challenged her, she might not have felt provoked to go to Duncan's party; and if she hadn't gone, she wouldn't have ended up threatening to kill him in an alleyway and getting suspended for it.

And that wasn't all: if Sharon hadn't asked Clinton about Duncan's invitation, Clinton wouldn't have phoned Duncan to protest about it. The argument between the two men in the gym just before the murder might not have happened, and then Christine and Alexis wouldn't have overheard it and reported it to the police. Then Clinton wouldn't have been under suspicion and everyone would have been spared a lot of grief.

Sharon stared sadly out of the big windows towards the sunlight and the river during this diatribe.

'I'm sorry, Judy, really. I couldn't help overhearing what Duncan was sayin' that time, and I just assumed he was talkin' about some invite to the bofe of yer. An' 'cos of that, I fort it was OK to ask Clinton. S'pose I should've known Duncan would be trying to nick someone else's bird – wasn't the nicest geezer around, was 'e? Anyway, at least I never told the cops that Clinton and Duncan were at each other's froats over you.'

'No, but you'd told those two tarts in the sauna and they weren't slow to pass it on the police.'

Sharon shook her head miserably. 'Nah, I never told 'em. But I did mention it to one or two people, and word sort of gets around. 'Fraid there was a bit of talk about you two, what wiv Clinton being black. Anyway, I should of just kept me big mahf shut. Then Duncan might not 'ave bin topped.'

'Hang on, now you're suggesting Clinton did do it.'

'Well, I dunno. I can't see it, meself, 'e's such a gentle sort of bloke. But you know, anyfing can 'appen, can't it? And it all seems to fit, dunnit? I know 'e was your bloke an' all that. But can you be sure it wasn't 'im? Really sure?'

Judy drained her glass. 'Well . . . not completely. But the CID are losing interest in him now – they've got the two lads who did the robbery. They've probably been in court this morning.'

'Really? An' they reckon they might 'ave done Duncan in an' all? Oo are they?'

Judy shrugged. 'Couple of minor villains from the estate where I work. I know them, actually. Both got form, but not for violence. Can't see them killing someone, but if the bastard running this inquiry wants to pin it on them, that's exactly what he'll do. Listen, Sharon, would you like the other half of this?'

She flicked the side of her empty glass with her fingernail, and Sharon stood up, grinning, to get refills. When she returned, her face was screwed up in thought.

'You know those coppers came round to see me, right? No offence to you, Jude, but rat-face and pig-face is 'ow I fink of 'em, way they be'aved. Anyway, they were goin' on at me abaht why I fort Duncan had left by the time I locked up and went 'ome.'

'Oh, yeah?' The second lager was slipping down smoothly, with none of the initial hesitation. Rat-face, pig-face and the rest of the police force seemed very distant.

'Well, I told 'em that Clint said to me that 'e fort Duncan 'ad gone – which is true.'

'Huh – bet they made a meal of that.' Judy put on an imitation of Slicer's self-righteous, insinuating voice. 'And he's got the perfect motive to say that, hasn't he, Miss Bunnie?'

'Yeah, sumfing like that. 'Ere, you're gettin' pissed. But the fing is, the more I fink about it the more I'm sure I 'eard the door click shut, so I was already finkin' Duncan 'ad gone before Clinton told me.'

'Yeah, but surely that door's clicking all the time with people coming in and out.'

'Nah, you gotter remember this was late on a Sunday and there was only, what, five people left, right? Sean went, and he 'anded 'is key in and I saw 'im go out the front door. Same goes for Christine and Alexis – two tarts is quite a good name for 'em, come to fink of it. Then when I was cleaning up in the bar and

115

going in and out of the office, I 'eard the click and just assumed it was Duncan leaving and not bothering to 'and in 'is key.'

Judy had slumped back in her chair and was concentrating on swilling her lager carefully round the glass without spilling it. 'Well, could someone else have been in the place?'

'Not wivout me knowing, 'cos I've gotter let everyone in.'

'But hang on. Clinton told me he'd heard someone in the changing room, upstairs, when he went in there after having a drink. He thought it was Duncan at the time, but now he thinks it could have been someone else.'

'So the only someone else it could 'ave bin was the guys who broke in – they must've come frew that top winder before the place was even closed.'

'Must have. Unless . . . listen, did you tell the officers who interviewed you about hearing the door click shut?'

'Not sure I did. They pissed me off sumfing rotten, see? Cos they was sayin' I'd given information to the robbers and wasn't doin' me job properly. An' they seemed more interested in Clinton than anyfing else.'

'That's bloody typical.'

Judy sighed heavily and shook her head, staring through the window, eyes screwed up at the brightness of the open sky above the river. Then she turned back to Sharon with a moist, dimply smile and held up her empty glass, eyebrows raised hopefully. 'Oh well,' she said cheerfully. 'Nothing to do with me.'

'Jesus, it's beginnin' to give me the creeps,' said Sharon, standing up with the glasses. 'Those tea-leafs must've been in the place while I was closing up by meself. If I'd gone right upstairs to check the gym they'd probably 'ave done me in an' all.'

Judy nodded heavily. 'That's right. Lucky escape. Better have another drink and forget it.'

CHAPTER 14

Slicer was so angry he gave a little jump every half-dozen paces, as if propelled off the ground by the force of emotion. He strode through the station, slammed the incident room door back on its hinges and threw his precious trilby into the corner. It landed on the tea-tray, upsetting a carton of milk.

'It's not just the juries who need sorting out in this town!' he yelled at Manningbird, who was sitting comfortably at a desk doodling on a notepad. 'It's the bloody magistrates as well!'

Manningbird raised his pale, mole-like eyes and looked at Slicer with one grey eyebrow lifted. 'Tell me something I don't know,' he murmured, turning back to his pad. 'Such as, what's got you out of your pram?'

Slicer flung his coat at the coat rack where it hung askew, like a corpse on a bush. 'We've lost 'em, that's what. We asked for remand in police custody, three days, and the bastard wouldn't have it. Sent them to Brixton instead, said we could interview them there.'

'Why'd he say no?'

'Said the law only lets him do it if there's a need, and he reckoned we hadn't shown there was one. Like hell, we hadn't – only need to solve a bleeding murder, don't we? Plus some crap about inadequate facilities, risk of oppressive treatment and all that subversive left-wing bullshit.'

Beyond raising the other eyebrow, Manningbird remained calm. 'Who was it?' he inquired mildly.

'Hugh Effing Dimwood, J.P., that's who.' Slicer's sharp features contorted with distaste as he spat out the name. 'Aided and abetted by David Effing Righter, who seems determined to represent every bloody suspect we've got on this case.'

Manningbird drew in his breath and screwed up his face, as if

117

a twinge of arthritis had just hit him. 'Tough combination, that. One poof, one commie. In fact, one commie and one commie poof, to be a bit more precise. Dimwit was put up by some militant trade union, from what I 'ear.'

'And Righter's an agitating tosspot,' muttered Slicer, suddenly noticing where his hat had landed and hurrying over to dab the milk spills off it with the sharply folded handkerchief from his breast pocket.

'Still,' said Manningbird cheerfully, pushing his chair back noisily and standing up, 'I shouldn't let it worry you too much.'

'No?' said Slicer gloomily, distracted by his dabbing. 'Why not? It'll be a pain in the arse going down to Brixton every time we want to squeeze their balls a bit.'

'I've been on the blower to our scenes of crime officer this morning, and it seems they've managed a nice little print. On the frame of the window where they broke in, apparently – very careless. They matched it up exactly this morning with the ones on White's file at the National Fingerprint Office. So that'll do nicely, as they say.'

'Oh yes?' Slicer rearranged his coat on the rack, primped his trilby into shape and hung it on one hand to admire it, head cocked, like a sculptor appraising his handiwork. 'So I wasn't wrong when I told the little sods last night that we already had their dabs – that'll save us a lot of bother in court, eh? Great stuff. Probably ties up the robbery, then – but what about the murder?'

Manningbird yawned and stretched complacently, showing off the spinnaker-like profile of his belly as his jacket rode back. His voice was artificially casual.

'I've also been talking to the forensic lab, and the footprint in the blood belongs to Leggit. They checked his shoes against it this morning, first thing.'

Slicer turned sharply round from hanging his hat on the stand. His eyes emitted a gleam of triumph and his mouth slid into a grin.

'No – straight up? Couldn't be better, eh? We'll have them trussed up like turkeys by the end of the week. Just wait till I see that little toe-rag again – there won't be any more crap out of him.' He mimicked Winston's street-wise accent: ' "See my brief, I'm saying nuffin'." '

118

He brought his hands up in front of him in the strangling position, his face reddening and twisting. But Manningbird interrupted his aggressive euphoria with a few caveats: it was a common make of training shoe, it would be some time before they'd complete their analysis of the pattern of wear and reach a definite conclusion. And unless more evidence turned up, White and Leggit would still be able to argue that they'd stumbled on the corpse rather than killed anyone.

'And there's another thing,' Manningbird added, sitting down again and reaching for his pad, which was covered in scrawls of blotchy Biro. 'Apparently it *is* a stair rod.'

Slicer stared at him blankly. 'You what?'

'A stair rod, Ron, believe it or not. Like Jim Stone was going on about. The metal bar they found in the pool of blood – remember? Sort of thing they used to 'old stair carpets down with, before the days of the fully-fitted Wilton. It's' – he squinted at his notes – 'a cheap Edwardian model, apparently. Cast-iron bar thirty inches long and 'alf an inch in diameter, wrapped around with a thin layer of brass-coloured metal, type as yet unascertained, to make it look like the real thing, to wit, brass. No decent prints on it, unfortunately.'

Slicer suddenly sat down as well, as if drained by his recent excess of feeling, and his eyes wandered around the floor as if he'd dropped a contact lens. 'Must have picked it up out of a skip,' he muttered eventually. 'Then they took it in with 'em, just in case.'

''Scuse me, sir.'

A porky young man in grey suit and mock-regimental tie bobbed obsequiously up to Manningbird's side clutching a notebook in which several words were written in large capital letters. The Superintendent looked at him irritably.

'What is it, Colin?'

'Sorry to interrupt, sir. Phone call from a woman living in Stock's block – apparently she saw a strange car near by on Sunday evening. Old banger, she said, foreign.'

'All right, Colin, log it, will you?'

Colin bobbed away to the other side of the room. Slicer, meanwhile, was looking out of the window, miles away, hands pocketed, rocking on his heels and nodding.

'Yeah,' he was saying quietly, as if learning a script. 'Lifted it from a skip, confronted by our Dunkie in the course of the robbery, bash him on the head – panic job. Then they try and disguise it.'

'There's one more problem with this rod, if you're listening, Ron. To do with the blood. Most of it'll probably match the blood type of our Dunkie, as you insist on calling the stiff. But part of the metal covering was damaged, leaving a bit of a sharp edge. There's some blood on that end too – but it's a different type.'

'Really?' Slicer turned round, enthusiasm vying with irritation in his features. 'So that might come from our little combo. Nice one.'

'Did either of those two toe-rags 'ave a cut 'and when you interviewed them the other night?'

Slicer grimaced.

'Wish I could remember. But it was Fatty Stone's idea to test for a second source of blood – he should have been on the lookout, see if he had a bandage on or anything.'

'We'll find out soon enough. Could be a problem with the forensic link, though. Apparently you need a stain the size of a ten-pence piece to do DNA testing, which would pin it to one person, definite. But there isn't enough of it for that, so they're going to 'ave to use another sort of test – not DNA.'

'How far does that one narrow it down?'

Manningbird shook his head and turned down the corners of his grey lips. 'Two per cent of the population, if we're lucky, forty per cent if we're not. All depends on the group. Our next problem is we'll 'ave to persuade our friends in Brixton to give samples, because unfortunately we're not allowed to just strap the buggers down and stick a needle in 'em. No doubt our radical brief will tell them to dig their 'eels in.'

'Mmm, maybe not,' muttered Slicer, tapping with a neatly manicured forefinger on one of his incisor teeth. 'If I remember rightly, we can make a big deal of it in court if they refuse.' He put on a plummy barrister's voice: 'Ladies and gentlemen of the jury, you may ask yourselves what the defendants are trying to conceal.'

'Worth bearing in mind, Ron. One thing, though – if we can't get blood off of 'em, a few fresh 'airs'd do. They can use the junk on the end of the 'air to do the blood type.'

Slicer stopped tapping his tooth and his neat moustache twitched slightly. He raised his hand as if it were clutching a football-

120

sized object. 'Oh, I think we could produce the odd fresh hair at the next interview, don't you, Chief?'

Manningbird's earlier cheeriness had faded as they spelled out all the difficulties, and he turned away to stare through the window into the yard and light a Silk Cut. He let a cloud of smoke float an inch out of his mouth, then sucked it sharply back in, like a chameleon swallowing an insect.

'Either way, Ron,' he said weakly, 'this blood isn't going to do it for us, not unless the luck's really running our way. The forensic's good, but not that bloody good. We still need more – some sort of break.'

Slicer walked up to stand close beside the Superintendent, adopting an identical pose in unconscious commiseration.

'Don't worry, Chief,' he said in the tone used with a disappointed child. 'We'll be seeing those two little buggers again in the morning and we'll really put the screws on them. Nothing like a good cough, eh?'

Manningbird turned to him crossly, emitting smoke from three orifices, like a holed exhaust pipe.

'Look, Ron, you ever 'eard of the Guildford Four? Eh? And all the rest of 'em? This is the bleedin' nineteen-nineties. Ethical interviewing, and that. We're going to get a result without the party tricks, right? No point in pushing it, eh?'

Slicer screwed up his face and raised his hands in mock-surrender.

'All right, all right, only a thought,' he said, switching from the cajoling to the placatory. 'Don't lose your rag, Bryan. Just thinking aloud. But if you ask me, a good prosecuting brief would make mincemeat of them. They're just waiting to be plucked. Begging for it.'

Judy raised her head from the cushion, but as soon as she did so her head began to throb. Each pulse of pain seemed to brighten the world yet drain it of colour, as when a landscape is lit by lightning. Blow after blow seemed to hit her behind the eyes, and she sank gently back on to the sofa again with a feeble moan. Then a sour belch forced its way up her throat, and she remembered the successive half-pints of the thick, urine-coloured lager and the increasingly rambling conversation with Sharon Bunnie. After that there'd been the peculiar looks she'd got while striding unsteadily home singing 'I'm Forever Blowing Bubbles'. (Where had she got that from? Probably those endless, cold, boring Saturday afternoons outside London football grounds.) Now she just concentrated on breathing deeply to summon the strength to sit up and face the pain once more. She would never drink at lunchtime again, ever. In fact, she would probably never drink again, at all. Simple as that.

For a while she thought that the agitated twittering noise she could hear was part of her hangover, but as she opened her eyes little by little she traced it to a bunch of sparrows sitting and quarrelling on the guttering outside the square bay window where the sofa stood. From her low vantage-point, she could occasionally see a beak, a cocked tousled head or a little horny foot scrabbling for a better hold. The jumpy little birds reminded her of the peaky teenagers who gathered round the blocks on the Chaucer Estate in the warmer months, smoking furtively behind their hands and noisily exchanging pushes and insults. A few light-grey clouds had moved across the morning's unmarked sky, but some of them were already stained with the pink of imminent sunset. She looked at her watch and saw it was a quarter to four.

Suddenly the phone rang, and the harsh jangling noise shocked her into the sitting position in one movement. As she stumbled across the room, the rush of agony in her head nearly knocked her down, but she managed to pick up the receiver and lean her ear against it.

'David Righter here.'

'Oh, yes,' she mumbled, propping herself against the wall and trying to focus her mind on an image of the lawyer's bony, earnest face.

'Sorry I couldn't help your Mr Pink very much the other night. I'm afraid your colleagues pulled rather a fast one, which isn't unusual, I have to say.'

Pompous git, thought Judy, as she struggled to push a few words out through the wall of pain. Typical bloody lawyer.

'Yes, no, all right. I mean, don't worry, I heard about it. From Clinton.'

'Are you all right? You don't sound very well.'

'Er, no, I'm fine – just a bit of a headache. But listen, how did you get my phone number?'

'They said at the station that you weren't on duty, so I tried

122

the phone book. There aren't that many J. Bests in SE23, you know.'

'No, s'pose not. Anyway, thanks for helping Clinton. I don't think he's the main suspect any more, in fact. They pulled in two other suspects last night.'

'Yes, I know. That's why I'm calling, actually. I'm representing them.'

'Oh, yes? How come?' Judy detected a hint of self-satisfaction in Righter's voice and wanted above all to get back to the sofa and nurse her head.

'Colleague of mine was duty solicitor during the night and was called to the station to see them. He handed the case to me for this morning's hearing because I already knew a bit about it.'

Nice excuse for stealing the thunder, thought Judy. 'Listen, why are you telling me all this?' she asked irritably.

Righter cleared his throat carefully, and a guarded, formal tone entered his voice, as if he were addressing an unsympathetic magistrate.

'Well, I saw them for a bit before the hearing, and I represented them in court. They were remanded to Brixton, by the way. The police wanted to keep them in the station, but the bench wasn't very impressed by the fact that they'd appeared in court unshaven, still wearing paper overalls. But that's not the real problem. The real problem is that for some reason best known to themselves they won't talk to me or the interviewing officers. They want to talk to you.'

Judy swallowed another gust of lager-laden fumes as it tried to escape from her stomach, and wondered if she was going to be sick. 'Me? Why? I can understand why they might refuse to talk to Slicer and company, but why not to you? Surely it's in their own interests, if they're in serious trouble, isn't it ?'

'Quite so – this is what I've told them. I think it's because they don't actually know me, but they do know you. That counts for a lot in the sort of world they move in – you know, you're mates with someone, you can communicate with them, they see things from your point of view. I've come across that sort of thing quite a lot. They seem to think they've got something vital to tell you.'

'Do they, now?' Judy closed her eyes hard, provoking more sparks of pain, and tried to think it through. 'And do they realise that what they tell me would only do them any good if I passed it on to you anyway?'

·'I don't know. The important thing for them seems to be that you're the one who hears it first. Maybe they want to show off, impress a woman, I don't know.'

'And are they expecting me to keep it secret from the CID, whatever it is?'

'That I don't know – you'll have to work it out with them. Anyway, they've filled in a visitor's form and are expecting you down there in the morning.'

Judy promised to think about it and put the phone down. Her head was still unsteady as she went to the bathroom and swallowed two painkilling tablets which snagged and rasped her throat as she tottered back to the sofa and collapsed on to it with a grateful gasp. The sparrows had flown off elsewhere, the sky was darker and the clouds were now the colour of gold and bruises. Another windy winter's night was beginning and she had no one to help her with a difficult decision. She wondered about ringing up her mother, but all she'd get was the usual vague counsel of caution.

She propped her head a little higher and sighed. The cautious thing – the thing she'd always done, in other words – was to sit tight, do nothing and wait for the dust to settle. She just had to stay clear of Wayne and Winston, leave the case to Slicer and the CID, and mind her own business until it was sorted out. Then she'd be reinstated and her steady little life as a WPC would resume as before. Her career would be damaged by the suspension, but if she didn't get promotion soon, well, it probably wouldn't be too long before some nice young officer who'd already been promoted would want to marry her and carry her off to be a housewife and produce snotty kids in Croydon.

But she found this chain of thought being gradually but inexorably pushed aside by a powerful feeling of protest and agitation. It was as if she'd been injected with a fast-acting stimulant, and she was now up and pacing the room, feeling hot in the chest and throat, the pain in her head evaporating. She was suddenly rummaging through the dark cupboard where she'd always pushed her feelings of resentment and rebellion, believing they could only do her harm and bring more discord to the house. Now she held them up and embraced them like long-lost childhood toys.

She thought angrily about the mixture of contempt and sentimentality she got from her male colleagues in the police force – contempt for her professional abilities, sentimentality when they felt they could protect her. She thought about the hard-drinking machismo which put her off her earlier intentions of joining the CID. She thought about Slicer, about his twisted, weaselly grin, and the arrogant, aggressive way he'd treated her. She thought about the Chief Superintendent's ingratiating smile as he'd told her she was being suspended, and about the whole unthinking, order-obsessed, uncreative police hierarchy. An image from the morning popped back into her head, of the girl's neatly joined ankles disappearing into the deep water of the pool. She reached out, snapped on the light with a brisk blow of the finger, and turned towards the suddenly bright room with a look on her face her friends would not have recognised.

'Sod the lot of them,' she told the furniture. 'I don't care if they do throw me out – I'm going to do it.'

CHAPTER 15

Judy zipped her anorak over her thick Fair Isle sweater – her 'social worker' sweater, as a male colleague had called it – and clattered quickly down the concrete stairs into the chilly evening, breath condensing in front of her. Above the street's pseudo-classical roof line, the light of a bright half-moon was diffused vaguely through a thin layer of misty cloud. Her Metro took three long twists of the key to start, and she felt that the grinding noise would bring people to their windows, that they would guess what she was up to and report her. Her stomach was queasy, and she was sure her voice would tremble when the time came to speak.

She'd decided on a route which would avoid the police station on the main road through Rotherhithe, and the engine lurched and sputtered as she drove along Dreadnought Close and turned right through Rotherhithe Village, wiping the condensation from the inside of the windscreen with her forearm. The tightly built little houses were silent and dark apart from a few slivers of light from curtain-edges, and the streets were deserted except for the occasional huddled figure crossing the light-pools of street lamps with a hunch-backed, shivering dog. She crossed the humped bridge over the canal and stopped at the junction with Surrey Quays Road.

There was nothing coming, but as she was pulling out a speeding car seemed to appear suddenly in front of her and she hit the brakes hard. The other car swerved and lurched, and as the prolonged hoot of protest tailed away Judy sat tight with her eyes closed, resting her forehead on the cold steering-wheel. She tried to tell herself that she was trying to solve a crime, not commit one, and that this jitteriness was ridiculous. All she was trying to do was pass on a useful scrap of information to her own colleagues, which was what any responsible member of the public would do. Another car came up behind her, flashing its lights, so she let the clutch out again and drove on towards Greenwich with exaggerated carefulness.

In the streets round the Royal Naval College a few teenagers were pushing noisily in and out of the pubs and a handful of winter tourists, arms linked against the cold, were looking hesitantly at the menus outside restaurants. Judy found a parking space in the little road leading up to the waterfront, and as she got out of the car she saw the black yard-arms of the Cutty Sark outlined against the sky, the rigging trailing down like spiders' webs. She walked past the dark bulk of the great clipper and the dimly lit glass dome over the lift shaft to the foot tunnel under the river. She heard the lift gear whining and whirring, and a muffled voice shouting and cursing somewhere in the depths. She remembered walking through the pale-tiled tunnel, eyeing the seeping puddles and fighting back claustrophobia. But now the little yacht Gipsy Moth was in front of her, her white hull illuminated eerily from the dry dock below, like a face in the dark with a torch held beneath its chin. Her two gangways were hauled to the vertical, and a notice told anyone curious about her voyage round the world that they'd have to wait until April.

Judy remembered Sir Francis Chichester's wizened, simian face in the newspapers and on the television when he died, and all round the deserted plaza she sensed the ghosts of dead sailors whose last contact with England had been on this muddy brown loop of the Thames. She shivered and pushed her hands deeper in her pockets as she walked over to the railings and stared at the river. The water seemed quiet and smooth, as if the tide was just turning, but the reflections of the red and white lights of the river bus pier shimmered and moved with the ripples created by unseen currents, and a hundred yards from the bank, beyond a group of moored barges, there gleamed a darker stream where the water ran faster.

On the far bank, among the eccentric rooflines of the modern river-front apartments, sat the glowing dome at the opposite end of the foot tunnel. Further back, with several tall, long-armed cranes clustered round it like a presidential guard, the silver shaft of Canary Wharf Tower rose beyond the dirty orange glow of London's lights and cut into the lower rim of the night sky, illuminated milkily by the moon. It was an expensive playground, thought Judy, where flash, well-upholstered people like Duncan and his friends were shouldering out the dog-eared people and crumbling buildings which had clung to this mudbank, unhelped and neglected, for the last quarter-century. Now that the place had been selected to usher in the future, they were being flicked impatiently aside, like insects off a honeypot: except that, suddenly, the money wasn't there, and the men in suits were standing around looking surprised and pained, making helpless hand gestures, and anxiously telling each other that the golden days had only been postponed by a couple of years. She heard a polite, attention-seeking cough, and turned jumpily to see someone sitting on a bench a little further along, next to a lifebuoy stand.

'Is that you, Ahmed?' she said in a slightly cracked voice. Her earlier headache had receded and was now just a mildly uncomfortable after-image across her forehead.

'Yeah,' came the reply in a stage whisper. 'We can't go on meeting like this, you know, Jude. People will talk.'

Judy looked round to check there was no one else near by, then walked over and sat down next to him. She was still on edge, but she noticed in a policewomanly way that the lifebuoy was missing from the stand in front of them, despite a warning that a life might depend on it staying in place.

'Thanks for coming, Ahmed,' she said. 'Sorry about the cloak-and-dagger stuff.'

'Yeah, what's this all about?' His voice was nervous too, and slightly playful, and the lights from the pier gleamed on his eyes and teeth as he flashed her an uncertain grin. A scent of aftershave hung about his dark face.

'I'm not after your body this time, I'm afraid,' she said quickly. 'I'm afraid it's just about this case, you know, the murder.'

'Yeah, I thought it might be.' He looked down for a moment, one hand fiddling with the fingertips on the other, and when he looked up at her again his smile was more formal and his eyes less bright. Judy hurried on.

'It's just that now I'm suspended I'm not meant to talk to anyone about it, and you said if there was anything you could do to help . . . well, there is. There's a couple of things Slicer ought to hear about, or someone in the squad, anyway. And you were the only one I thought I could ask.'

'Fire away.'

She told him about her lunchtime discussion, leaving out the overdose of lager and its after-effects, and explained Sharon Bunnie's certainty that she'd heard the door click as someone went through it – someone she'd assumed at the time was Duncan leaving the club.

'From what she told me, she didn't make that very clear to Slicer and Stone, and she doesn't want to go back to them now. Either she didn't remember at first, or maybe it was because they needled her and got her back up, or maybe it was a bit of both. But she was very definite about it today, and if she's right, it might mean someone else was in the place – another suspect, possibly.'

Ahmed's smile was gone, his forehead creased.

'You're assuming these two we arrested from the Chaucer broke into the building much later?'

'For the time being, yes, I am assuming that. Personally, I can't see them doing the murder, somehow. But my problem is that now I'm suspended I can't march in and tell Slicer that he might have missed something important – I've been formally warned off. Which is why I got in touch with you – to make sure that someone on the investigation does know about this possible extra person in the place. I just hope you're not going to grass me up.'

Ahmed was nodding as he listened, watching his foot tapping on the ornamental paving beneath the bench. Now he looked at her and grinned wryly.

'Nah, don't worry,' he said. 'I can keep a secret. Might call in the favour one day, though.'

'Thanks, Ahmed.'

A couple emerged from the shadows under the prow of the Gipsy Moth and moved towards the riverside railings. They were so closely intertwined that they nearly lost their balance; but once they were wedged against the railings they got on with giggling, kissing noisily, and groping under each other's coats. Ahmed looked embarrassed, and as he caught Judy's eye he jerked his head towards the pier.

As they strolled away down the river-front, eyes averted, hands in pockets, and keeping a good five feet between them, the smell of Indian food wafted past them. Judy glanced at Ahmed and thought of all the old wharves now being converted into posh apartments – Java Wharf, Cinnamon Wharf, Coriander Building.

Ahead of them, downriver, where the new toy-box architecture gave way to the old refineries and chemical plants and derelict landings which bordered the Thames from here to the sea, two chimneys were pumping out plumes of white smoke.

'I know what you mean, though,' said Ahmed as they passed under the Cutty Sark's white figurehead, their footfalls echoing crisply off the granite setts. 'About Slicer, I mean. I can just see him getting so pissed off with that receptionist girl that he doesn't listen to what she's got to say. You know, because she's annoyed him or he's got some other bee in his bonnet. You know what he was saying this afternoon?'

'No?'

Ahmed snorted and shook his head before continuing, as if he couldn't quite believe what he was going to say.

'Well, you know we had this bloke Pink in at first?'

Ahmed stopped walking and talking in sudden embarrassment, then tried to continue normally

'Yeah, course you do, he's a mate of yours, isn't he?'

'I'm never going to hear the end of that now, am I?' said Judy, failing to keep the bitterness out of her voice.

'It's fine by me, Judy – don't get me wrong. Anyway – at first the boss is dead set on him being the main suspect, you know, because of all the trouble over you, the argument, and all that. So, apparently Pink says when he's interviewed that he heard someone on the way out of the changing room, someone he thought at the time was Duncan – which fits in with what your Sharon says now about hearing the door click and thinking at the time it was Duncan, doesn't it? Anyway, at first Slicer's not interested in what Pink might have heard, because it doesn't fit in with his theory. You know, it's a suspect trying to throw in a red herring. But now he's switched to these other two because of the wallet and all that, White and Leggitt, and so suddenly he's interested. You know what he said at the conference this afternoon?'

'Go on, thrill me.'

'He said we could persuade Pink to say he'd seen someone in the changing room who looked like White or Leggitt, in return for getting us off his back. Not just *heard* something, which is what he actually said, but seen someone. Amazing, isn't it? He didn't put it quite as crudely as that, but that's what he meant. I

130

know you've got to cut the odd corner in this game, but that's going a bit far, don't you reckon? The Super reckoned so too, slapped him down a bit. And when you think about it, it wouldn't even help us much – we've already got the forensic to say those two were in the building, and just having a sighting of them wouldn't be evidence that they done the murder as well as the robbery.'

'He's a right bastard, that one, between you and me,' muttered Judy as they entered the narrow walkway between the river and the heavy black railings of the Royal Naval College. Behind the railings, low floodlamps threw a bleached light up into the spreading, vein-like branches of the scarred plane trees, like a glimpse into the underside of some diseased organ.

'I could agree with that,' Ahmed said hesitantly. They glanced at each other and grinned in complicity, squeezing against the railings to let a pair of dark-coated women pass the other way. Judy wanted to ask his advice about the prison visit, but asked him instead about the afternoon's conference.

Ahmed was talking freely now, and he told her about the break-in at Duncan's office, Wayne wearing the missing jacket, the footprint, the fingerprint, the second type of blood on the stair rod, and the decision to find out if Wayne and Winston's blood matched it.

'There's going to be some pretty heavy pressure on those two, all right,' he concluded. 'I wouldn't like to be in their shoes.'

'You reckon they did it?'

They passed a sign warning of danger from anglers casting their lines, and an eddy in the river produced a sudden gentle bubbling close to their feet. Judy peered over the railings, as if they hid an eavesdropper. Ahmed grimaced, moving his head uncomfortably.

'I dunno. You see, I reckon if they were in there squashing that geezer's head like that, there would have been splashes of blood on their clothes. Or on Pink's, if he'd done it. And there weren't any, according to the forensic. Course, when I said that at the conference, Slicer says the two of them must have thrown their clothes away, burnt 'em or something. Well, if they were bright enough to do that, how come they didn't throw their shoes away? As things stand, we could only prove they went in there and stood in the blood, not that they did it.'

'OK, so if they didn't do it, who did?'

Ahmed shrugged his shoulders. 'Apart from your bloke, there aren't any other suspects. We've talked to all his family and friends – close ones, anyway – without so much as a sniff. There was this break-in at the victim's office, but there's nothing in it to suggest a connection – unless the City police are hiding something from us. There's just a couple more colleagues of his we've got to interview tomorrow, and none of them can throw any light on it. House-to-house only produced one old bag who reckoned she saw a black guy and a white guy sitting in a car near the club at about the right time. Which just increases the problem those two have got.'

'Really? Is she reliable, this old dear?'

'How do I know? Wasn't me spoke to her. For all I know, it's pure imagination. You know what it's like round here sometimes.'

'Did you interview someone called Grania at Duncan's company?'

Ahmed nodded. 'Certainly did. Bit of a memsahib on the quiet.'

'Did she tell you that she used to go out with Duncan? And that he took her over from a bloke called Eddie?'

The railings between them and a floodlamp in the college grounds produced a flickering effect as they walked, and when Ahmed suddenly stopped he was striped with shadow, like a man behind bars. They stood facing each other next to a stone obelisk commemorating a naval hero of Georgian times, the noises of the river seductive and calming behind them.

'No, she did not.'

'Probably nothing in it. Just something I learnt in the one evening I spent with that lot.'

Ahmed shook his head as if to clear it, and his voice was angry and reflective.

'I shall have words with memsahib Grania tomorrow. Little cow. This could put a whole different light on things.'

'Don't get carried away – I never got the feeling there was any particular needle in it. They all seemed to be in and out of bed with each other all the time, to be honest.'

'Yeah, but you can never tell when it suddenly gets serious. Bloody hell, Judy, how can the police investigate if people don't tell them things?'

'You know as well as I do – they've all got something to hide,

132

we're not very good at asking the questions, and they don't like us much these days anyway. Not even the toffs.'

Ahmed looked up at the obelisk for a moment, as if it was going to bring him enlightenment. They started strolling again, and after a minute Judy cleared her throat nervously.

'Listen, Ahmed, you promise you won't tell anyone what I'm going to tell you?'

He grinned. 'I can't afford to, not now I've told you all the inside details – I'm in it as deep as you are.'

'I'm going to see Wayne White and Winston Leggitt in Brixton tomorrow. Apparently they want to talk to me.'

Ahmed was silent for a moment, pushing back his bush of black hair.

'Well,' he said eventually. 'They're not talking to anyone else.'

'That's right – not even their solicitor.'

'Yeah? Sounds a bit odd. I suppose it's because you know them and all that. Local contacts – triumph of the home beat system, you might say.'

'Yeah, 'cept I'm meant to be keeping clear of this inquiry.'

'So why are you going?'

They started walking again, the grandly illuminated domes and colonnades of the College now in view on one side. Judy talked about how she'd always obeyed the rules, been good at home and school and in her job, but she wasn't going to obey them this time. She didn't care if she got into trouble, because her career was already in reverse. She was angry at the way Clinton had been treated, and she wanted to be sure they didn't try to pin it on him. She wanted to make sure the right person was arrested for Duncan's murder. And – she didn't mind admitting it – she wanted to defy Slicer. She wanted to prove him wrong.

'So – all sorts of reasons, really,' she said. 'For once I'm going to stop being a good, efficient little girl who does what she's told, and take a risk. And if I run across rat-face, that's just too bad.'

'Good for you, Judy,' said Ahmed weakly, as if this female self-assertion was a strain on his system. 'You go for it, then.'

'But will you back me up? Keep a secret?' Judy looked anxiously into his cola-coloured eyes, remembering the article she'd read in a women's magazine about never telling male colleagues your personal problems.

'You bet.' He laughed and clapped her on the shoulder with

133

nervous heartiness, as if they'd just landed successfully on half the undercarriage or driven through a red light together.

'Sorry to be paranoid.'

'In this job, you have to be. Fancy a drink?'

In front of them was the Trafalgar Tavern with the river lapping mildly at its illuminated white and yellow façade. A board outside advertised whitebait suppers and through one of the windows they saw a waiter in a white jacket moving among the tables with a tray.

'Why not? I'm getting a bit sick of all these pillars and black railings.'

She tapped her foot against a decorative wrought-iron depiction of ropes, pikes, crowns and shields.

'Yeah, we could have done without all that bullshit in the part of the world where I came from,' said Ahmed, leading the way into the pub's elaborate hallway. A neatly built man wearing a check suit and a dazed smile was coming down the wide stairway from a wedding party upstairs, arm in arm with a satisfied-looking woman in a turquoise frock.

'Can't get away from the courting couples tonight,' said Ahmed. 'What you having?'

When he returned from the bar with the drinks they wedged themselves into a space by the open window.

'What's that in your glass?' said Judy suspiciously. Ahmed looked out of the window before replying in a studiedly casual voice.

'Ginger beer. Very nice too.'

'What? Ginger beer? How d'you get away with that in the CID?'

'They all understand when I tell 'em. It's because I'm a Muslim, see?'

His eyes met hers and he shifted uncomfortably from one foot to the other. Judy put her drink down and took him by the arm as if to escort him off the premises, but he shook her off with an embarrassed grin.

'I've got to go into pubs, haven't I, or I couldn't do the job. I used to drink a bit, but it was just getting out of hand. And my family found out about it and started giving me stick.'

'Well,' said Judy, lifting her gin and tonic, 'explains why you're a bit more on the ball than some of your mates. Cheers.'

CHAPTER 16

Dr Trotter came through the door of the Chief Superintendent's office and bustled across the carpet with a speed that was improbable in one so tubby. He had covered the five yards to the desk, the lapels of his double-breasted grey check suit flapping around the soft contours of his embonpoint, before Manningbird and Slicer had fully risen to their feet. They stared in disbelief at his paisley-patterned bow tie, subjected his moist little hand to the sadistic squeeze reserved in police circles for potential adversaries, and slumped back into their chairs, exchanging a covert glance of cynical amusement. But their visitor remained standing at the other side of the desk, rubbing his hands and looking quizzically round the room.

'Now then, let's see,' he was saying, in a precise, fussy voice. 'Perhaps we could manage something a bit less formal, a bit less shall we say, hierarchical? What about two of us on the sofa over there, eh, and you could bring one of those chairs to the other side of the coffee-table, couldn't you, Mr Slicer? Mmm?'

Slicer's eyes flared wide with hostility, and his mouth was open, about to deliver some crude rebuke, when hesitation struck him. He closed his mouth again and looked at Manningbird, who cleared his throat and suddenly seemed to be trying to see over his paunch to the shine on his shoes. Slicer looked back at Trotter, whose bright little eyes flitted busily from one to the other of them.

'Mmm? Mmm?' he repeated.

Slicer open his mouth again and addressed his superior officer. 'Er, who's in charge of this briefing, sir?'

'Well, er,' said Manningbird, raising his eyes from the floor and looking round the room.

'May I suggest we proceed on a mutually interactive basis,

135

behaving as partners in the venture rather than trying to impose a system of authority?' Trotter's voice was smooth and insinuating. 'I always feel that a desk forms something of a barrier to communication, don't you? A defensive weapon – perhaps an offensive one, sometimes, mmm?'

After a last outraged glance at Manningbird, Slicer slowly dragged the heavy swivel chair across the carpet, studying Trotter poisonously as he did so. Trotter did not look like a man who gave himself a hard time or failed to look after himself. Everything about him was rounded and pampered. His blond hair, though thinning, was gleaming and silky, and his cheeks, though well advanced on the journey down into his neck, were pink and impeccably shaved. His moist, pernickety mouth seemed designed for sucking cocktail cherries off sticks, and the back of his hands were succulently padded with pale flesh.

'Who is this poofter?' muttered Slicer as Manningbird brushed past him on his way to sit down on the sofa, as instructed.

'Shut it, Ron,' mumbled Manningbird, adrift between shame and anger.

The meeting got under way with Trotter giving them a little summary of how Scotland Yard and the Home Office, as part of a piece of research, had asked him and his colleagues to make a contribution to a number of serious investigations, intervening at an early rather than a later stage. The sort of psychological profile of the possible offender which he could offer had already been useful in producing a breakthrough and a successful conclusion in a number of long-running investigations into serial crimes which had otherwise ground to a halt – the Catford Chopper and the Horse Guards Rapist, to name a couple they'd almost certainly heard about. Now the idea was to see if they could offer any help at the very beginning of serious inquiries, including those into single, one-off crimes, perhaps suggesting 'alternative emphases and perspectives and perceptions before the inquiry became fully ongoing'.

'Mr Trott,' interrupted Slicer with a truculent snort, rolling his narrow shoulders in preparation for a scrap. 'I could name you any number of rapes I've solved without the help of any perceptions and emphases from any psychologist.'

He masticated the final word with slow distaste, like a sick dog chewing a wad of grass. Trotter's tidily manicured fingers fluttered placatingly.

'Absolutely, absolutely, no question, of course,' replied Trotter. 'This is just one extra tool we can offer to the investigator, which he may or may not need. After all, when we form a certain way of looking at things it's sometimes not easy to convince us otherwise, mmm, yes, no? Other possible avenues of thought, perhaps, a few if-then rules which might be applied to the principal personalities involved?'

'What's a sodding if-then rule?' demanded Slicer, his face colouring dramatically. 'If you don't mind me asking, Dr Trott?'

'Trotter. Oh, you know,' said Trotter, closing his eyes and putting his head on one side like a cheeky bird, apparently impervious to the danger he was in. 'Such as in ooh, car mechanics, say – if there's a spark in the plug, then the coil's all right – that sort of thing.'

Manningbird had recovered his presence of mind and came between the two to give Trotter a rough outline of the case – the gory scene in the gym, the robbery, the pathologist's report, the scientific information so far.

'D'you have any suspects yet?' asked Trotter, narrowing his eyes and pouting moistly as he scribbled notes with a thin silver pen.

'Certainly do,' said Manningbird smugly, settling further back into the sofa with his hands folded on his midriff. 'They're in Brixton Prison right now, on an 'olding charge.'

'Who might these gentlemen be? Unless they're ladies, of course.'

Slicer snorted like an impatient horse, but Manningbird held up a grey hand of warning and continued to do the talking.

'Couple of local petty criminals. One of them left 'is dabs – fingerprints, that is – on the window. The other left his footprint in the pool of blood.'

'Mmm, exceedingly colourful. Do they have any known history of physical violence against the person?'

Manningbird looked at Slicer, who turned the corners of his mouth down and shook his head. Trotter asked if they knew much about the victim, including his friends, his job and his sex life.

'Filthy,' interjected Slicer, swiftly. 'We know that for a fact.'

'Not a great deal,' said Manningbird, giving Slicer a dead glare.

'Ambitious, dedicated to his job, no obvious enemies. Except, that is, for one gent who we've now more or less eliminated. Reasonably popular at work, as far as we can tell. Socialised with his colleagues, 'ad several girlfriends – including one of our own WPCs who's a member of the club, as a matter of fact.'

'Really? Obviously not the fastidious type. Are you planning to find out more about his friends and background? And his sex life?'

Slicer cut in. 'What's the point, now we're nearly home and dry? And d'you mind not insulting our WPCs?'

'Come on, Ron,' said Manningbird, closing his mole-like eyes wearily. 'You're not exactly complimentary about them yourself. I 'eard what you said about Judy Best and the Old Kent Road at yesterday's conference, remember. So let's listen to what the man 'as to say.'

Trotter's glittery eyes were snapping from one to the other, his little jowls wobbling. 'Mmm, do I detect a spot of conflictual intra-disciplinary interaction? I've always felt, *entre nous*, that teams on major inquiries could benefit from a little systemic consultation.'

Manningbird looked at him sideways, heavy-lidded. 'If you're asking, does my colleague 'ere get up my nose from time to time, the answer's yes. But it's an occupational 'azard, and I'll straighten 'im out in the pub later on. As for young Dunkie, d'you 'ave any ideas? Failing a sudden attack of remorse and a full confession from our present suspects, the fact remains we've still to get sufficient evidence to pin it on 'em.'

'Mmm.' Trotter leaned back luxuriously and fixed his eyes on the collection of plastic helmets, baseball hats and other eccentric headgear which the Chief Superintendent kept on his shelves instead of books. Then, slowly and delicately, he inserted the point of his pen in his left ear and began speaking, rapidly and precisely.

'A few preliminary thoughts, maybe, subject to amendment after more detailed investigation of the facts so far. Point one: great physical strength – although that may not be the case if the stair rod was used to stun the victim first, as it were. Two: unusual sadism and cruelty – the deliberate crushing of the head and face, indicating a desire to obliterate the person's very identity, to extinguish his entire personality. Three: as a motive for the foregoing, great hatred, indicating, to my mind, that the victim was known to the assailant and had taken against him, possibly over some period of time. Alternatively, the victim was not especially well known to the assailant, but the assailant had somehow come to *represent* for him all the deprivations and antagonisms of his life. Either way, it's unusual for a killer to try to destroy the victim's features in such a brutal way. That's only usually done to strangers in organised warfare or terrorism. Four: we might be talking, literally, about a psychopath – someone devoid of the normal human emotions of empathy, someone without a concept of the suffering of others.'

Slicer, who had been fidgeting impatiently throughout, jumped to his feet at this point, thrust his hands into his pockets and bounced over to stare out of the window.

'Suffering – I'm suffering all right,' the others heard him mutter. Trotter's only reaction was to transfer the pen to his right ear with a narrow-eyed wince of pleasure, and continue.

'Five: if my speculations so far are correct, we might be dealing with a stalker – someone prepared to take the time and make the effort to conceive and follow an elaborate plan, watching and waiting until the victim is in the chosen situation before making his move. Six: that implies a solitary lifestyle, a person probably living on his own, possibly without much family or many friends, with the time and leisure to make such plans and preparations. Seven: there is some evidence from criminological studies to suggest that an offender of this kind may become, shall we say, somewhat attached to his activities. In other words, he may kill again, if he hasn't already killed before. And finally, eight: it occurs to me there may be something symbolic about the location here. A sporting rivalry spilled over into murderous hatred, for example? Mmm? Who knows?'

Manningbird continued to stare opaquely at Trotter for several seconds after the end of this speech, his head swaying gently, like a nodding dog in the rear window of a car. Then he gave a little start, realising it was finally his turn to speak. Slicer was still at the window, huffing and bouncing on his heels.

'In other words,' said Manningbird eventually, in a mesmerised monotone, 'a right bleeding nutter?'

'Got it in one,' said Trotter with satisfaction, nodding vigorously and examining the yellow-black blob accumulated on his ballpoint. 'In layman's terms, a right bleeding nutter.'

Slicer turned from his study of the contractors' lorries grinding down the grey winter high road and faced them with a vengeful expression. 'Call it copper's instinct if you like,' he said sarcastically. 'But that's more or less what we said right from the start – isn't that right, Chief?'

CHAPTER 17

The visiting-room at the prison, with its battleship-grey tables arranged in rows under the vibrating shine of the strip lights, resembled both an examination hall and a kindergarten. There were older people seated at the tables, hunched and defeated-looking, examining their folded hands, anxious not to be recognised. But all around them were women wearing cheap, smart clothes and too much make-up, some of them trying to control small children with wheedling voices and faces streaming with tears or snot. There were babies in pushchairs, their mouths clamped round the teats of bottles which rolled from side to side on their chests as they stared about them with pop-eyed surprise.

Down at one end, two prison officers with peaked caps and moustaches were watching the scene with wary contempt, hands behind backs, passing the occasional remark to each other. How familiar it was, Judy thought, as she sat waiting at table eighteen, unmade-up and dressed in her usual off-duty jeans, white sweatshirt and black leather jacket, a monochrome contrast to the garishness of the other women. The place reminded her of the social security offices where she'd occasionally been called to deal with disturbances – the same unhealthy-looking skin, the same whipped-dog eyes. She remembered putting an arm-lock on an old man who was shouting toothlessly about his giro cheque, smelling his soiled-mattress smell and feeling how thin and brittle his bones were as she propelled him out on to the cold pavement and told him to go home.

The officers looked at the clock, looked at their watches, nodded to each other, and opened a door at the end of the room. Men emerged like sheep from a crowded pen, stumbling against each other and looking uncertainly around them until they got their bearings on one of the hunched figures or waving women.

At first Judy didn't spot Winston's athletic figure in the anonymous mêlée of grey prison uniforms, but there he was, suddenly,
with rather less bounce and roll in his walk than usual, and less
cheek in his grin.

'Hi, Jude,' he said humbly, looking at her like a submissive
child and fiddling in the pocket of his blue and white striped
prison shirt for a scrappy gold packet of tobacco. Evidently his
mother had not yet brought him some of his own clothes.

'Look, Winston,' said Judy coldly. 'This is completely out of
order and I'm staying no more than ten minutes. What's it all
about?'

All around them men were already leaning forward on the
tables, smoking and talking and gesticulating intently, making
excuses and complaints, faces contorted in the effort of impressing
their point of view on the outside world. The noise-level rose,
and a child screamed repeatedly as a prisoner with a lined face
and ragged hair tried to embrace it. Winston took his time rolling
and lighting a cigarette, his face clenched in concentration.

'It's like this, see,' he said finally, taking a deep drag and
cocking his head on one side, eyes narrowed judiciously. 'I've got
plenty to say, right, but I'm not saying nuffin' to that scumbag
Slicer. No way. Out of the question.'

'What's wrong with Detective Inspector Slicer?' asked Judy,
preserving a straight face and an innocent voice. 'He's the officer
running the inquiry. Anything you want to say you should say to
him.'

'What's wrong with 'im?' Winston's voice went squeaky with
indignation and his face contorted as if someone had waved a
stinking haddock under his nose. 'He's bleedin' violent, for a
start. He's got no respect for nobody. And he's a bleedin' racist.
That's just for starters. Know what he called me?'

'I don't want to know, thanks very much, Winston.'

'Sooty, that's what. I'm not taking that from no one, I tell you.
There's a law against it, and coppers got to obey the law like
anyone else, to my way of thinking. And he's been putting the
screws on my mate Wayne. He's not as hard as what I am, I don't
mean to boast, like, but it's the truth, and 'e'll be saying something
stupid next time that fucking reptile 'as a go at 'im, pardon my
French. People like 'im should have a public 'elf warning on 'em.'

'Have you been able to talk to Wayne since your arrest, then?'

'Nah, they been keeping us apart. 'Cept at the beginning when they put us in next door cells. They wanted us to start rabbiting on about it while some officer sits outside making notes. Like we was born yesterday. I just kept telling Wayne to say nuffin' and ask for his brief. After that it was another of the old tricks what the filth pulls, telling one of us that the other's gone and coughed. I tell you, nuffin's too low for that scumbag Slicer. He'll be in here having another go at us this afternoon, you wait for it. Bastard.'

Judy leaned back impatiently on the hard chair, seeing Winston's eyes drop furtively to her breasts as her jacket slipped back. She leaned forward again and crossed her arms.

'Winston, you're hardly going to get me on your side by insulting other police officers. Why don't you tell your solicitor what you want to say? He's the one who's going to have to defend you in court.'

'Dunno 'is track record, do I?' Wayne spread his muscular palm as if producing a scientific truth. 'Brief I usually get has left the business. Yeah, well, he's doin' a bit of time, actually. So this geezer's a total stranger. Don't know if I can trust 'im.'

'Look, Winston, whatever you tell me won't do you any good unless I pass it on to your solicitor or to Mr Slicer, or both.'

'Yeah,' said Winston, leaning forward confidentially and making his point slowly so she wouldn't miss it. 'But the fing is, coming from you, they're going to believe it, aren't they? If it just comes from me, they'll think it's just another nigger making it up to save his own skin.'

He leaned back again to find that a toddler with a threadbare duffle coat and a blotchy pink face was standing stock-still at the side of their table, staring at him as if he was a Martian. Wayne twitched with irritation.

'Look, piss off, sonny!' he snapped. The child's face collapsed in terror and it stumbled away, screaming.

Judy tried to ignore this minor drama as she reflected on Winston's reasoning. He clearly believed that the institutions of authority operated according to principles that were different from those he was familiar with: everyone listened to each other, believed each other, and stuck together. He probably thought that was how the respectable world, the world of front gardens and standing orders and little shaped carpets round the base of

143

the toilet, achieved solidarity and protected itself against the criminals. If he could just get her, his only link with that world, on his side, then the rest of the respectable world would come over too. She suppressed the urge to tell him about the double-crossing, arm-twisting and bad faith she'd come across in the police force, to describe the way Slicer had treated her.

'Come on then, let's have it,' she said.

Wayne leaned forward, his features seeming to swell and shine with charm and persuasiveness, and cast a quick glance to either side to check that no one would overhear him.

'Look, you know we did the break-in, right, and nicked the money? We'll put our hands up to that one, all right? But you gotta back off on this murder business, all right? No way did we top no one. No way.'

'How are you going to persuade our Mr Slicer about that? Especially since one of you left your footprint behind in the victim's blood? I knew him, you know: he was a friend of mine.'

'No, really?' Winston's eyes sprang even wider. 'Jesus, Jude, I'm really sorry to hear that. Close, was he?'

'He was once, but not for long,' said Judy grimly.

'Sort of ex, then? Got yer. That's bad luck. But, listen, Jude, it wasn't us, honest. I tell yer, I got the shock of my life when we saw the poor bugger. We just shined the torch into the gym, see what's what, like, and there he was, lying there, all that strawberry jam. I nearly frew up, honest. We was so upset, we thought about reporting it ourselves. Then we thought we'd better just mind our own business, know what I mean?'

'Yeah? I notice you weren't too upset to take the poor guy's key and raid his locker. What was it, leather jacket, wallet, anything else?'

Winston put his face in his hands for a moment, then came up looking contrite and spread his palms. 'What can I say, Jude? Completely out of order. Can't deny it. But it was Wayne spotted the key on a little shelf in the gym there, and he seemed to think it was the obvious thing. Complete toe-rag, that kid, know what I mean?'

'That's right, Winston, blame it on your mate,' said Judy crossly. 'But as far as I'm concerned you're the senior partner in this job. What's more, I can't say I'm very impressed by these

144

little confessions – they've already got the forensic to prove all that.'

Wayne leaned forward and caught her forearm urgently, as if prompted by all the forearm-grabbing and hand-clinging going on at neighbouring tables. He was so close she could smell his breath, sour with nerves and tobacco, and see the tendril of red veins in the corner of one eye.

'Nah, the main thing is, Jude,' he said in a dramatic stage whisper, 'we saw the geezer what done it, that's what.'

Judy pulled her arm away and preserved an impassive face. A quick picture passed behind her eyes of Wayne and Winston crouching in the shadows, watching the murderer, furtive and bloodstained, making his way out of the building.

'What d'you mean?' she asked calmly. 'Did you actually see it happen, or what? You just said you came on the body afterwards.'

'Nah, we didn't see 'im actually on the job, like. No weapons rising and falling, like the films, an' that. Nah, we saw him 'angin' around outside, dinn' we? Befo:e the place closed down for the night. Before we went in.'

Judy folded her arms more tightly and smiled sceptically. 'Come on, Winston,' she said. 'Is that really the best you can do?'

'Nah, Jude, listen to me, will yer?' There was pain and desperation seeping into his eyes now, nibbling at his voice. ''E was carrying something in his 'and, know what I mean? Something like a stick or a metal bar. A weapon, wasn't it?'

'Hang on a minute, Winston. When did you see this guy? And where?'

''E was 'angin' about in the doorway, must have been, what, round about nine. We rolled up too early, didn't we? We was told the place shut at half eight on a Sunday, not half nine, so we was 'angin' about, sitting in the .notoi mostly, a few yards down the road. And this geezer rolls up wearing a track suit, looking dead shifty and carrying this piece of gear. We thought it was a squash racket at first, what with it being a squash club an' that.'

'How did he arrive, by car?'

Wayne was rolling another cigarette, relaxing again now that he'd regained her interest. 'Didn't see one – could have parked it round the corner. We thought he'd gone into the club, but when I took a stroll down the road 'e was still 'angin' about just outside the door, in the little porch place.'

145

'Did you see him again, after that?'

Winston scratched his head and looked away, fidgeting with a pack of cigarette papers on the table. 'I fink it was 'im. Fact I'm sure it was. Trouble is, we weren't so close the second time. There were these two white tarts came out the club and gave us a funny look, sitting there in the car, so we moved out the way, down the end of the club, see, down near the river where there was no one about, to wait for the place to close. We saw a few more people leaving, and he was one of 'em. You know, about ten, fifteen minutes later.'

'And was he carrying the stair – er, the weapon, whatever it was?'

Wayne leaned forward and breathed on her again, brown eyes glittering. 'Nah, 'e wasn't. Finking back, 'e definitely wasn't.'

'And could you give a description of this person?'

'I already did, din' I? White geezer, tall, taller than me, brown hair, short, could be blond, black track suit – or somefing like it, you know what it's like under those street lights, can't tell shit from salami.'

Judy looked away and tried to think as salvos of noise burst continuously around her. All over the room, prisoners were still gesticulating and persuading, visitors looking more weary and reproachful, children falling asleep or fighting among themselves. Down at the end, one of the officers glanced at the clock and yawned widely enough to swallow a human fist.

Unless Slicer had been very careless, she thought, Wayne and Winston wouldn't have been told about the weapon they'd found. So it seemed unlikely Winston was making something up to fit in with what he knew. The tale seemed too cumbersome to be a lie. On the other hand, he might have remembered seeing the rod lying there in the blood and invented his story around it.

'How would he have got through the security door into the gym?' she asked. 'Everyone has to be let in by the receptionist.'

Winston shrugged. 'I dunno. If it's just got one of them buzzers, you can just stick something in the crack to hold it open.'

'But it would just keep buzzing until the latch was closed, and the receptionist would cotton on.'

Winston gave her a jack-the-lad grin. 'I used to repair those things when I 'ad a job once – check it out, Jude. You're the detective, aincher?'

146

She began to get up, but he grabbed her again, round the wrist this time. She thought of all the welts and bruises and minor damage you saw on the women on the Chaucer Estate, and looked down at him icily. He quickly let her go.

'You believe me then, don't yer Jude?' he said pleadingly. 'You'll put 'em straight? I can't afford to get done for a big stretch – I got responsibilities. What about me old mum?'

'Can't recall you worrying about her too much in the past, Winston,' said Judy. 'Using her flat as a doss-house and a place to deal dope.'

'But you'll get that Slicer off my back, eh? I don't want to talk to that geezer again, know what I mean?'

'I don't think Mr Slicer would take that much notice of what I say,' said Judy, smiling tightly. 'But I'll see what I can do.'

She stepped out of the prison gatehouse, hurried past another queue of waiting families, and turned into the main road. One of the prison officers had given her an over-inquiring look as she'd waited for her money and keys to be handed back at the search point. The same man had also stared at her on the way in, and she wondered if he'd recognised her, perhaps from the magistrates' court. Now she looked around impatiently for a phone box, eager to get on with her plan, and saw one two hundred yards further down the hill.

She had nearly reached it when there was a sudden squeal of tyres and she jumped round to see a burgundy-coloured Cavalier performing a lurching U-turn, causing a bus to brake and beep its feeble horn. The car roared along her side of the road in low gear, bounced two wheels up on the pavement and came to a halt five yards away. Even before he'd erupted from the car like a pilot in an ejector seat, she knew it would be Slicer.

'Were have you been, Best?' he demanded, red in the face, striding up to her menancingly. Black or white, copper or not, their tools of communication, sooner or later, were the grabbed arm, the shouted threat, the raised hand. She stood dazed and furious, not replying. The prison officer must have phoned the station – unless Ahmed had given her away.

'Have you been in that bloody nick?' shouted Slicer, planting his hands on his hips. Judy fought the automatic impulse to confess and submit and placate, and put her hands on her hips as well.

147

Passers-by were stopping to look and smirk at this theatrical confrontation.

'I don't want to talk to you,' said Judy in a low, vibrating voice that was strange to her. 'I'm suspended from duty, in case you don't remember, so what I do in my private life is no business of yours. Now if you don't mind I'm going to make a phone call. All right?'

She turned and made for the phone box, but he grabbed her by the arm and pulled her round to face him again. She lost her balance and staggered, but his grip on her arm kept her upright as he thrust his pulsating face close to hers. Her eyes were sprayed with fine spittle as he yelled at her.

'Suspended or not, Best, I'm warning you to stay away from everything to do with this case, or you'll be on a charge of conspiracy to pervert the course of justice. Understand?'

Judy looked deep into the dark eyes, searching behind the surface for a moment for the source of this aggression. Then the need to get away took over, and she shook his hand off with a grunt.

'And you,' she snapped back. 'You'll be facing a complaint of assault if you don't keep your hands to yourself. Got that?'

She strode to the call box without looking back, but her hands were trembling so much that the receiver rattled against her skull as she dialled. There was an immediate answer.

'Is that the squash and weights club?' she asked, her voice unsteady.

'What's that?' an ancient voice replied tremulously. 'This is the foot clinic.'

Judy slammed down the phone and tried again. This time she hit the right buttons and Sharon Bunnie answered. Yes, said Sharon, why didn't she come down straight away?

Slicer glared for a while at her leather-jacketed back, running his hot palms down the side of his suit, then glared at the bystanders. A skinhead with torn jeans and a seaweed-green swastika on his forehead stared back and spat heavily on the ground. Slicer raised his forefinger and opened his mouth, then changed his mind, ran the forefinger under the lower edge of his trim moustache, and sauntered deliberately back to the car. Stone, doughy and impassive, was waiting in the passenger seat, whistling tonelessly and drumming his fingers on the outside of the door.

CHAPTER 18

The low clouds were clearing and the wind getting up again as Judy stopped her dirty Metro outside the parade of shops in Blackheath where Christine Bottomley worked. This was another part of the world, occupied by people of an altogether different income bracket. The paving stones weren't cracked, the shops had clean windows and bright paintwork, and tubby old men in check caps strolled comfortably in and out of them with gently panting Labradors and proper shopping bags with leather handles. Back down the hill, in the low city landscapes where Judy spent most of her time, the old men were skinny and hatless, and tripped and cursed their way along the gritty streets with jumpy little mongrels and torn plastic carriers. And the women here – by the time Judy reached Vamps Hair and Beauty Studio, she felt she'd already seen half a dozen of them wearing navy pleated skirts and court shoes, climbing in and out of large estate cars with precocious children in knee-length shorts called Benjamin.

As she stepped through the door she seemed to hit a warm wall of conflicting perfumes, with the bitter tang of setting lotion just coming out the winner. A young peroxide blonde with pancake make-up looked up at her expressionlessly, and Judy was reminded of the eyes of a dead prostitute she had once seen hauled out of the river.

'I'd like to see Christine, please.'

'She's still at lunch,' said the blonde, staring first at Judy's unkempt, windblown hair, and then at her scuffed white trainers.

'I'll wait, then, if you don't mind.'

'Have you got an appointment?'

'No, it's a personal thing, only take a few minutes.'

The blonde shrugged slightly, picked up an emery board and began rasping at her nails.

'Suit yourself,' she said, her fishy eyes fixed on her task. 'Have a seat.'

Judy sat down, her mind immediately picking at the case again as her eyes wandered impatiently round the shop. There were trolleys containing deep plastic shelves of toothed rollers and lengths of floppy yellow rubber, there were little baskets full of pink combs and implements like miniature bottle brushes, and there were postcards of Florida shorelines and Tenerife sunsets taped on a cupboard door. But it was the door of the club she had in her head, opening and closing, clicking and buzzing. Why hadn't anybody thought of it before? Or if they had thought of it, why hadn't they acted on it? It seemed that Winston's criminal mind was rather more agile than those of the detectives. She and Sharon had needed only a couple of minutes to demonstrate that the club's security door wasn't the barrier everyone had assumed it was.

If someone walked through the door, leaving the strong spring to close it, it was easy for someone else, standing in the little lobby outside, to place a wedge against the jamb and prevent the door from clicking back into place and locking shut. The buzzer went quiet as soon as the receptionist's finger came off the button, the door looked closed to the casual eye, and there was no warning to indicate that it wasn't. The wall to the left of the door was solid up to waist height, with a two-foot wide glass panel above that level, and when Judy used the plastic tag on one of the locker keys to jam the door, Sharon could see her from the reception desk through the glass panel. But when Judy stood back a couple of feet and used a squash racket as the wedge, stretching out her arm below the level of the glass, she was out of sight of anyone inside the building. On a quiet night, with no one else about, she could have kept the wedge in place, peeked through the window to check when Sharon moved away from the desk, then pulled the door open and sneaked inside. By putting her hand against the door as it closed under pressure of the spring, she was able almost to silence the clicking noise of the latch.

Judy sighed impatiently, earning a stab of a look from the blonde, and picked up a tattered copy of *Country Life*. She studied the uneven teeth and priceless pearls of Arabella Stoke-Bodgers, younger daughter of Sir Rupert and Lady Stoke-Bodgers, and flicked through the pages of expensive mansions and black-and-white photographs of cock pheasants and snipe. Still no Christine, and her attention drifted to snatches of conversation escaping from under the row of blue beehive-shaped hairdriers.

'Salt water's definitely the best thing for your gums,' said one voice, sad but firm. 'Works a treat.'

'South America? Ooh, that's lovely,' cooed another. 'There's certainly plenty of it.'

'Malaria? Oh yes, I know everything about malaria.'

The blonde abandoned her nails to smile fulsomely at a departing customer, a tall woman with a new henna-coloured hairdo who offered a credit card with the words: 'American Express – voila.' As she left, the door was held open for her by a new arrival in an expensive-looking belted suede coat and a leopardskin-patterned chiffon scarf. Judy immediately recognised her – the woman she'd seen in the changing room a week or two before the murder, talking sotto voce to her friend about exotic underwear and unusual sexual practices.

'Someone to see you, Chris,' said the blonde, resuming her manicure. Christine had bobbed black hair, delicate skin and features, and there was no sign in her large empty eyes that she recognised Judy.

'Miss Bottomley?' she said in her pleasant-but-firm voice, keeping back tempting remarks about not recognising her with her clothes on. 'I'm a police officer working on the Duncan Stock case – remember we told you we might want another word?'

Christine looked guiltily around her as she pulled off her scarf and coat, revealing tight black leggings and a pink sweat-shirt with the words 'Body Talk' stretched across her breasts. Behind her the blonde's eyes had come brightly alive and watchful. The dumpy hairdresser further down the room was also sneaking interested glances, in between pulling strands of the hair of a startled-looking woman through the holes in a sort of plastic skull-cap. Judy hoped no one was going to ask for her warrant card.

'Could we go somewhere private for a moment?' she said, keeping the smile on. 'Won't take a moment.'

Christine finally opened her pink painted lips and spoke in a stilted, mock-cultured voice quite unlike the south London chatter which Judy remembered from the changing room.

'Oh, yes, certainly,' she said. 'Would you like to step into the tanning studio? Fortunately I'm vacant at the moment.'

Judy followed Christine's tightly-packaged rump through a door at the back of the shop. They emerged in a dimly lit, brown-carpeted room which smelt slightly of damp and contained what looked like half a dozen outsize metal coffins on little legs.

'Good God, are those the machines which make you brown?' said Judy.

'Yah,' said Christine, looking at her as if she belonged to another century and lifting the lid of one of the sunbeds like a saleswoman showing off the latest domestic appliance.

'And you just lie down in there and close the lid?'

'Yah,' said Christine again, smiling incredulously. 'You just strip off and pop in. And you come out all brown.'

Judy shook her head, sat down on a hard chair next to a moribund busy Lizzie and explained why she wanted to ask more questions. She noticed as she talked that her lies had already ceased to bother her.

'So I'd just like you to think back to when you came out of the club. Did you see anyone, anyone at all?'

Christine bit her lip prettily and sat down too. 'You mean, up in the gym? I told your nice Mr Slicer all about the argument when he came to see me the other day.'

'No, not the argument. Forget about the argument for the moment – I mean later, when you were leaving the club.'

'Well, we were walking home, 'cos we only live about a quarter of a mile from the club, and there were a couple of blokes sitting in a car just up the road, looking, well, sort of suspicious, you know? One of them was a – well, coloured. I told Mr Slicer about that as well, but he didn't seem very interested at the time. He said he'd be coming back himself, actually.'

'I'm sure he will, Miss Bottomley,' said Judy smoothly, looking hard at the floor for a moment. 'He's got other fish to fry today, I'm afraid.'

'Oh, well,' said Christine, recrossing her legs and clasping her scarlet-tipped fingers round one black knee.

'But was that all you saw outside the club? What about just outside the door?'

'You mean, in that little lobby place, with the notice-board? Ooh, I don't know. There are quite often people there unlocking bicycles or looking at the notices. You know, there are all sorts of things pinned up there, like adverts for flats and the opening times of the swimming pools.'

'But this was a Sunday night, surely you'd have noticed if there was anyone there?'

Christine screwed up her features and turned away for a moment, as if to think. Judy noticed how a curl of hair grew down between the tendons of her neck, below the straight line of her bobbed hair. When she looked round again, her eyes were confused, frightened, over-eager to please.

'Yes, maybe, I think there was someone there.'

'Description?' asked Judy gently.

'I don't know, I really don't. I was nattering to Alexis at the time, I'm afraid. We're always talking, us two. Have you asked her?'

'No,' said Judy, heaving a frustrated sigh and standing up. 'I'll be doing that next. Think about it a bit more, and someone'll be back to take another statement, OK?'

A buzz of gossip halted raggedly as they came out into the shop again, and Judy walked to the door in an awkward silence. Three strides along the pavement, she turned and saw that Christine was already surrounded by her colleagues, talking and gesticulating defensively, like the eyewitness of a crime in a media crush.

Judy headed for the phone boxes at the end of the shopping parade. The evidence from Christine was not much help, but she didn't have the patience to go searching out Alexis as well. Something in her mind had fastened ever more firmly on Winston's description of the man outside the club, and she was remembering more and more about Eddie Nutting, Duncan's tall, curly-topped colleague from work. There was his volcanic temper on the squash court, the mismatch afterwards between his smiling, bobbing head and the poisonous gleam in his little eyes. There was his sarcasm about Duncan at the party, and the fact that he'd been succeeded in Grania's affections by Duncan: Ahmed was right – you never knew when these things, under a calm surface, became murderously serious. She also wondered if it had been Eddie, not Grania, who had turned suspicion on her, away from himself, by reporting Duncan's sexual assault on her in the alleyway – didn't he live down in Wapping, and mightn't he have been passing that way, bound for the Docklands Light Railway? As she lifted the receiver to arrange a visit to the City of London, a

remark of Grania's at the party suddenly came back to her –
something about the orgy before the massacre. As she waited for
the switchboard to answer, she noticed gratefully that the phone
boxes up here smelled of cleaning fluid rather than urine.

Slicer was in a better mood when he got back to the incident
room and reported to Manningbird. He'd seen both Wayne and
Winston in the company of their solicitor, David Righter, and on
his advice they'd both agreed to give blood. Winston had a plaster
on one of his fingers, but refused to say how he got the cut. The
police surgeon was calling in at the prison later in the afternoon
to take the sample and send it on to the forensic lab in Lambeth.
Wayne had been tearful and trembling, and Slicer was confident
that he'd crack before long. Rather less satisfactory was the business of Judy Best.

'Garbutt was right,' he said. 'It was her all right. We found her
walking down Brixton Hill just as we arrived.'

'What did she say?' asked Manningbird wearily, pushing away
a pile of statements and rubbing his colourless, subterranean eyes.

'Just a load of bollocks and cheek. She didn't admit to going
in to see the spade, but he didn't make any secret of it once we
got in there. Kept saying we'd have to speak to his home beat
officer if we wanted to find out any more. Makes you puke.'

'What did Righter say?'

'He knew about her visit too. Dare say he arranged it. Bleeding
political agitator. Swears it wasn't his idea, of course – says he's
got no idea what Leggit's playing at either.'

'Looks like we'd better 'aul her in for another chat.'

'Nothing would give me greater pleasure,' said Slicer, displaying
his twisted grin. 'We could drop in on her first thing in the morning, maybe. Rate things are going we'll have her on a criminal
charge before long.'

Manningbird gave Sliver a long, sceptical stare, then exhaled
long and hard, stood up, and walked over to the window with his
hands in his pockets. From the rear, his bulky body looked like
a crumpled bean bag, and a tuft of grey hair stuck out over one
grey ear.

'I've been thinking,' he began.

'Haven't we all,' said Slicer sarcastically. Manningbird ignored
him and carried on.

'About that trick-cyclist, Trotter, this morning. I think we might 'ave to cast the net a bit wider, just in case our two friends in Brixton don't fit the bill. I've been looking again at some of the statements from Stock's colleagues and friends.'

'Oh, yes?' said Slicer with insincere brightness. 'Any right bleeding nutters among them, you reckon?'

Manningbird turned and riffled through the two-inch pile of standard police forms.

'You never know your luck, Ron. Ahmed's not 'appy they're coming clean, see? Not giving 'im the full story about various liaisons and leg-overs involving Mr Stock and 'is friends.'

'Ahmed!' snorted Slicer, wrinkling his nose. 'You surprised? 'Course they're not talking to him, bleeding Tandoori pillock.'

Manningbird held up a waxy-grey hand.

'Careful, Ron – race, colour or creed, remember? Everyone on the team's entitled to their 'unches. Anyway, he's re-interviewing some of them, and there's a couple more just arrived back there today. I'm thinking you and me might 'ave to take a closer look at a couple of these City slickers.'

'What, you mean see if any of them have got plasters on their hands?' said Slicer, angry and sarcastic. 'Let's just wait for the lab results on the blood, eh? Any of that crowd of yuppies up there got cuts on their hands, they probably did it opening bottles of vintage champagne.'

Manningbird sat down heavily and sighed, patting his baggy pockets for cigarettes.

'Don't make a song and dance about it, Ron,' he appealed. 'Christ, this case is going to make me drop off me twig – I'm looking forward to a pension, I can tell you that.'

He lit up and disappeared with a little moan into a fog of blue and grey smoke. His voice sounded softer as he continued.

'So let's just forget about your two toe-rags for a while, take a closer look at Stock's address book, that kind of thing, OK? Now for Christ's sake come and 'ave a look at these bleeding statements.'

CHAPTER 19

The sandwich bar was called Colin's Snacks, but the owners were
Italian. Most of the lunchtime customers had gone by the time
Judy arrived and sat down next to the window. A black-haired
young woman in a white apron looked up from wiping the worn
Formica tables to give her a weary nod when she asked for a
cheese and tomato sandwich.

'Un panino formaggio e pomodoro per questa svergognata!' the
waitress shouted, her voice surprisingly strong. The stringy man
dodging about behind the glittering coffee-machine, taking near-
empty bowls of tuna and cream cheese out of the display cases,
muttered under his breath. Judy settled back under a fading poster
of Lake Garda to wait for Lynne. If she could get anything useful
from her, she'd decided, she'd go straight to Manningbird first
thing in the morning, bypassing Slicer.

She had nearly finished her sandwich when Lynne arrived, bust-
ling nervously through the door in a bulky green belted overcoat
and patting her hair into shape. It was all tinted billows and
curlicues, as if she had freshly emerged from Vamps.

'Ah, there you are,' she said, panting slightly as she undid
various knots and buttons. 'Recognised you straight away. It isn't
half blowy out there again, you know.'

'It's the greenhouse effect, Lynne,' said Judy, grinning. 'Warm
winds all over the world from now on.'

After a minute of adjustment and redisposition of handbag and
outer garments, Lynne ordered a cappucino, settled her chubby
forearms on the table, and looked at Judy. Her fresh lipstick was
slightly smudged in one corner, her rounded face seemed tight
and tense, and her eyes were cloudy and preoccupied.

'I'm glad you phoned me, actually,' she said. 'Because I was thinking about phoning you. Or that nice young officer I gave a statement to on Tuesday. Mr Ahmed.'

'Oh, yes, why was that?'

'Well, it was because I found something. After Mr Ahmed and the other police had gone, this morning, I was doing a final clear-out of Duncan's desk. I thought it might be important.'

Lynne leaned over the chair beside her and started another lengthy tussle with her possessions, this time involving the straps and buckles of her handbag. Judy watched, half-irritated and half-amused; she must have three mortice locks on the front door and a heavy-duty fastener on her bra.

'Where in the desk was it, Lynne? The police should have had everything out of there.'

'Well, yes, that's what I thought,' said Lynne, finally coming up pink-faced with a folded square of paper, already scuffed and marked after a few hours' friction with her lipsticks and powder compacts. 'But there it was, on the bottom of one of the drawers – the lowest one, where all the files are. I didn't notice it until I actually pulled the files out. There were a few other bits of paper as well, and lots of dust and paper clips.'

She unfolded the paper and passed it to Judy. The company's name and the words 'internal memorandum' were followed by a short, unevenly typewritten text.

Dear Dunc,

Just a short note to welcome you to your new job – and to give you a warning. We know why you've been put there and we know what you're up to. We know who your first target is, and we're not going to stand for it. It's gone far enough, and we'll resist it with everything we've got. This is a decent firm, so just remember that. There are other ways of saving money. From your loving colleagues.

Underneath it, in the bold handwriting Judy remembered from the card Duncan had given her, was the single scrawled word '*Bollocks.*' Typical, she thought: cool and aggressive.

'Mmm,' she said, staring at it for a few seconds before folding it up again and running her fingers along the sharp creases. 'What d'you make of that, then? And how does it fit with Duncan's desk being broken into over the weekend?'

157

'God knows how it fits with the break-in. Even the police don't seem to know what that was about. I suppose whoever it was wasn't after anything like this – only money.'

'Or maybe he was after it, but didn't find it.'

Lynne screwed up her forehead, slow to follow the line of thought.

'S'pose so. Removing evidence, you mean? But what I can't get over is, it must be someone I know, sort of doing something creepy and secret in the same office, sending threats to people. Makes you feel you just don't know what nasty things your neighbours are up to.'

'What makes you say it was done in the office?'

'Well, it was typed on one of the secretaries' typewriters – it's easy to see, if you compare. Not sure which, though, they're all the same model. And it was done by someone who can't type, you can see that.'

'Yes, it's very clumsily done. So who does that bring it down to?'

'Just about everyone in the department who isn't a secretary, I suppose. That means about twenty people.' Lynne flashed the corners of her mouth up and down in an imitation smile.

'I thought nothing moved at Banks and Heritage without you knowing, Lynne?'

Immediately Judy realised her edginess had pushed her into a mistake – the sort of mistake Slicer and his kind probably made all the time. She quickly chased the remark with a placatory smile, but a just-perceptible veil of offence had already crossed Lynne's eyes.

'Well, this is hardly the kind of thing people talk about or make copies of, is it?' she replied huffily. 'Threatening the boss like that.'

'You know, Lynne,' said Judy, extra-sympathetically, trying to recover lost ground, 'this really is such a coincidence – amazing, really. This sort of thing is exactly why I wanted to see you.'

'How d'you mean?'

'Well, the inquiry's not going too well, between you and me. The officers in charge seem to be trying to pin it on the two kids from a local estate who robbed the club's office the same night – you've probably seen something about it in the papers. And I

158

ought to tell you straight away that I'm not part of the inquiry team.'

'Oh?' Lynne leaned forward, her wary face looking suddenly more lively at this whiff of transgression. 'What brings you here, then? You being a naughty girl or something?'

Judy's laugh came out with an unwanted coyness. 'I don't think so, no. I'm just making a few informal inquiries on my own, that's all. Because I knew Duncan and met one or two of his friends, I thought they might feel a bit easier talking to me. Such as you, for example. And I was just wondering generally if anyone in his office might have had a motive. Anyone with a grudge against him. And here we have it, in black and white.'

She tapped the folded paper with the back of her fingernail. Lynne sipped at her coffee, the brown froth from her cup forming a tide mark across her sticky pink lip.

'Well,' she said, studying Judy hesitantly through the sugary-smelling steam. 'Everyone knows he wasn't exactly the most popular bloke, but I don't suppose anyone said that in their interviews with the police. They don't like the boys in blue very much in this game, you know. Too many of them sailing a bit close to the wind.'

'Yes, that's what I thought. Duncan started to twitch the moment he was introduced to me. But who was it who didn't like him?'

Lynne shifted uncomfortably and put down her coffee cup, looking at the round electric clock on the wall.

'Well, you know what it's like when anyone gets into a powerful position – face to face, everyone rather sucks up to them, but when their back's turned, it's a different matter. Everyone runs them down and rubbishes them. It's just fear, I suppose. They know this person controls their life, really, and they hate it.'

'Exactly. So if you're feeling under pressure anyway, and you get the idea he's about to start sacking you, you might just start doing something a bit silly or desperate, like writing this memo?'

Lynne nodded sadly. 'That's right. Has to be. It's a cut-throat world round here these days, not like it used to be, what, even ten years ago. It couldn't be Grania, though. He walked all over her, one way or another, poor thing, but I don't think she'd get violent. Or even make threats. Bit of a mouse, really.'

159

'I wasn't really thinking of her. But I was going to ask you about Eddie Nutting.'

A new wariness seemed to enter Lynne's manner. 'Eddie? He's a bit of a maniac from time to time, but aren't they all? They're all bright young things here, you know, all a bit highly strung. I've seen them come, seen them go, but there's never been anything like this, anything so serious, you see?'

Lynne paused to finish her cappucino, eyes averted, and dab her sticky lips carefully with a lace-edged hanky.

'All right, I know I've got my opinions about everyone, you're right. I tend to shoot my mouth off given half the chance, but I don't want to say too much, really. I'll just get out of my depth, that's all.'

Judy sensed that she'd lost her, and decided quickly against cajolement. She pushed back her feelings of disappointment, smiled, and patted Lynne's bare forearm placatingly, surprised at how far her fingers sank into the cool, pale flesh.

'I know,' she said. 'It must feel like I come pushing my nose in asking you to point the finger at all your colleagues, and it's not really like that. I just wondered if there was anything obvious you could tell me. I won't press you any further. Don't tell anyone else in the office about this memo yet, OK? Give me a call if any connection turns up between this and the break-in on Duncan's desk. And I'm assuming it's OK for me to pass it on to the inquiry team?'

Judy unfolded the piece of paper to read it again, holding it up between them so they could both look at it. But Lynne was suddenly distracted by something out in the street. She half-turned to her left, with a sickly little smile and a hesitant wave, and Judy turned just in time to catch the eye of Eddie Nutting, walking past on the pavement only a few feet away, with another man beside him. Eddie, his curly hair tousled in the wind, was just finishing a little wave and a smile as sickly as Lynne's, while the other man was already walking on. But Judy thought the smile on Eddie's face was contradicted by a steely look in his deep little eyes, and she felt a little jolt of fear as she hurriedly folded the paper away, hoping he hadn't seen it. It was like being smiled at by a shark.

The breeze seemed suddenly to have gone out of Lynne's ample sails, and she was fussing with her belongings again.

'Oh dear, we should have gone somewhere a bit more out of the way,' she muttered. 'They're a bit late back from lunch, aren't they, those two? Anyway, I must get back. They were giving us a jolly funny look, don't you think? I'll just tell them it was social, that I'd met you at Duncan's party and just bumped into you. It's such an awful business, everyone in the office is so tense and edgy. Nobody's themselves, really. Oh, well, we'll just have to see what happens.'

Judy tucked the memo into her inside jacket pocket and resigned herself to hearing no more from Lynne. If only she was acting officially, she could put the pressure on and demand some answers, but as a freelance – a civilian, in effect – she was hamstrung. She felt suddenly dispirited, resolving to go home and sleep on what she'd discovered. She'd go to Manningbird in the morning with the letter. They ought to be grateful to her, but if she got into trouble, well, too bad.

'There's just one more thing,' she said as Lynne stood up to struggle into her coat. 'Just as a personal favour, d'you know who it was who saw me and Duncan in that alleyway? After the party?'

A playful smile returned to Lynne's cheeks again, but only for a moment. 'I was wondering if you'd ask about that,' she said. 'I'm afraid it was Grania. I think she was feeling the pangs a bit that night, if you know what I mean.'

Judy struck the side of her head lightly with her hand and smiled ironically.

'D'you know, that was my first thought – that it was her. It was something about her attitude towards me that night. Then I decided it must be Eddie, because I thought it must be on his way home and, well, other reasons.'

'Really?' The word came out with a grunt as Lynne's large white hand finally popped out of the end of her sleeve. 'We had a bit of a laugh about it in the office the next morning, I'm afraid. Duncan's latest conquest, sort of thing – although he got rather a flea in his ear, didn't he, this time? Poor old Duncan, the sky was the limit for him.'

'A bit of a laugh, eh?' said Judy warmly. 'Well, your colleagues have been doing the three wise monkeys in their police interviews, from what I hear, but dear Grania did manage to tell them about me giving him a flea in his ear, as you put it, and they gave me a hard time. Potential suspect, you see, after I'd threatened him. I'm actually suspended at the moment, because of that.'

With a decisive jerk, Lynne pulled the belt of her coat into a knot and picked up her handbag. 'I'm sorry, love,' she murmured. 'Grania's really upset too – keeps on bursting into tears. See you again, I hope. Good luck.'

Judy sighed as she watched Lynne's broad green back sailing away down the pavement towards the square. She felt suddenly exhausted. She could be at home in a hot bath, reading a novel, instead of trudging round London like a hard-up sales rep. She turned towards the counter to ask if she could have another coffee, but thought better of it when she saw the look of mute appeal in the waitress's dark, overworked eyes.

She paid and left, zipping her jacket against a sudden swirl of wind which pulled her hair back from her forehead and pushed its way into her mouth, chilling her teeth. Across the sky rushed ribs of cloud whose colour varied from black to gunmetal to milky white. In between them came slanting shafts of glowing sunlight and glimpses of turquoise borrowed from the shallows of a tropical ocean. One cloud was coming over much lower than the rest, like an attacking aircraft, the sun splitting its vapoury lower edge into the colours of the rainbow.

She was watching the drama of the sky so intently that she forgot the busy city pavements around her, where people flapped along, grimacing and clutching their hats. Then suddenly she walked hard into a large man in a grey coat with a dirty velvet collar standing at the window of a computer shop. He gripped her arm for a second as they both reeled and tottered, then looked down at her with a mirthless yellow-toothed grin and a gust of winey breath. For a second his grip tightened, and he seemed to debate holding on to her before suddenly letting go and walking away. But the look of blank anger in his eyes and his sweetish, tramp-like smell stayed with her, and she wondered what happened to the losers in this windy temple of money and status. Did they ever lurk in basement carparks and kill their bosses with spanners? Or did they just accept defeat and go home quietly to Orpington to slump in armchairs and fiddle around in greenhouses?

*

It was an hour later that the phone rang in the incident room. Detective Sergeant Stone, staring blankly out of the window with his mouth set like a crack in a pie, took his feet unwillingly off the desk and lifted the receiver.

'DS Stone,' he grunted irritably. 'Yes, that's right . . . Oh, yes . . . Which one . . . Oh, yes – and what do you mean, in danger?'

He gestured urgently for Ahmed to pass him a pad and pen, tucking the mouthpiece under his voluminous chin like a toy under a pillow. Ahmed watched anxiously from the other side of the table.

'And where is she now? . . . What d'you mean, after her? . . . No, don't hang up just yet, sir . . .'

Stone threw down the pen in frustration, took the receiver away from his ear, and held it close in front of his face to swear at it briefly and fluently, as if it was one his more persistent petty offenders.

'Not Judy?' said Ahmed immediately.

'Yeah, stupid cow – how did you know? Anyway, that was one of Dunkie's colleagues – wouldn't give his name. Said she's in danger from the guy who killed him, up in the City somewhere. Then the stupid sod hung up. Posh voice, sounded panicky.'

'What do we do?'

'Better tell the chief. I thought the bleeding murderers were in Brixton nick. This'll teach her to bugger about, silly tart.'

163

CHAPTER 20

It was only when she had left the Underground station and was halfway along Brunel Road to the estate where she lived that Judy realised she was being followed. It was dark now, but not yet late enough for the streets to be filling with people on their way home, and she thought at first she was the only one making her way along the narrow pavement. But as she turned round by the Adam and Eve pub to check for traffic before crossing the street, she saw the tall figure, fifty yards behind her, a dark anorak hood drawn round his head. Then a sudden gust threw a spray of fine grit at her face and she ducked sideways to protect her eyes, hearing the wind swish through the cold dry twigs overhead. 'Mortgage rate too high?' read a notice threatening to flap free of one of the roadside tree trunks. 'Phone us and find out.' When she looked furtively back again half a minute later, he was only forty yards away, and on the same side of the road.

She started walking faster, her heartbeat seeming to keep time with her footfalls and her neck feeling tight with the surging of blood. She wondered what she could do if she needed help, if Eddie attacked her. On the right were some blocks of flats, their dimly lit landings deserted. On the other side of the road was a new terrace of houses with mock-Tudor fronts and only the occasional light showing behind a net curtain or a pink fluffy blind: he'd be on to her and silence her before she'd rung the first doorbell. She ought to simply turn round and use her half-dozen judo holds and wristlocks to arrest him herself, here and now, but she thought again of his shark-like eyes and his awful fury on the squash court, and doubted that she could handle him alone. She could just run into the road, maybe, and wave her arms and flag down a car or a van, but there suddenly seemed to be no traffic. She wished she was on duty, in uniform, with the awkward but

164

comforting weight of the police radio clipped to her belt and the mouthpiece on her shoulder. Help, in the form of a whooping area car with two large bobbies in it, would be only a couple of minutes away. As it was, she was alone.

Then she remembered the call box a bit further down, where the road rose slightly to cross the neck of water which linked the river to the dock basin near her flat. She put her hand in her pocket, fingered some coins and the phonecard she'd used for her earlier calls, and glanced behind again: still forty yards. She'd just have time to get through to the station and shout a quick message, even if she had to hold the door of the booth closed. And then, if necessary, she could fight and run until help arrived.

She was close to a jog as she went up the slope, with the high, impassive bulk of the gasometer, like a figure of judgement, rising now on her right in the grainy glow of the street lights. A van appeared on the bridge, coming towards her, but it was moving so fast it had gone by before she thought about trying to stop it. But no matter, she was at the phone box now, jerking the door open, spilling some of her change as she pulled it out of her pocket. She even had the coin in her raised hand, moving as if to drop it in the slot, before she realised with a jolt that the booth contained no phone. Either it was being refitted, or it had been ripped out, but there was no apparatus there. Just a dark board with a couple of holes in it which stared at her like blank, black eyes. She stood open-mouthed for a moment, her mind revolving helplessly in neutral. A useless thought flashed up briefly: you don't get call boxes like this in Blackheath. And then, falling back on the simple instinct to run for home, she set off out of the box like a greyhound from a trap, pushing the door back violently and half-colliding with it as it rebounded off its hinges.

All she had to do was turn right along the side of the dock, skirt it for a hundred and fifty yards, and then she'd be away from this stretch of lonely, open ground and in amongst the houses, where people would see what was going on and come to help her. Her jeans and trainers allowed her to run well, better than she would have done in her uniform skirt, but she could hear him running behind her now and remembered those lean, hairy thighs on the squash court. Her tongue was dry with fear as she veered off the pavement and checked her pace to take the steps down to the waterside with a rapid, stuttering stride. In the light of the milky globes lining the water's edge, a group of mallards, not yet gone to roost, swam rapidly towards her, expecting a shower of bread scraps or the crumbs from a crisp packet. And then she stumbled.

Judy saw the dark paving bricks coming up towards her face, taking an interest in their herringbone pattern for a sudden fraction of a second. She managed to put her hands down to stop herself from falling full length, feeling a nail tear and grit grinding into the ball of a thumb. But it was too late: by the time she was upright and trying to run again, he was at the bottom of the steps and flinging himself towards her, arms stretched out like some long, leaping monkey. The impact of his body on her shoulders propelled her, staggering, towards the waist-high black railings which edged the basin, and she heard herself gasp like a shot-putter as her stomach slammed into the thick metal bars.

Although she was winded, her hands closed instinctively around the bars and she dropped her body downwards to check the momentum which could take her – both of them – over the top and into the water. Her back formed a hump, and she felt his weight slide up it, his hands scrabbling for a firm hold around her arms and body, his breath rasping and grunting near her ears. Then a powerful hand was closing on the back and side of her neck, forcing her head down until her eyes were jammed against the railing. My neck's going to break, she thought, and the memory flashed into her mind of the man at Duncan's party, powerfully forcing someone's head down on to a table.

The picture produced a violent surge of revulsion: she wasn't going to be treated like this, stalked and chased and jumped on. With all the force remaining in her breath-starved body, Judy bucked, like some victim of the African plains trying to throw off its predator. To her surprise and delight, the grip on her neck slipped off, the weight on her back slid forward towards her head, and her attacker uttered a cry of alarm.

'Oh shit!' he said, in a strangulated, upper-class voice.

When Judy bucked again, more wildly this time, his body slid quickly, twisting and thrashing, over the railings, his legs cartwheeling over and thudding into the brick wall just above the black water. Her leather jacket was yanked forward over her head, smothering her and jerking at her armpits as he hung for a moment by the hand which gripped its lower edge. Then he

166

dropped into the water with a docile plop, and the hungry ducks scattered, pumping hard with their webbed feet and looking back in alarm.

Judy collapsed backwards on her rump and sat there gasping for air and wondering dizzily if someone was going to arrive to help her. She looked up and saw lights come on in the tall upstairs windows of a house on the other side of the basin, but a few seconds later the lights disappeared as a woman reached up and swished shut the floor-length curtains. Higher still, the lights of a plane were swinging round from the north to follow the river up to Heathrow. Then, above the sound of her own stertorous breathing, she became aware of someone else making sounds of distress. From somewhere below her came gasps of cold and shock punctuated by splashes and coughs, and she pitched herself forward on her hands and knees and crawled to the edge.

The man she saw in the water, looking up at her in the milky lamplight, wasn't Eddie. Streaks of blond hair were plastered over his forehead, his mouth was contorted with the obsession for air, and for several seconds she thought it was a total stranger who'd attacked her. Then he spoke, and the conjunction of the voice and the face prompted her to recognise Jeremy: Jeremy Heritage, as in the family firm.

'Help me out,' he demanded hoarsely. 'The water's freezing, actually.'

The wind gusted suddenly, with a noise like someone flapping a blanket. It set off a line of ripples across the dark surface of the water, sent some dry leaves scuttering along the deserted dockside, and scooped another handful of stinging grit into Judy's face. The pain made her mind go numb with anger.

'You can fucking well drown!' she screamed at him. 'Go on, drown!'

Jeremy looked pained and surprised, as if this was a quite unreasonable reaction to what had just happened. He opened his mouth, but before he could speak his teeth rattled like a sudden roll of castanets, and he closed it again to concentrate instead on making an ungainly, splashing turn in the water. Then he started to swim clumsily along the wall of the basin, the padding of his anorak restricting his arms to lunging, flipper-like movements. Judy got to her feet, the pain across her lower ribs making her wonder if they were broken, and walked slowly along the railing

167

above him, looking intently down at his progress, as if she was coaching him in a pool.

'You killed Duncan, didn't you, you bastard?' she shouted, her voice shrill and wavering. There was no reply from below, only a steady splashing and gasping.

'You're all a bunch of bloody nutters, aren't you?'

Again no reply; her body was flooding and weakening with a sense of relief that she was unhurt by this maniac, and she wanted to stop, grip the railings, and weep. But she knew it wasn't over yet.

'You're under arrest, you know that?' she yelled. Jeremy had grabbed hold of one of the chains looped along the basin wall, and was manoeuvring himself on to an iron ladder leading down into the water. As he pulled himself upwards like some bedraggled monster from the depths, she was suddenly possessed by the fear that he would overpower her once he was on dry land. As his trunk appeared above the rim of the basin, she rushed at him and kicked him full in the chest.

Jeremy let go of the ladder with one hand and grabbed her foot as it bounced off him. She overbalanced and lunged for the railing as he transferred his other hand to her leg as well and pulled down with his full weight, grinning up at her sadistically, his teeth large and even. The tug of war lasted a few seconds, during which she focused with brief clarity on the plaster on the forefinger of Jeremy's right hand, remembering what Ahmed told her about the stair rod. Then she screamed wildly as she felt her hands slipping off the smooth, painted metal, and glimpsed above her a sign on a pole which read 'Danger – Deep Water'. She kicked at Jeremy's face with her free foot, but he tucked his head protectively on his chest and launched himself backwards into the water again, clutching her leg like an ape swinging on a liana. The back of her head bumped on the brickwork as she slid fast over the edge and splashed down into the black water.

For a moment her mind was emptied by the shock of the icy immersion and the thin, chemical taste of the water as it flooded chokingly into her nose and mouth. There was sudden silence, and she could not tell if her head was above or below her feet. Then she felt Jeremy's hands let go of her leg and start groping around her shoulders, trying to get a grip on her head, and she quickly remembered that he was trying to kill her. He wanted to hold her under the water, to push her down into the black depths until she drowned. Her limbs milled slowly in the instinctive effort to stop sinking and fend him off, and she heard the sound of air escaping from her mouth, like a child blowing bubbles through the bathwater. She opened her eyes, expecting only blackness, and saw in surprise how the round light of one of the lampposts was floating and shimmering, like a full moon, beyond the bubbling surface above her. Then she felt one of her legs scrape against the wall of the basin, her head broke the surface, and the terrifying heaviness and silence of the water gave way to the lightness and noise of the open air. She could hear people shouting somewhere near by.

As she sucked air back into her lungs, she was filled with relief and a new desire to fight. Then Jeremy's fingers clawed across her eye as he lunged at her, and suddenly she knew what she should do. She took a second great swallow of breath and ducked down deliberately, as deep as she could go. She twisted like a fish to get both feet against the basin wall, with her knees tucked up near her stomach. Then she pushed off hard, and swam blindly through the blackness, thinking with horror of slimy underwater creatures and sunken ropes or supermarket trolleys which might grab her or snag her and hold her down here until her strength failed and her lungs filled with water. When she surfaced ten yards away she carried on swimming hard towards the middle of the basin, hoping she could get to the other side fifty yards away, before the madman could reach her.

Her jacket dragged like a sea-anchor, and her trainers prevented her getting a grip on the water. But after half a minute of exhausting face-down thrashing she allowed herself to look up, gagging for air, and slow down. She could hear more shouting, and people were running along the side of the basin. There was no sound of pursuing splashes behind her, so she trod water and turned round. She was thirty yards from the edge now, and Jeremy had just emerged at the top of the ladder and begun running heavily back towards the road, his pursuers fifty yards behind him.

It looked like the police had arrived. Judy twisted round again and swam back to the ladder breast-stroke, exhausted by the release from danger and suddenly aware that her hands and feet were going numb. Several running figures passed in front of her along the edge of the basin, shouting and gesticulating like the Keystone cops. One of them stopped by the ladder and stood there, hands on hips, while she swam the last few yards.

'Hello, Mr Slicer,' she shouted breathlessly.

'What the hell are you up to this time, Best?' came the answering snarl.

Judy's hands made contact with the top rung of the ladder, but they were like unfeeling stumps, unable to get a grip. She hung there, gasping like a walrus to get her breath back.

'Solving your bloody case, that's what,' she muttered defiantly between gasps. 'Give us a hand out of here, will you?'

With an old-womanly tut of irritation, Slicer leant over and grabbed her outstretched arm. She struggled up out of the water and leant against the railings, shivering and panting, her face the colour of flour and her hair in rat-tails. Some of the aggressive irritation went out of Slicer's face as he stared at her, his little moustache twitching. Here comes the sentimentality, she thought with weary resentment.

'Bad time of year for swimming,' he said eventually, grudgingly pulling off his overcoat and draping it round her at arm's length with averted eyes, as if he were covering an unattractive streaker at a rugby match. 'You'll die of cold in this wind unless you get out of those clothes.'

Judy looked at him suspiciously, wondering if he was going to get her to strip here and now, under his coat. 'Where's the suspect?' she asked, teeth chattering uncontrollably, a large pool of water gathering around her feet.

'I expect the others have got him,' said Slicer, crossing his arms over his body and rubbing his shoulders as a new gust struck at them. He looked away for a moment, towards the river, then looked back at her, his eyes uncertain.

'Who is it, anyway?' he asked sourly. 'We just got this call from one of Stock's colleagues.'

'Another posh nutcase called Jeremy,' stuttered Judy between shivers. 'Christ, you must have interviewed him, why weren't you on to him?'

'I suppose you think he's the murderer, eh?' said Slicer aggressively, the wind ruffling up his smooth hair like rising hackles.

'Course I bloody well do – why d'you think he tried to get me soon as I was getting close?'

'Well, I'll believe it when I see the evidence. And if it is him, I shouldn't get too big-headed about it, Best. You're well out of order and you know it. We'd have been on to him in a day or two, rest assured.'

After her mistake over the identity of her pursuer, Judy felt too insecure to argue. Besides, she was almost in convulsions with the cold.

'Come on,' she said. 'I need a run to get warm, and he's my arrest, by rights.'

'What you doing trying to drown him, then?' he responded sharply, eyes glinting.

Pulling Slicer's coat around her, Judy set off in a stumbling, arthritic jog. Across the road, beyond the lock which separated the basin from the river, she saw the revolving blue light of a police car. Slicer was muttering at her shoulder about pneumonia and hypothermia as they ran towards it.

The car was parked on a paved riverside area which looked as if it might lead to an escape route along the Thames towards the warren of waterfront streets in Rotherhithe. Only when they reached the car was it clear that the paving, dotted with occasional benches, formed a cul-de-sac: the place was designed for hardy pensioners to take the air, and any access along the river was blocked by the blank wall of a building on the one side and the entrance to the lock on the other.

The car's engine was still running and the driver was sitting in front with the door open, talking into the radio. Ten yards further on a knot of officers, uniformed and plain clothes, were leaning against the railings and peering over into the river, their backs turning brighter and bluer every few seconds in the revolving light. A wet anorak was lying on the paving near by, a puddle of water seeping out of it like blood.

'Christ, is he in the drink again?' said Judy, pushing up to the railing between two other officers and staring down into the sucking, surging river. A red-and-white lifebelt and a piece of timber the size of a railway sleeper were being tossed about like toys on the brown waves, thudding against the concrete river wall below them.

The man next to her was Ahmed, who turned to study her for a moment as she stared wildly across towards the lights and

171

construction cranes of Wapping, dominated by the silver pencil-shape of Canary Wharf Tower.

'You all right?' asked Ahmed.

Judy, soaked and shivering, nodded jerkily.

'You know who it is, d-d-d-don't you?' she mumbled.

'Yeah,' declared Ahmed, nodding hard. 'It's that outsize berk Heritage, the one I interviewed this morning. I told the gaffer he was dodgy. Why, you know him as well? From that party?'

'Yeah, s-s-s-seen him at the club once or twice with D-D-Duncan.'

'When he saw he was trapped down here, he went straight over the side like a bloody suicide case. Look, there he is, can you see? Doesn't stand a chance in this tide.'

Beyond a huge wooden mooring point which stood in the river, guarding the mouth of the lock like a small island, Judy could just make out a bobbing head, twenty or thirty yards out. It looked like just another piece of flotsam being rushed downriver by the ebbing tide.

'Shouldn't we be in there after him?' she asked, her speech slurring and jarring as she gave up any attempt to prevent her body from shaking violently in the bitter wind. Another siren was approaching behind them.

'You must be joking,' said Ahmed indignantly. 'We dropped the lifebelt right on top of him and the silly bugger swam away from it. There'll be a launch here any minute . . . Look, you're in a bad way, I'm getting you back to that ambulance.'

Ahmed took her firmly by the shoulders and steered her back to the road where the ambulance had just pulled up. Her teeth were chattering like a football rattle as the bespectacled woman crew member sat her on the bench in the back of the vehicle and started pulling off her sodden, clinging clothes.

'What happened, then, darlin'?' the woman asked matter-of-factly as she wrapped Judy's shuddering white body in two red blankets, and started massaging her hands and feet. 'Fancied a dip, did yer?'

As the ambulance drew away, the police helicopter arrived over-head, clattering and circling. For a moment its spotlight swung over to the bank and fastened like a brilliant leech on the car and the group of officers at the riverside railing. Slicer and Ahmed buried their faces in their elbows until the blinding light let go of them and began swinging to and fro across the river. The machine was hovering now, the roar of its engine rising and falling as it struggled to hold position against the heavy wind. Suddenly the beam stopped searching and fastened on a point a quarter of a mile downstream from the mouth of the lock.

'Looks like they've found him, sir,' said Ahmed excitedly. Slicer gave him a sour look.

'Make life simpler if they didn't,' he muttered back.

Two fast police launches were now ploughing across the rough water from the river police headquarters at Wapping, the lights on their wheelhouse roofs aimed at the spot below the helicopter. The launches began circling and manoeuvring tightly, and the group on the bank could see figures moving urgently on their decks. Then one of them swung away and headed home, banks of spray flying up and glittering in its own searchlight as it crashed against the tide and waves. Shortly afterwards the message came through on the car radio that they had the suspect on board, half-full of water but still alive, and they'd probably find him in the London Hospital with a police guard in an hour or so.

Judy was taken to Guy's Hospital where they gave her hot drinks, decided her ribs were bruised rather than broken and put dressings on her scratched face and grazed hands. By eight o'clock she was back in her flat, talking to Clinton on the phone.

CHAPTER 21

'Mad bitch,' muttered Slicer for the tenth time as he and Stone edged along the Embankment in the fuming, tooting evening traffic. 'She's not happy with a leg-over and a shouting match with young Duncan, oh no, that's not nearly enough aggravation for one week. She waits for him to get topped, and then she's off waving her fanny about again and getting into trouble with one of his mates. And who ends up sorting it out and hauling the pair of them out of the bloody drink? We do, that's who. They're like a lot of stupid kids. She's bad news, that one, and the sooner she's out of the force the better.'

Stone shifted the Cavalier another ten yards forward, revving the engine unnecessarily to let off his impatience. The overheated air in the car was thick with body odours and laden with petrol fumes.

'Only trouble is, he's our main man now,' said Stone, wincing slightly as he shifted in his seat. 'I mean, he's hardly likely to try and drown a plonk and then swim across the sodding Thames at high tide just because she cut him up at the traffic lights or wouldn't talk to him in the pub. I mean, he's got to have something on his mind, hasn't he?'

'You never know with these toffs,' said Slicer, drumming his fingers on the dashboard. 'They're meant to set an example to the rest of us, but their private lives are like something out of a zoo. Look at that toff, whatsisname, got done the other day. Total degenerate.'

Slicer drew up his top lip in disgust, like a beaver about to attack another log, and wound down the window to stare tensely out at the joggers and tired tourists labouring past Cleopatra's needle under the bleached brilliance of the street lights. The car filled with more fumes and the hum of a hundred overheating

174

engines, and they ground on in without speaking until something in the traffic jerked Stone out of his sullen immobility, convulsing his potato-like features.

'Christ, did you see that?'

A bearded cyclist in a skew-whiff woolly hat was wobbling along outside a bus, waving a fist at the driver and yelling about giving way. The driver stared straight ahead as if the cyclist was invisible.

'Bloody pedal-pushers, ought to be lined up and shot,' said Slicer, his mood not improved. 'She's probably a cyclist herself, our Judy. But too save-the-whales for my liking. Thinks she's solved the inquiry for us, cheeky cow, and Ahmed's already claiming he got some sort of gut feeling about Heritage this morning. A plonk and a Paki, eh, Jim? What in God's name is the world coming to? That's what I want to know.'

'Don't worry, Ron,' said Stone insincerely. 'We'll see what this Jeremy has to say tomorrow. Make our minds up on the evidence, eh?'

Slicer uttered a cross between a squeak and a grunt, and silence fell between the two men again. Half an hour later, eyes smarting and noses clogged from the rush-hour dirt, they pulled up outside a red-brick mansion block in Fulham and parked behind a dilapidated Fiat. As he climbed out of the car, Slicer squinted at the white hood-shaped porches and the little black-railed balconies on the upper floors.

'What you might call traditional territory,' he said sourly, pulling from his pocket the keys they'd collected from the custody officer at Wapping police station. 'I thought the only people who lived in places like this were frail old ladies with loads of loot.'

The lock turned smoothly in the panelled oak door and they entered a gloomy hallway which smelt of dust and lavender. It had an elaborately moulded dado rail on the wall, a sick-looking aspidistra on the table and the rumpled remains of an Oriental carpet lying on the dry parquet. As they started up the stairs, a tiny figure in a black coat appeared unsteadily from the rear shadows of the ground floor, clutching an oversized handbag; two myopic bushbaby-eyes peered anxiously at them.

'What'd I tell you, Watson?' grinned Slicer cleverly as they headed upstairs past the scuffed, turd-coloured anaglypta.

'You're such a clever dick, sir,' said Stone in a tone so pleasant even Slicer couldn't take offence. 'Have you noticed the stair carpet, though?'

'What do you mean, have I noticed the stair carpet?' said Slicer indifferently, inserting the Yale in the door of flat 3.

'Oh, nothing, really,' said Stone. 'It's just that it's new.'

The two men stepped inside and went from room to room snapping on the lights. The interior of the flat corresponded uncannily with the exterior of the block. It looked as if it had been suspended in a time-warp ever since its first Edwardian occupant moved in with a heavily sprung, chintz-covered three-piece suite, dark red velvet curtains and an armful of engravings of long-horned cattle standing moodily among lochs and mountains. Here and there was a discordant modern note: a huge TV and a tower of stereo equipment in the living-room; an unwashed pile of Habitat-style crockery and cutlery in the sink; and, on the wall facing the rumpled bed, the poster showing a blonde standing at the net with a tennis racket, hitching up her skimpy skirt to expose two firm mounds of tanned buttock.

In the small dining-room, an ugly mahogany sideboard was piled with a battered traffic cone, a yellow lantern, several bent brass plaques, a bus stop sign and other bits and pieces apparently stolen from public places. On the mantelpiece was a small tarnished silver cup with 'Under 14s swimming' stamped unevenly on the side, and several dirty crystal decanters containing low levels of liquids the colour of peat or furniture polish. The rooms looked as if they had been cleaned about two months ago, and had the over-heated, institutional smell of a boarding-school day room. Slicer moved slowly from one room to the other, nostrils crinkled fastidiously, nodding sagely now and then.

'I shouldn't go too near those pyjamas, sir,' warned Stone from the threshold of the bedroom. 'And those socks in the corner don't look too clever.'

'Thank you, Jim,' said Slicer with smooth menace. 'We're here for a preliminary look round, not to expand our small repertoire of jokes. So just get on with it, will you, without touching anything? You could start by sticking your head under the sink.'

Slicer poked round the bedroom: a few large suits and tweedy sports jackets in the wardrobe, some professionally laundered Viyella shirts and baggy lovat-green sweaters in the heavy mahogany chest of drawers. Under the sturdy, thick-mattressed bed there were a couple of dusty suitcases, a pair of outsize carpet slippers and a black track-suit top. He looked at it for a moment, grunted, looked briefly round for a matching pair of trousers, but couldn't find them. He tossed the top on the bed and moved to the front room.

'Looks like he inherited all this as a job lot from his grandma,' he said as he passed through the hall, under a fading yard-wide photograph of knob-kneed, sprig-haired nine-year-olds gurning at the camera outside some turreted institution. There was no reply from Stone.

In the living-room Slicer looked at the bookcase in the alcove beside the black marble fireplace. Among a few neglected-looked textbooks on geography and economics, he found a volume showing the best routes up various University buildings in Cambridge, including an account of how an Austin Seven had once been suspended underneath one of the town's most beautiful bridges. There was a book about going round the world on a motorcycle, and another about the many and varied methods devised by various civilizations over the centuries of torturing and killing people. Slicer started flicking curiously through the illustrations, wincing and ooh-ing under his breath, but forced himself to put the book back and turn his attention to the handsome roll-top bureau underneath the shelves.

The lid squeaked and clattered back to reveal a tousle of papers, cheque book stubs and old envelopes. On the top was a notice of coding from the Inland Revenue, a red-printed final reminder about a telephone bill, and a postcard of a naked, smiling girl standing on Bondi Beach. 'As you can see,' said an awkward hand in block capitals on the other side, 'everything's big in Australia. Heading north tomorrow. Yrs Simon.' Slicer was wondering how deep to dig into the pile on the desk when his eye fell on the nearly full waste paper basket near by.

He went down on one knee and tipped the contents on the floor, pushing a blackening banana skin to one side with distaste. He spread out the old *Daily Express*es and rolled-up bits of paper and noticed that one of them was more tightly rolled than the others, as if it had been discarded with special vehemence. Slicer picked it out, got up from the floor to the chair, and carefully prised it open. It was a note, hand written in black ink with a fountain pen and headed 'Friday 11.15 a.m.', on a Banks and

Heritage memo form. The writing, though still large, was evidently dashed off in hurry and anger, and the skein of creases on the paper made it all the more difficult to read.

Jeremy: Where the hell are you? A party's no excuse for this kind of lateness – everyone else has managed to get here after last night. Things like this are happening too often and I want you in my office at 10 on Monday to get a few things straightened out. And there's someone I want you to meet. You'd better cancel this Yorkshire trip – tell them someone else will come up later.

The D at the bottom was written in an aggressive flourish. Slicer had just finished reading it slowly a second time when a shadow fell across it and he looked up, startled, to see a huge figure looming over him with a raised weapon, about to strike.

'Have some of this, sir,' grunted Stone, bringing the stair rod down fast over his shoulder and halting it six inches from the natty parting in Slicer's slick hairdo. Slicer ducked away and cursed.

'For Christ's sake, Jim,' he snapped, his voice wavering after a moment of real fear. 'There's enough fucking psychopaths around without you joining them.'

'Sorry, sir,' said Stone cheerily, po-faced. 'I just thought you'd like a taste of what young Dunkie saw before the night closed in, as it were.'

'Don't try to be intellectual, Jim, it doesn't suit you. Where did you get that bloody thing, anyway?'

'I just popped out on to the landing to have a look at the upper flight of stairs. They haven't replaced the carpet there yet, so it's still got rods like this. I'll lay odds it matches the one in the gym, eh? Young Jeremy will've nicked it while they were putting the fitted carpet on the lower stairs. He likes nicking bits and pieces, judging by the collection of public property in the next room.'

'Mmm,' said Slicer, frowning. 'We'll forensicate it in the morning. And this.'

He passed the piece of paper to Stone, taking the stair rod in return. After a half-minute of silent examination of objects, the two men looked at each other.

'Could be the motive,' said Stone grimly. 'And could be the weapon.'

'Yes,' said Slicer, savagely bouncing one end of the rod on the splintery wooden floor and staring vacantly across the room. 'Un-bleeding-fortunately, you may be right. We'll see what the little bastard has to say for himself tomorrow. Or perhaps I should say big bastard, given the size of him.'

There was a brief buzz, like the last throes of a trapped wasp. Slicer stopped bouncing the rod and raised his eyebrows at Stone.

'Entryphone,' said Stone. 'I'll get it.'

He lifted the handset in the little hallway, noticing the greasy crust on the earpiece and holding it an inch away from his head.

'Jeremy?' said an anxious voice.

Stone's little eyes widened and he opened his mouth to speak. Then he changed his mind at the last minute, produced a strangled little gulp, and gave the entry button a long, careful push. He replaced the handset as if it was made of bone china.

'It's the bloke who rang this afternoon,' he told Slicer in a stage whisper, coming back into the living-room on the balls of his feet as if a baby was sleeping in the corner. Slicer gave him a filthy look.

'You look like a sodding elephant on a tightrope,' he said biliously. 'What bloke? And why are you whispering?'

'The bloke who warned us about Best,' said Stone, stopping flat-footed in his tracks, offended. 'Same voice. He's on the way up. Don't want to scare him off.'

Slicer sighed and put the rod down on the floor.

'Don't be a prat,' he said. 'OK, let's have him.'

Slicer positioned himself by the front door and gently opened it, leaving it slightly ajar, while Stone hovered just behind him in the doorway to the kitchen. Over the sound of Stone's stertorous breathing, they could hear footsteps trudging slowly up the stairs. Then the door was pushed open a couple of inches.

'Jeremy?' came the voice again, posh and quavering. 'You there?'

The policemen didn't move. But when the door was pushed wide and a tall young man with thin curly hair came through it, Slicer stepped forward and grabbed him by the left elbow. Stone then lunged to grab his right arm and they propelled him fast into the front room. The top of his thighs hit the back of the sofa and his upper body jack-knifed over it.

'Ooof!' gasped Eddie Nutting. 'What the hell's going on?'

'We're police officers, that's what the hell's going on,' said Slicer, a vindictive edge to his voice. 'So perhaps you can tell us what you're doing here.'

Eddie, torso hanging upside down like a fruit bat, screwed his face round to squint at them, his little eyes full of fear.

'I'm a friend of Jeremy's,' he said breathlessly.'Where is he?'

'You ought to know,' said Stone indignantly. 'You're the one who rang us and didn't give your name.'

'How do you know?' asked Eddie, twitching and struggling a little against Slicer's grip.

Stone, who had walked round to the front of the sofa, now bent over and thrust his pale, globular face close to Eddie's inverted one, which was beginning to turn a veiny purple.

'Because I don't forget a voice, sir,' he sneered, testy and triumphant. 'Especially a lah-di-dah voice like yours.'

'Let me go or I'll be sick,' declared Eddie, like a child suddenly tiring of a party game. 'I've just eaten a big Chinese meal.'

Slicer immediately let him go and stepped back, glancing down at his suit as if to check he wasn't too late. Eddie straightened up slowly and walked carefully over to the corner under the huge TV, where he sat down in an armchair, taking deep breaths. There was a silence.

'You don't know what's happened, do you?' said Stone, his accusing expression suddenly brightening.

'No,' gasped Eddie, through an ominous hiccup.

By the time Slicer had explained the afternoon's events Eddie had lost some of his high colour and was staring at them with a dropped jaw, muttering 'Oh God,' from time to time, with little bobs of the head.

'Oh God,' he muttered. 'I was right, then. Swimming is just about the only thing he's any good at.'

'Right about what?' asked Slicer, who had sat down again by the desk and was weighing the stair rod in his hands again.

'Right that it was Jeremy,' said Eddie, looking beadily at Slicer. 'I always knew he had a screw loose – well, several, actually. But I thought he was up in Yorkshire by Sunday.'

Slicer looked hesitantly at Stone, who raised his hands defensively.

'That's what he told Ahmed this morning,' he said. 'Claimed he travelled up on Sunday night, just when it was all happening in the gym. They were checking with the hotel this afternoon.'

'Must have gone up Monday,' said Eddie. 'I thought he was a bit jumpy when he came in this morning, especially when he heard your man wanted to talk to him. Had this bandage on his hand, too, said he skinned it on the engine of his old banger, trying to start it.'

'Yeah, but why did you think he was after Judy Best?'

'We were walking back to the office when we saw her in a caff with one of our secretaries, waving some piece of paper about. Jeremy went even quieter, and when he got back to the building he suddenly said he had to go off and buy some cigars. I've never seen him smoke a cigar in my life.'

'Yes, but why does that add up to suspicion?' said Slicer testily, shifting in his chair.

Eddie looked up, fingering his pockmarked face nervously.

'I wasn't sure. No one likes to sneak, do they? But there'd been a bit of an atmosphere between those two recently. Jeremy the old world, Duncan the new, that sort of thing. Silver spoons versus portable telephones, and we all know who's winning that match, don't we? The three of us were down in some pub near where Duncan lives recently, and Jeremy threatened to chuck him into the river. Had a few beers, but he seemed serious about it. Throbbing vein on the forehead, the lot. Few more weeks in the job, and Duncan would've stopped socialising with us at all, I expect. Conflict of interest.'

Slicer reflected for a moment, then turned to pick the memo off the desk and hand it to Eddie

'How would this fit in with what you've been describing, then?' he asked.

Eddie read it, looked up, read it again, then handed it back, his little eyes glowing and his head bobbing.

'Oh dear,' he said. 'It all fits, I'm afraid. Like a glove.'

'Go on.'

'Well, it's true Jeremy was late in on Friday. Didn't show till after lunch, in fact, arrived in a filthy mood and just grunted at everyone. And Duncan had to go off to meet a client for a lunch and a meeting. Poor old Jeremy, he must have thought he was for the chop.'

'Think he was right?'

Eddie flopped his head from side to side, weighing the thought.

'Hard to say. Maybe it was just Jeremy's paranoia. Normally you wouldn't get a note – just a call to the office and you'd be out of the building five minutes later, never to return. So maybe it was just going to be a reading of the riot act.'

'Who would he have been going to meet?'

Eddie shrugged. 'No idea, I'm afraid. I say, though, this all rather clinches it, doesn't it? What sort of sentence will he get, poor bugger? This'll finish his old dad off, that's for sure.'

'Life,' said Slicer with satisfaction, folding up the memo again and slipping it into his inside pocket. 'Let's get back to the station and you can give us a statement.'

Eddie was leading them down the stairs when he suddenly half-turned with a shy grin.

'By the way,' he said. 'How is young Judy? Not too wet, I hope? Must say I had a weak spot for her straight away.'

'Christ,' said Slicer, looking disgustedly at Stone. 'Not another one.'

CHAPTER 22

Grania sat down, blew some wisps of orange hair out of her eyes, and sipped her gin and tonic with relish. She'd spent most of the morning at the police station giving them another statement, then traced Judy to the squash club to apologise for following her and Duncan into the alleyway and telling the police about it later. Judy had accepted the apology and now Grania had accepted the invitation to stop for a drink.

'Jeremy must have decided to follow you when he realised Lynne had told you about the threatening memo,' she said in her accelerated, breathless voice. 'Gosh, it must have been terrifying.'

'Well, I certainly thought he was going to drown me,' said Judy, reaching for the back of her head to test the bruise with her fingertips. 'What worries me is that if he'd succeeded he'd probably have gone after Lynne as well – on the grounds that she and I were the only ones who really knew about the memo.'

Grania screwed up her straight, freckly nose. 'Hideous,' she said. 'To think one was working with a murderer all that time. And a writer of poison-pen memos – explains the break-in, at last. Duncan, you, Lynne. That would have been three people he'd killed.'

Sharon Bunnie, who was leaning on the bar reading the *Evening Standard* and serving drinks to a few lunchtime squash players, called over to them in her high sing-song.

''Ere, Jude,' she said. 'You seen this in the paper? There's this geezer reckons murderers are like drug addicts.'

'What geezer?' asked Judy. 'Read it out, will you?'

Sharon cleared her throat. ' "Killing may take over the lives of multiple murderers as a kind of addiction, a leading psych – er-wotsit, said today. Some killers appeared to have much in common with addicts, particularly compulsive gamblers, Professor Michael

Dimchurch told a conference of criminologists. Some multiple killers spend many hours in fantasy, selecting victims and choosing weapons and locations, he said. One man detained after two murders was planning twenty more, and his activities followed an addictive pattern. He roamed his local area at night, spying on and selecting potential victims. Over time, he became more confident and began to take greater risks," blah, blah, blah . . . How about that, eh?'

Judy and Grania looked at each other, then looked away and reached simultaneously for their drinks. Judy stared out towards the river as she drank her orange juice, remembering the blackness of the water and its thin, chemical taste. It was an ordinary reassuring sort of day outside, with standard white clouds and spells of weak sunshine. It was hard to believe what had happened yesterday, or that winter was just beginning.

'There's one thing that puzzles me,' said Judy, turning back to Grania, whose face looked haggard and sad. 'Why didn't anyone in your office suspect it was him? There must have been signs it was all building up, aggro between them and so on. There must have been something, as well as the memo, surely?'

Grania began massaging her forehead and appeared to be studying the spills and cigarette burns in the carpet tiles.

'You're right,' she said. 'I suppose none of us wanted to even think it, let alone actually say it. Everyone knew Jeremy was a bit of nutcase. But everyone felt quite loyal to him, you know, because of the family firm and all that. We all knew he didn't fit in, that he'd only really got the job because of the family connection. His dad had already been screwed when the Swiss took over, and it was only a matter of time before Jeremy got screwed too – and not only Jeremy, I might add. We all know they're going to let others go soon as well.'

'You mean, sack them?'

'That's what it's called in the world outside. Your feet don't touch the ground. You don't go back to your desk, the security men see you off the premises, and your personal belongings are delivered by courier in a bin liner. One of the reasons they promoted Duncan was that they knew he wouldn't mind being the hatchet man. Positively relished it, in fact, and he must have been starting with Jeremy.'

'But if that's what was going to happen, surely he wouldn't have written a note and made an appointment like that?'

Grania shrugged. 'Who knows? Jeremy didn't show up until lunchtime – bit under the weather after Dunc's bash the previous night. And Duncan had to go out for the rest of the day so he probably decided to do it on paper, just to make sure.'

'But if he was going to sack him, he didn't have to do it precisely at ten on Monday – he could have just done it when he next saw him.'

Grania spread her hands and tucked her head on one side. 'Well, that's the benign version, I suppose. Wacker was saying this morning that Jeremy must have been totally paranoid and all Duncan wanted him to do was meet the head of the Edinburgh office who was in town for the day – sound him out on moving to Scotland. Believe that, though, you'll believe anything.'

Judy shook her head and sighed. 'So Duncan may have been killed over a misunderstanding,' she murmured. 'Poor Duncan.'

Grania snorted and reached for her glass. 'Poor Duncan, my foot. I bet he was going to do me next, in spite of everything, you know, between us. Bastard. They'll have to find someone else to do the dirty work now.'

She finished her gin with a gloomy flourish and pushed her hair back from her face with both hands. Judy thought she was going to start crying and went and bought more drinks. When she came back there was a pink background to the freckles on Grania's cheeks and her voice was speeding up.

'Tell you something I really remember about Jeremy, soon after I first met him about three years ago. There were loads of us round at a friend's house one Saturday, down in Wimbledon, watching the rugger. Jeremy wanted us to do something else, can't remember what it was, go and have a tug of war on the common or something daft, and suddenly the picture on the TV started sort of wobbling. No one knew what it was until someone went outside and found Jeremy who'd made a lasso from a piece of rope in the shed and was trying to pull the TV aerial down with it.'

She paused, spluttering with sudden laughter and shaking her head: 'He's mad, when you think of it, he was doing that sort of thing all the time. Eddie's known him for ages and he's been telling us all sorts of things I didn't know about him.'

'Such as?' Judy settled more comfortably, feeling a first trace of curious pity enter the fear and anger she felt about the ungainly young man she'd last seen spluttering and doggy-paddling in the black water of the basin.

Grania told how he was the younger of two sons, always in the shadow of his more fortunate and successful brother, who was something big in estate management. He didn't do well at exams and wasn't much good at sport either – in spite of his size, he never went higher than the third rugby team at school. He was always getting into punch-ups in pubs and pulling off crazy and dangerous stunts. He'd swim across Windermere on New Year's Day, for instance, to impress the other house guests. It was all to attract the attention his family wouldn't give him, Grania reckoned, embarking woozily on her third gin; or perhaps it was a bit of ancestral madness.

But Jeremy's most dramatic stroke was riding his motorbike across the Sahara, breaking his leg in a crash and nearly dying of an exotic ailment like beriberi or green monkey disease while in the care of Nigerian villagers. That only made his mother more disappointed in him, although his father was then stirred into getting him the job at Banks and Heritage. But his colleagues never much took to him, not least because he drove a broken-down old Fiat, read the *Telegraph* or the *Express* instead of the *Financial Times*, and showed little sign of what Grania called 'getting up to speed'. He'd once brought a girlfriend he'd known since childhood to an office party, only to have her stolen from him by another in-house Lothario, a rival to Duncan.

'So if he thought his job was going to be taken away too, that would have been the last straw,' said Judy, who'd moved on from orange to tomato and was wondering how much fruit juice the human system could take.

'Yah,' said Grania. 'Something like that. He must have got that memo on Friday afternoon, just when he had that stinking hangover and there'd been all the aggro with Duncan already. And when he decided to bump Duncan off, he must have followed him here – unless he already knew he came here on Sunday nights or something. Listen, could you do me a favour, Judy?'

The bleak biography of the man who'd tried to kill her had made Judy feel suddenly exhausted, and she wished Grania would call it a day and push off back to Chelsea or Limehouse or wherever she belonged. But she nodded and leaned forward, automatically adopting the mode of sympathetic policewoman. Grania's pale green eyes were slithery with drink and sadness.

'Could you show me, well, you know, the place?'

Judy was blank for a moment, then realised what she meant. Coming to the club had given Grania the chance to see the place where her ex-boyfriend, lamented despite his betrayal and neglect, had lifted .his last weight. She probably needed all that gin and rabbiting to build up to this.

Judy took Grania's arm and guided her upstairs, noting the fine, slippery quality of the silk in her blouse and the bony delicacy of the limb beneath. Even the bodies of these toffs, their very skin and sinews, were somehow different. The gym was still locked and unlit, and the two women stood outside in the corridor and looked through the glass of an aquarium emptied of its usual shimmering, gasping inhabitants. Grania stared incredulously at the idle machines, the wire pulleys, the black weights, the ominous little padded seats and benches. When she noticed the dark, shroud-sized stain on the floor by the multigym, she raised two hands to her face and emitted a quiet 'Oh', which was immediately amplified and repeated like a stammering laugh by the empty, echoing corridor.

'Don't worry,' said Judy gently. 'They reckon he was unconscious before the weights were dropped on him.'

'I know,' whispered Grania. 'But it's just so weird, so horrible, to do that to another person.'

Her face was the colour of a wax candle, and she kept one hand clamped across it as they came back down the stairs. Then, at the bottom, she suddenly declared she was going to be ill and ran unsteadily into the women's changing room. As Judy walked wearily back into the bar, Sharon looked up nonchalantly, licked a finger, and turned over a page of her paper.

'I fink I'd better order a cab for poor ole ginger eh, Jude? What you reckon, about ten minutes?'

'All right,' said Clinton langorously, his arm muscles sliding and bulging as he stretched up and grasped the top rail of the bedhead. 'Now we've got that little item out of the way, you can tell me the latest.'

'It didn't feel very little from where I was,' murmured Judy, reaching out for the bottle of sparkling wine on the bedside table and filling their glasses with a wavering hand.

'Cheers,' said Clinton, grinning his widest grin as they clinked glasses amid the warm, sweaty odours of the bed.

'Right,' said Judy, smacking her reddened lips. 'The latest. Well, my colleague Mr Ahmed rang me this afternoon. The suspect's confessed, but he's still in hospital recovering from exposure, which is hardly surprising. Apparently it was him who broke into Duncan's desk after he topped him, looking for the anonymous memo he'd sent him. Must have missed it, though, 'cos that's the one Lynne found later at the bottom of the desk and passed to me. Nerves, I expect – in a hurry. Breaking into his own desk as well was quite good cover, though.'

Clinton snuggled back in the pillows, sipping from his glass. 'Guy's a headbanger, you ask me. What else?'

'What else? Well, his colleagues have suddenly stopped being Trappist monks and are falling over each other to give statements about his bizarre behaviour. I can see a plea of diminished responsibility coming up here. Meanwhile Righter's going to ask the magistrates to let my two friends from the Chaucer Estate out of the nick tomorrow, and you too, my son, as they say in the police force, are well in the clear.'

She ran her hand over his head, and he grasped her wrist and bit the ball of her thumb gently.

'Reckon I could get damages out of them?'

'Dunno. You'd better speak to our Mr Righter about that.'

'Thing I don't get is why none of your lot was on to Mr Jeremy a bit sooner.'

'Well, he wasn't there to be interviewed in the first trawl because he was up in Yorkshire for this two-day business trip. Then his mates thought he looked a bit strange yesterday morning, which is when Ahmed interviewed him, but no one said anything. It was only in the afternoon that Ahmed realised his alibi was duff for Sunday night – he said he'd been in the hotel up north from ten o'clock, but apparently he only got there well after midnight. And by yesterday afternoon it was too late – he was already playing ducks and drakes.'

'But this guy's a raving psychopath, and his mates just reckoned he was *a bit strange!*'

Judy yawned and took a slow drink of wine.

'Yeah, well, I think his friend Eddie was the first one to face up to things, 'cos it was him who rang the incident room to warn them I could be in a spot of bother. Between you and me, I thought it was Eddie who was after me – got the shock of my life when I saw young Jeremy's face staring at me from the pond.'

'Why did you think it was Eddie?'

'All sorts of reasons. But I should have cottoned on to Jeremy sooner, you know. There was this time I was at the club for some coaching, and he was hanging around the gym in a suspicious sort of way – that's probably when he got the idea about the weights. Anyway, I'm just glad that when Eddie rang Slicer and his troops, they had the bright idea of looking for me at home first, instead of setting off for the City or somewhere. Otherwise I'd be feeding fishes at the bottom of the basin now.'

Clinton reached out a consoling arm to her bare white shoulders. Judy put their glasses on the table and snuggled up to kiss him. Then she pulled away and raised herself smilingly on hands and knees above him.

'What about you, then, Sherlock?' said Clinton indistinctly, nuzzling her breasts. 'S'pose they want you in the CID now?'

'Not likely.' Judy murmured, her pale hair falling round her cheekbones as she reached down with her hand. 'I'd rather spend my time finding what makes people tick.'

'Aaah – you've just found it,' gasped Clinton gently, his arms fluttering feebly on the sheet. 'So what's all this girls on top stuff?'

'I'm not having you on my bruised ribs again,' she said gently, sinking slowly back on to him. Clinton closed his eyes and let out a long moan.

'Oooh, officer,' he whispered. 'That's a perfect end to a terrible week.'